BROKEN PROMISE

The Promise Me Series, Book 2

By

Tara Fox Hall

Published by
Melange Books, LLC
White Bear Lake, MN 55110
www.melange-books.com

Broken Promise ~ Copyright © 2012 by Tara Fox Hall

ISBN: 978-1-61235-472-9 Print

Cover Art by Caroline Andrus

Broken Promise
By Tara Fox Hall

Shocked at Danial's betrayal, Sarelle returns to her old home to consider her options. Yet even as Sar plans a reconciliation with Danial, Terian arrives, confessing his desire. When Theo witnesses Terian and Sar kiss, he angrily confronts Sar, leading to startling consequences. Will Sar's heart choose Danial, Terian,…or Theo?

About the Author

Tara Fox Hall's writing credits include nonfiction, horror, suspense, action-adventure, erotica, and contemporary and historical paranormal romance. She is the author of the paranormal action-adventure *Lash* series and the vampire romantic suspense *Promise Me* series. Tara divides her free time unequally between writing novels and short stories, chainsawing firewood, caring for stray animals, sewing cat and dog beds for donation to animal shelters, and target practice.

Other works by Tara Fox Hall at www.melange-books.com:
Surrender to Me
Return to Me
The Origin of Fear in Spellbound 2011 Anthology
Kink and *The Oath* in Wicked Christmas Wishes Anthology
Promise Me, Book 1 of the Promise Me Series

Author Contact
www.tarafoxhall.com

Chapter One

I woke up around midnight, groggy but content, and went into the bathroom. In the bright light, there was blood on my underwear, enough for me to realize my period had started.

God damn it! Were the forces of nature against me? My period had been late, and now I'd gotten it just as I was beginning a whole week with Danial all to myself.

By the time I'd showered and voiced more than a few curse words, I started to cramp. That was expected. I'd broken the cardinal rule to never have vigorous sex the day before a period. I wanted to lie down but Danial had drunk a fair amount of my blood the night before. Instead of resting, I went to the kitchen in search of food and vitamins.

"Sar!" Cia squealed as she ran over to me. "Congratulations! Danial told us this evening that you gave him your oath. It's almost like a double wedding!"

"Thanks." I hugged her, trying to ignore my cramps and how much I didn't want anyone to touch me. "Where are the dogs?"

"Out with Ivan for a run," she said, laughing. "He says they're better than him at catching mice now."

I tried to laugh, but it came out as more of a grimace. "Good."

I didn't feel any better even after eating some cereal. If anything, the pain was worse. "I'm going back to bed. Have a good night."

"Are you okay? You look sick."

"I got my period today, of all days. It's no big deal—"

A sharp pain ripped across my abdomen. I crumpled with a gasp. Cia grabbed me before I hit the floor and helped me to a chair. I sank down in it just in time for another pain to hit, shallow breaths tearing out of me.

"Something's wrong! Call 911! Call Doctor Camlyn!"

She turned and bolted for the phone. I tried to stay in the chair, but my stomach muscles hurt too much to sit up. I slowly eased myself to the floor and stretched out. It was better that way. The pain was manageable there.

"Sar!" Cia screamed. She was at my side in an instant, pulling me up.

I tried to tell her that hurt more, but she either didn't hear me or didn't listen.

"I called Doctor Camlyn. He'll be here in an hour; he said it's likely food poisoning. He gave me instructions to help you throw up—"

An hour? "Call 911!"

She shook her head. "That won't help. The closest hospital is an hour and a half away. The local EMT's don't know there's a house back here and there's a spell—"

"Call them and have someone lead them here!"

"Doctor Camlyn's office is less than an hour away. He'll be here the fastest. Just hold on—"

She cut off, scenting the air rapidly. Another wave of pain hit me, making me cry out as I eased back down to the floor.

She looked down, suddenly terrified. "Lay still. I don't know what else to do."

"Get Theo," I groaned. "This isn't food poisoning. The pain's too bad."

She was already dialing. "Theo? Get here as fast as you can. There's something wrong with Sar!"

I felt a sudden wetness, as if I'd peed myself. My eyes traveled down my body to see blood soaking my legs.

I'd miscarried. I'd been pregnant with Danial's child.

Everything went grey.

* * * *

I woke a few minutes later when Theo slammed into the house and tore into the room.

"What happened?" he said, crouching beside me.

"She fainted. There's blood. Doctor Camlyn's on his way, but he said it'd be an hour—"

"I'm miscarrying," I gasped.

Cia's mouth fell open, her eyes wide in surprise. Theo's expression held nothing.

"You knew," I whispered to him. "You knew this might happen? And you said nothing?"

"Help me get her into the bedroom," he said to Cia. "I'll lift her, but I want you to try to keep her as still as you can."

He picked me up as if I were light as a feather. Cia helped him bring me to Danial's bed, our bed, the same bed our child had likely been conceived on. The child that was bleeding out of me. Oh, God...

"Sar, hold onto me. Cia, get some towels and take off her pants. We need hot water and a washcloth. We need to make her as comfortable as we can."

Cia darted out of the room.

"Sar, stay here with me," Even under strain, he was still commanding. "Stay awake."

"I'm here. The pain's not too bad now."

Cia came back with the water, washcloth, and towels. Theo lifted me as she laid the towels underneath. Then she began taking off my pants, and the pain came back worse than before.

"Stop, don't move me. It hurts—"

"Sar, hold onto me. I've got you," Theo said, his arms like granite around me.

I held onto him as if my life depended on it. Cia got off my pants and began to clean me off.

As the pain lessened, I was embarrassed to be half-naked in Theo's arms. "Don't look," I whispered to him. "I feel so—"

"Shh, save your strength. You can make all the wise-ass comments you like when this is over."

Cia went to get fresh water and a new washcloth.

Theo nudged me hard with his hand. "You have to keep awake."

I didn't answer. God, I was so tired.

"Theo," Cia said, scared.

"What?"

"The bleeding. It's not stopping."

A jolt of fear hit me, waking me. Why was there so much blood? Was I dying?

"Call Danial, if you haven't already," he said calmly. "He should be on his way back by now. Tell him everything we've done. See if there's anything else he wants us to do for her."

Cia nodded and left, giving me a long anguished glance.

"Stay awake. I need you to stay awake."

Panic hit me. He thought I was dying, too. "Please save me," I whispered.

"I can't. I don't know what to do, damn it! Danial will be here soon, be calm—"

Danial couldn't save me. He didn't have the power to make me a vampire... A shiver went through me. "Don't let him give me to Devlin."

"You're talking crazy! What—"

"Not even to save me from dying! I don't want Devlin having power over me. Promise me!"

"Danial's not giving you to Devlin. He would never do that."

"He gave me a child without telling me it was possible he could. Don't let him—"

"I give you my word. Devlin will never touch you, no matter what happens," he growled. "Now, keep still and talk to me. Tell me about your pets; describe them and tell me their names. How many do you have?"

"Three . . ." I yawned. "Three cats, two dogs." I yawned again.

"Their names. Tell me their names."

I started to drift and didn't answer.

"Sarelle!" he yelled in my ear.

"I hear you," I said groggily, coming back to myself. "Stop yelling."

"Where's Cia? What is taking her so fucking long?"

I began to drift again, and bit my lip hard. I wasn't going to end this way, I didn't want to become a vampire...wait. There was another option.

"Theo, change me," I whispered.

He went utterly still. My rapid panting was loud in the small room.

"You're oathed to Danial," he said, pushing my sweat-damp hair back so he could look me in the eyes. "I'd need his permission."

"Please, save me—"

"You wouldn't survive. I'd have to give you a mortal wound in animal form. Even a strong person doesn't always make it. And I've never done it before, never even tried to do it—"

"Try it, please!" I said desperately. "Please, Theo! I don't want to die or be vampire."

He looked at me for a long moment, his blue eyes unreadable.

Spellbound, I watched as they suddenly changed from blue to the light yellow of his cougar form.

The bedroom door burst open. Doctor Camlyn and Cia came in.

"How long has she been like this?" Camlyn asked, crouching beside me, and moving my legs apart.

"About forty-five minutes," Cia said.

"Sarelle, when did the bleeding start?" he asked quickly.

"A little before midnight."

"Hold still for me."

I winced when he inserted a cervical clamp. Theo held me tightly, his eyes again blue, as Cia stroked my shoulders.

"The bleeding seems to have stopped, but we need to get her to my office so I can perform a D&C on her."

I nodded, dazed. I'd been right. I had been pregnant.

"Cia, stay here. Call Danial and tell him to meet us the office—"

"No way in hell I'm staying here!"

"You're staying," Theo growled at her. "Tell everyone Sar is sick and we've taken her to the doctor. You need to keep everyone calm, especially Danial."

She wanted to argue, but when she looked at me, her resolve seemed to vanish. She nodded once. "Okay."

Theo carried me as Camlyn helped Cia wrap me in the sheet from the bed. I tightened my grip on him as he picked me up.

Stephen drove us to his office. The ride seemed to last forever. Theo sat in the back holding me. I felt very weak, but I was in a lot less pain. After we arrived, Theo carried me inside and laid me on an examining table, covering me with the sheet as best he could.

"I'm going to be right here. Don't worry."

I gave him a weak smile. Camlyn came in, dressed in scrubs. "Wait outside, Theo. This might take awhile."

"I'm not leaving her," he growled.

Camlyn nodded and turned to me. "Have you given Danial your blood recently?"

"Last night. And it was a fair amount."

"Then I can't give you any anesthetic. You might go into a coma."

I closed my eyes. "Please, just do it."

"Don't bear down, and try your best not to move." He sat down, put my feet in the stirrups, and began the procedure. Theo turned his back to the doctor and held my hands, leaning over me to keep me focused on him. But I couldn't ignore the vacuum sound or the sensations as Camlyn did what he had to. It was unpleasant but not too bad.

"Scream if you need to," Theo said, his eyes worried.

"You're not being comforting—" I cut off as the first wave of real pain hit me, crying out as my back reflexively arched off the table.

He leaned into me quickly, his arms going around me. "You're safe. Hold on to me."

I screamed more before Camlyn was done, even though there'd been less pain than I'd worried there would be. When it was over, I wanted to sit up, but Theo wouldn't let me.

Camlyn washed his hands and returned to my side, bringing me a glass. "Let her sit up, Theo. Drink this, Sar. It'll help hydrate you. Do you have any pain?"

I took the cup, thankfully drank the cool contents, and handed it back. "No, not really." I ached a little inside and felt nauseous, but I guess that was to be expected.

"Have you been with anyone besides Danial in the last three months?"

"No," I said defensively. I understood why he asked, but I still didn't like it. Besides, I had questions of my own. "Why did this happen?"

"This wasn't your fault. You can go home. You need to keep off you feet for the rest of the night." He turned to leave.

Of course, it wasn't my fault. "Tell me the truth. How did I get pregnant with Danial's child?"

He stopped and spoke without turning to me. "You know the particulars of how."

I still felt weak, but now that the worst was over, I was angry. "Answer me, damn you!" I would have gotten off the table if Theo still hadn't held me. "Danial told me vampires can't have children!"

Camlyn sighed and turned to me. "I don't know. He took those ancient potions even when I warned him there might be unforeseen side effects. At his request, I tested him to make sure they weren't changing him to the point where he might be able to get you pregnant. His last results were negative. This shouldn't have happened. I'm sorry."

The door closed softly behind him.

Theo flipped open his phone and called Danial. I inferred from what was said that he'd be there in a few minutes. I thought about Camlyn saying he was sorry and remembered that night in the kitchen when he'd said similar words to Danial.

Your results were negative, Danial. I'm sorry.

And it all fell into place. The potions Terian had made for him. Devlin and Danial talking that night I overheard them at the door. The cryptic message on voicemail from Devlin. Theo's face when he saw me on the floor. He hadn't been surprised I could be pregnant, but Cia had been stunned.

Your strategy is compelling, Danial—

Devlin had known, too.

All those conversations I'd thought had to do with his lack of ability to make vampires—it had never been about that. Danial had planned this from the beginning, from when he'd met me. Maybe I wasn't the first human he'd tried it with. I'd been stupid thinking he loved me for me. Who was I, anyway? A widow of small means willing to give herself to a stranger. And I'd sealed my fate last night when I'd given him my oath. My tears trickled out.

"Don't cry," Theo said gently, hugging me. "You're going to be okay."

"No," I choked. "I am not okay. And I'm not going to be."

"Sar—"

"You knew. You knew and you didn't warn me!"

He disentangled himself from me and retreated to the wall. "I didn't know you were pregnant. But when I saw you bleeding, I knew what was happening to you. I've seen another woman—a werefox—miscarry when she changed form not knowing she was pregnant."

"Why did he do this? Do you know?"

"He loves you. He would never want what happened tonight to happen to you. You heard Camlyn. He's been checking regularly to make sure that he wasn't able to get you pregnant. This was an accident."

"Maybe he didn't want this, but he sure wanted me to get pregnant! And he never said a word to me about it. All this time, all this effort, and he never told me, never asked!"

"You don't know that. You need to talk to him and ask for the truth."

"Why bother?" I said bitterly. "He never tells me the truth."

"It's true he loves you."

I turned away from him. "No. That's what I don't know."

His footsteps retreated, the door closing as he left. Alone, I tried to make sense of all of it.

The more I thought, the more certain I was that Danial wanted a child. This hadn't been a by-product of those potions he'd taken: it had been the goal. And I'd had no idea. Why would he want a child with me? Why now? He was a vampire, for God's sake. I'd never heard of one wanting a child.

Why had I miscarried? Instead of being sad over it, I was guilty to be grateful. If I had a child, I didn't want it to be an accident or because of anything other than my choice.

The door opened. I froze.

"Sarelle, are you awake?" Danial asked.

He knew I wasn't sleeping; he was being polite. "I'm awake."

He came to the table and put his arms around me. If he had said anything at that moment, I think I would have screamed at him, told him to get out and never come near me again. But he just held me.

As time passed, emotional turmoil eclipsed my anger. I turned to him and buried my face in his chest, long, choking sobs ripping out of me. He held me tightly and stroked my hair. He made no noise, but I felt his tears on my forehead as they fell. Eventually I ran out of tears and lay in his arms, my nose stuffed, my eyes sore and red.

"Let's go home."

He picked me up very gently, wrapping me in the bed sheet, and took me out to the waiting SUV. Theo drove us home and Danial carried me to our bed, laying me down on fresh green sheets. He then left without a word.

I took a deep breath, relieved the blood was gone and that he'd left me alone.

The door opened and Cia came in. She sat on the bed and hugged me. "I'm so sorry."

"Me, too."

"I'm here to help you out of those clothes. Doctor Camlyn doesn't want you to shower tonight or take a bath—"

"Please, I'd rather do it myself. Just bring me a washcloth and some warm water."

"Fine. But don't get up, except for the bathroom."

"I promise I'll stay right here in bed. I'm exhausted."

She brought me the water, washcloth, and some pajamas from the wardrobe. "I'll be right outside. Call me when you're done."

After she left, I slowly cleaned myself up. It felt good to smell the scent of soap and to feel the warm water on my skin. I put on the new pajamas and got into bed. "I'm done."

She came in and gathered up the soiled laundry and water. "Just yell if you need anything. I'll be right outside. "

"How is he?" I asked her, hating myself for caring.

"He's very upset, almost wild. He blames himself for what happened. He and Theo are outside talking, but he'll be in as soon as he calms down." She patted my arm. "He didn't want to upset you any more than you were."

Good, Danial was to blame. I was glad we were on the same page about that.

She left and I laid there thinking about what to do. I'd been through hell and was dead tired, so I didn't get very far before I fell asleep.

When I awoke, I was no longer alone. Danial was beside me, holding me close, snoring softly. It took me a long time but I eventually fell back asleep. In that time, I decided what I had to do.

Chapter Two

When I woke up the next evening, I felt much improved. I still ached, but no longer felt so weak. Sleeping for twelve hours had helped. I checked the time; it was seven p.m. Danial's arms were still around me. I'd never figured out how he could do that and not have his bottom arm be uncomfortable. Maybe now I never would.

I gently moved him, and went into the bathroom. I used the facilities, and checked myself over. I was no longer bleeding. Good. That would make things easier. I stepped into the shower, and proceeded to use all the available hot water. I stayed there until the water turned cool, letting the water wash over me, trying to wash away what had happened. I wanted the last twenty-four hours to be a dream, to go back into Danial's arms and have everything be like it had been before between us. I wanted a life here with him.

But what had happened was real. I had to deal with it. That meant I would have to have it out with Danial, and I didn't need Theo to tell me it was not going to end well. Regardless of what he said, Danial had lied to me yet again, and I needed some time apart from him.

Packing up some cold weather clothes was the first order of business. I was tempted to wait until Danial left me to feed or work. I told myself that was cowardly and it was better to be up front about what I needed now. I had given him my oath. I owed him more than to sneak off when he wasn't looking. There was also the real possibility that he might not let me leave. I'd deal with that in real time, mostly because if he really wanted to keep me here, I wouldn't be leaving.

I went to the closet, and got down my bags. Opening the wardrobe, I surveyed my winter clothes. What to take and what to leave? I settled for the basic stuff; a few sweaters, a few pairs of jeans, a few flannel shirts. I folded them up, and that was one bag. I had extra socks and undergarments at home, so I didn't need to waste space on those. I went into the bathroom with the other, and grabbed my deodorant, and other toiletries, and put them in the other bag. My vitamins were in the kitchen, but I wouldn't be needing them.

I turned and went back into the bedroom. Danial was still asleep. Again, I was tempted to leave him there sleeping, and sneak out. I reminded myself I wasn't going to do that. All being spineless would do is postpone the messy scene we were going to have. It was better to get it over with now.

Thinking of all the times we'd kissed each other awake, I was already upset. I put my bags down, sat on the bed, and nudged him gently, saying his name. "Danial."

"I'm awake, Sar. I've been awake since you first started packing," he said, opening his eyes. There was raw anguish in his words. "Are you leaving me?"

I couldn't look at him. "No, I'm not leaving you, Danial. But I do need to go back to my house for a while. I need some time to work through what I feel."

"And you can't do that here with me," he finished. It was half statement, half question.

"I need to be alone," I said.

"Sar—" Danial began.

"Danial, my getting pregnant was no accident. It is clear to me that you planned this out. You wanted me to get pregnant. That's what the potions were for. And you never told me anything about it. Why?"

My accusation hung in the air between us. Danial's guilt was evident on his face.

"Why, Danial?" I asked.

When he finally answered, there was no anger, only a lot of sadness. "Because I love you, Sar. I want your child, our child. I want to be a father again."

"No," I said abruptly. "That's not it. Try again, Danial."

"Sar, that's why, I swear—" Danial said vehemently.

"That may be how you feel, but why now? Why not wait until we've been together longer? I met you three months ago!"

"Because it's so difficult, with me being vampire. Even if we try for years, it may not happen for us." He took a breath, letting it out with exasperation. "And you don't have—"

He stopped, but I knew what he had left unsaid. My sadness deepened into despair.

"Because I don't have many years left?" I finished quietly.

"You'll live many more years, Sar," he replied quickly.

"You and I both know what we're talking about here, Danial. Years left to have a child. Years my body will be young enough to make one. I'm thirty now."

"Yes. I'm sorry, but…yes." Danial got to his feet and moved toward me, opening his arms.

I held up a hand, telling him to keep his distance. "But you left out the most important 'why', Danial. Why didn't you tell me?"

Our conversation had begun quietly, but each exchange now was louder than the last. I hoped that everyone within earshot had left already. I didn't want Cia or any of the others to hear this.

"I would have, when I knew that I might be able to father a child," Danial said delicately, stopping in his tracks. "I didn't want you to know until I could find out for sure if it was possible. I was scared, Sar."

"Scared of what?"

"What if I mentioned the subject to you, and you decided you wanted a baby, and the potions didn't work? All my tests were negative." He paused. "I know doctors can make babies now without copulation, but I didn't know if I could handle you being pregnant, and knowing it was someone else's baby and not mine, not with the way I feel about you."

He looked at me hopefully, willing me to believe him.

I wanted to believe him. Yet I knew him well enough to know that he might be distorting the truth.

"You told me that first night we had sex that vampires couldn't father children, ever. Yet you seemed to have found a way around that with a potion. So is it even true that you're sterile?"

"It's true for the most part." he said reluctantly.

"FOR THE MOST PART?" I yelled at him. "Have we been having unprotected sex all this time?"

"Sar, I couldn't have gotten you pregnant that first night we slept together, not without a human male sharing our bed to do the deed." Danial was defensive now, and also getting angry.

He had no right to be angry. I was the one who'd been lied to. I got angrier.

"So you went and got some magical fertility potion to slip me when I wasn't paying attention?" I yelled back at him. "What about trust? I trusted you!"

"Sar, get control of yourself." Danial was composed, but his eyes were tinted red again, his anger bleeding through his calm exterior. He folded his arms across his chest. "I am the one who took the potions, not you. I am the one who was playing with fire and hoping not to get burned."

"Did you think about what would happen if it worked?" I shouted at him. "Who assumes all the risk then? Me!"

"I would never put you in harm's way. The weekly tests were to make sure this wouldn't happen. I didn't want a surprise pregnancy for us, much less to have you go through what you just have. You've got to know that—"

He was working hard to placate me. I was having none of it, not this time, not about this.

"You don't know; that's my point here! Terian said there were no dhamphirs that he knew of, that the information on them was conflicting, unreliable."

"So we are back to Terian, are we?" Danial's eyes were glowing red now.

"Leave him out of this, Danial—"

"You brought him into it, Sar. You trust his words as gospel, yet you distrust mine?"

"He knew about dhamphirs, Danial, because he thought that he was one—"

"But he is not! What he told you about himself has nothing to do with what our child would be, or could be!"

I decided to go for the big guns. "You have no way to guarantee that your baby wouldn't rip me apart being born," I said icily.

"I would never let that happen, Sar," Danial said, his red eyes sliding away from mine.

"But you don't know for sure," I said softly. "Do you?"

"I'm not a monster, Sar," Danial said wearily. "Weres of all kinds have children all the time. Nothing is different, unless the mother decides to stay in animal form for her pregnancy and deliver that way. Nobody dies, or is hurt." His eyes were darkening, the redness fading.

"But you aren't werefox," I said in a more normal voice. "You are vampire."

"Our baby would be half human, half vampire," Danial said quickly. "There is no reason to believe that it would be any different from a normal baby, or that you'd have anything other than a normal pregnancy and delivery. The hardest thing to do would be getting you pregnant—"

"Why didn't you tell me you wanted children?" I asked searchingly.

"I already told you—"

"Sure, that's part of it, Danial, but I want to know the rest of it. You didn't let me know you were even thinking about this, or that it was even possible. Tell me the reason why."

"Why?" Danial said exasperatedly. "I already told you: out of fear."

"This was more than you being afraid I might want a baby and you wouldn't be able to give me one. Tell me the truth."

Danial sat down and put his head in his hands, all the fight leaving him in one long breath. "I was afraid I'd be able to give you one and you wouldn't want one," he murmured.

Our eyes met. The despair in his eyes mirrored my own.

"I was afraid you'd act like you did when I asked you to stay with me the first time you visited. I thought you'd be happy when I offered you a home here, but you reacted as if I'd told you that you had to give up your dogs or something drastic like that."

"You were asking me to give up something significant," I replied coolly. "My life, Danial. My life as it was up until I met you. I had a home of my own—"

"I offered you the world," Danial said bitterly. "You hemmed and hawed, making it seem as if you were giving up a rich life to live in squalor with me, when the exact opposite was true."

"Life isn't all about being rich," I said angrily. "I had to do what was right for me."

"And I did what was right for me," Danial shot back. "I know you, Sar. You leap forward for something in the heat of the moment and in the next second, you draw yourself back into your shell. What is this, if not your attempt to run at the first sign of trouble in our relationship?"

"You lied to me, and tried to get me pregnant. Worse, now you're admitting it was to trap me. What kind of relationship is that?"

"That's not it at all," Danial said angrily. "I just didn't want to be

18

put off by you. I do want a child, our child. I would want it no matter what. We have a chance, Sar. I don't want to lose it."

"We have time, Danial."

His words tore out of him. "No, we don't, my love. Do you know how short ten years seems to me? Twenty years? It goes by so quickly, Sar. I don't want to lose you. I can't make you vampire, can't keep you with me against the flow of time. I don't think you'd agree anyway, even if I wanted that. Devlin would have to do it, and then he'd have power over you." He stepped toward me "I would never give him that, Sar, never."

I backed away. "I don't want to be vampire. I told you that from the first."

"I don't want you to be, either. But our child, he or she would be part vampire. They would live a long life, maybe even have my immortality, if what the legends say is true. They would be part of you and part of me. I could hold onto you, onto what we had—"

The world I'd built with him was rocking on its foundations. The grey boxes that Danial kept, containing all his mementos and memories from his long immortal life. Pictures and tokens weren't enough for him to remember us. He was looking to make a living memory, something that wouldn't fit in a box. We weren't the same; I was going to die and he was going to live forever. In that split second, I understood that difference more completely than I ever had before.

"—I can't lose you, Sar."

"Danial, it's over between us," I said tearfully. "We're over."

Chapter Three

"No, we're not ending this way," Danial said, his eyes now entirely red. "I love you, Sar."

"Not enough to take what I could give you. I gave you all of me, and that wasn't enough," I said sadly. "I'm sorry."

I turned to leave, and Danial grabbed me, pulling me into his arms. I struggled with him.

"Danial, let me go!"

"That's it? How can that be your choice?" He held me, even as I continued to struggle. "How can you just say it's over between us, just like that?"

"Because you always want more! It's always got to be the next step, before I am even comfortable with the last one!"

He held me tighter. "Shh. Please, Love, I'm sorry. I never wanted you to be hurt."

"Let me go, Danial," I said quietly.

"I can't let you go, Sar. I won't. Just as you can't seem to face my agelessness, I can't face the years stretching out in front of me without you, not after how good these last months have been. I've been so happy knowing you, loving you—"

He will never let you go. Theo's words, spoken months ago. Here was that threat, unspoken until now.

I had only one card left to play, and I played it. "Danial, I'm going to my house tonight, to think things over. Maybe we can reconcile, after I spend some time alone. You can force me to stay here with you, but keeping me prisoner is the only way you'll stop me from leaving."

Danial instantly recoiled from me, his eyes narrowed. "I would never make you stay with me against your will. Leave now, if you wish to."

That was a big relief. "I'll call you when I'm ready to talk."

"Do you have any more rules you think I should be aware of?" he said nastily.

"Yes," I said simply. "I meant what I told you Christmas Eve, despite everything that's happened. I just need a little time."

Danial didn't reply.

I reached down, picked up my bags, and left the room. My dogs were lying on their new beds near the couch. I crouched down next to them.

"We've got to go," I said emotionally, my voice breaking. "Come."

I got up and walked to the dining room when I realized that neither one was following me.

"Ghost! Darkness! Come!"

Both dogs came reluctantly. When I opened the door, Ghost whined, and Darkness circled, but neither would go out the door with me.

When had I last walked them myself? Back before the snow had gotten so deep. Ivan had been taking care of that for me.

I located their leashes in the hall closet, and clipped them on. Though both dogs whined, I led them out to the SUV, and got them both to jump in the back.

"You'll be fine," I said comfortingly, as I got in and started the engine. "We'll be fine."

As I drove down the driveway, I looked back at the lighted house in the rearview mirror, and everything I was leaving behind. A few tears slipped out. I wiped them away angrily.

The trip back to my old home took forever. Adding to the time was a quick stop at the local all night supermarket to pick up groceries. Who knew what waited for me in the fridge at my house? I hadn't been there for more than a month. Thinking about that, I got some Chinese food to go. I was starving now and I was not going to feel like cooking when I finally arrived home.

I finally made it back to my house close to midnight. To my surprise, there was a light on inside. My spirits fell: I would have to deal with Suri. She might think I was here to pick up my cats, to finally bring them to Danial's home. We'd talked about it a few days before.

That conversation seemed a lifetime ago.

I drove the SUV into the unheated garage, remembering the tractor was parked beneath the house in the heated garage, in preparation for plowing. Good thing, too, as the slowly lightening sky looked whitish, like snow would begin falling at any moment.

I parked the SUV and walked into the house with the dogs. The cats instantly surrounded me, joyously meowing. I picked them up, cuddling them and telling them how much I'd missed them. Then it dawned on me how uncomfortable I was.

My house was cold. The thermostat said it was fifty-one. I turned the heat up to sixty-five, making the furnace kick on. That would get things moving in the right direction.

"I guess we should make a fire," I said resolutely. "Then bring in groceries."

After giving each of the dogs a Cheweez, I began making a fire. Someone had made one recently, but it had gone out and the ashes were cold. Once some flames were flickering steadily, I went about settling my things, bringing in my groceries, and packing them away. I ate my Chinese food, sharing with the dogs, and then put away my clothes.

Taking stock of my cupboards, I was glad I'd taken the time to stop for food. Except for some chunks of meat, there was nothing in the fridge. Hadn't I taught Cia to cook?

Belatedly, I remembered Cia had moved back to Danial's land, in preparation for mating to Aran. She had most likely taken her supplies with her. For whatever reason, her replacement Suri wasn't here.

It was, however, a good possibility that Suri might eventually show up. If she did, I made up my mind to tell her she was free to stay or go back to Danial's. Despite the awkwardness of Danial and me, I was hoping she'd stay. I hadn't been truly alone now for a while, and I was unused to the feeling. There was too much quiet; no sound of the phone ringing, or someone calling out hello, that they'd taken over for someone who'd completed their shift for the night. Thinking that over, I passed out on my sofa, exhausted, comforted by Jess and Cavity purring on my lap.

I woke up several hours later, just after dawn. After feeding everyone and cleaning litter boxes, I built up the fire again, and then debated what to do next. Although I was tired and it was now early morning, I decided to go for a walk. The dogs needed it, and so did I. I was still too wound up to really sleep, not to mention the crick in my neck from dozing on the couch. A walk in cold weather might be just enough to get me some good rest. I wasn't hungry at all.

The morning was brisk and clear, sunlight streaming down. I blinked in its bright light, and then stalwartly started across the field, figuring to make about a mile total before returning.

I'd forgotten how deep the snow could be, or that I might need snowshoes. We got as far as the edge of the forest. The harsh winter wind had blown the snow into knee-high drifts, and my pants were soaked through. Worse, my dogs were both leaping in circles around me, and I was out of breath. I might have been thin enough to fit into all my jeans, but I was still very out of shape. Calling the reluctant dogs, I headed back to the house. When I got inside, I took off my wet clothes, dressed in some flannel pajamas, and bedded down on the couch with a blanket rather than face my empty bed. I was asleep in moments.

I woke late in the afternoon, and got dressed. When I went to build up the fire, I noticed that my wood rack was better than half-empty. Pulling on some gloves, I began carrying some up. By the time I was done, I was painfully aware how much my physique had atrophied. I hadn't lifted anything heavier than a soup pan in two months.

Exhausted again, I showered, fixed dinner, and then watched some TV. I had a lot to choose from; the TiVo was full to the brim. I'd never remembered to stop recording my various shows. I erased a bunch I'd seen at Danial's, which left me the pick of a few new movies to occupy my mind tonight. I watched part of one movie, and then Darkness began to snore. I laughed to myself and looked down at the dogs, asleep at my feet.

My smile disappeared. It was past time to go to bed. No one would be feeding my pets tomorrow for me. I would need to get up early and feed them. Plus there would be other work that needed doing, work only I would be here to do.

I'd just woken up five hours before, but I sank into my bed gratefully. As I lay back, my eyes fastened on Danial's red shirt, the one he had said he'd wear for me one day. It was lying on my dresser, neatly folded, from where I'd mistakenly left it while gathering my winter clothes to bring to his home. I got up, grabbed it, and brought it to the bed. The cloth smelled like him, which got me sobbing again.

I didn't want to be here alone. I wanted to be with him. I loved him and I missed him; missed feeling his body here next to mine, missed his arms around me and his soft sighs when he slept, the one time he truly let down his guard.

When I ran out of tears, I washed my face and changed my pajama top for a dry one. Then I set my alarm, tucked Danial's shirt underneath my pillow, and fell into an exhausted sleep.

* * * *

The next morning was hard. I hadn't gotten up at six a.m. for a long time. Luckily, strong incentive was there in the form of dogs whining, cats meowing, and freezing cold air. I got the fire started again, the pets taken care of, and then went back to bed for a few hours. Even doing my best, I couldn't adjust in one day.

Later, after I'd showered, and had breakfast, I sat and thought about everything again. I went over what had happened and all that Danial had said to me the night before. I had several big questions to answer before I would be able to decide whether to go back to him, or break things off for good. Sure, I'd told him we were over last night, but that had been just my anger. I had meant what I said when I'd promised to be his, and my word was important to me. Besides, I loved him. If it was at all possible, I had to try to work this out, no matter what he had done.

The questions weren't easy. What did he want from me really? What was I willing to give him? How far was I willing to bend before I said 'no'? What did I want and need from our relationship, and from my life?

What Danial really wanted, if I believed everything he said, was to keep me with him, still human, still able to give him blood and have me not age, so we could truly be together. That was impossible, so he wanted me to have a child with him so he could keep me alive through the child. I understood that easily enough. Women had done it all the time for men who went off to war through the ages. I didn't fault him for my miscarriage. He couldn't have known any more than I had that I was pregnant. He had been getting tested all along. I kept coming back to just one unsettling question: What would Danial have done if he'd known he could father a child, and I'd told him I didn't want one?

Would he have forced me to do it? Would he have let it go? Most likely the correct choice was neither of those, it was number three; he would have asked me and told me how important it was to him. Then he would have given me time to think about the idea, and decide that it wasn't that bad.

Was I willing to give Danial a child? Not right now, probably not anytime soon. But in the next few years, maybe. He was right in one regard, it was not going to get any easier to have a child the older I got. That train of thought made me more worried; what if I miscarried again? What if the potion itself was flawed?

After some consideration, I dismissed that. Terian didn't dabble in magic; he had an online business, according to Danial. He wouldn't have given it to Danial if it hadn't been one hundred percent right.

Maybe Danial hadn't taken the potion for a long enough duration. Dr. Camlyn had said pregnancy shouldn't have happened according to the tests.

I took a deep breath, considering a darker option. I'd never been pregnant before, never tried to be. Maybe there was something wrong with me.

I got up from my chair and called my gynecologist for an appointment. His office said that he had no openings this week, but they would fit me in next week on Tuesday. I wrote down the information on a piece of paper, and went back to my thinking.

What I needed from Danial was straightforward, at least. I was done with the artifices, the deceit, and the subterranean goings on. He was never going to keep anything hidden from me again, whether it was small, large, or seemingly nothing to do with me. There would be full disclosure from him, or no Sar.

What I wanted most was a life with Danial; being loved by him and living with him, Cia, Theo and the rest of the weres. I had to know that everything he told me was the whole truth. An oath from him saying that he promised not to keep things from me would suffice. And while he was at it, he could give me a promise that he would be faithful to me, too.

My logic was sound, but it made my heart sink. I'd demanded full disclosure after Terian had first attacked last fall, clueing me into key facts Danial had hidden from me. Danial had promised then to have no secrets. Being interested in making a child and actively working toward having one while letting your spouse believe that not only were you not interested in children, you couldn't physically have any, was a hell of a secret to be keeping. If he could lie to me about something so important, he could lie to me about anything. How could I ever regain my trust in someone who had been so duplicitous?

Tired of thinking in circles, I got up and made myself lunch. I needed a break. Afterwards, there was one other overdue task I still needed to complete today.

Every winter, my protocol was to lock two gates at the far end of the cornfield, preventing snowmobilers from tearing around my field late at night in the winter. With all that had happened in the fall, I'd never gotten around to it. I hadn't remembered until I'd seen it standing open during my first walk yesterday. Snowmobile tracks and a discarded beer car had given me further inducement for some quick action.

After some searching, I located the padlocks and chains. During the dog walk, I chained and locked the two gates, taking satisfaction that the snowmobile tracks would be covered over soon in the next snowfall. Returning home, I threw the beer can into recycling, gave my dogs a Cheweez, and then watched some more of my TiVo.

No one had called since I'd arrived two days ago. I thought about calling my mom, but I couldn't face her, Kat, or anyone else right now. I just wanted to be alone, to try to decide what to do.

* * * *

The next day was much the same for me, though I was sorer from the physical work. I hadn't had any more bleeding, so I concluded that my body was healing okay. I thought about calling Dr. Camlyn to ask his ideas about why the miscarriage had happened, but I didn't want to talk to him, either. Some of that was pure anger, because he had to have an inkling of what Danial had been up to. Why hadn't he said something to me? Didn't he have a professional code of ethics that would make him notify me? Maybe not. No doctor automatically called and told men that their lovers or wives had stopped taking birth control pills. It was the same thing, I guessed, in a way.

The next day was the same, and the next. Despite my anger with Danial, I wondered what he was doing, if he was thinking as I was, deciding what he wanted, or if he was missing me as much as I missed him. I assumed he'd gone back to work, now that our honeymoon had fallen through. I picked up the phone to call him a few times, but never dialed. I wasn't done thinking yet.

* * * *

That Friday night, a little after five p.m., I was outside on my deck, gloomily thinking that this was the first Friday I had spent alone in two months. I told myself I was doing okay, even if I was miserable. After all, I wasn't inside crying, or listening to sad songs, I was out here, getting some air and listening to the trees creak in the wind.

For being the end of December, the weather was almost balmy. A warming trend had happened, melting the deep snow I'd struggled in at the beginning of the week. I was actually enjoying being out here on my deck, in my heavy jacket, watching the sunset. Or what was left of it by the time I'd walked the dogs, and gotten a load of wood. Ghost and Darkness were lying at my feet. Every so often, we would hear a shot in the woods as the last small game hunters reconnoitered for the day. All hunting save coyote ended at sunset, but there were always a few people who stayed too long in the woods, either on accident or on purpose.

As the light faded and the stars came out, the shots ceased. The screech of an owl sounded far off in the woods, echoing like a woman's scream. Unnerved for some reason, I decided to go in. There was no point waiting out here in hope that Danial would show up with flowers and the biggest apology this side of the county.

Much to my surprise, I was suddenly proven wrong when a dark colored truck suddenly pulled into my driveway. Hope rose within me that it was Danial. I quickly squashed it. I was the one who'd told him to stay away from me; who'd said I needed time apart. Talk about weak will. Did I really want to have another fight, or worse, be dragged back to him if this was Theo?

The truck idled in my drive, but no one got out.

Could it be Cia, come for a visit? I hadn't heard from her since I'd told Danial it was over. She'd clearly thought that I was making the wrong choice, and was withholding her friendship. Upset with that conclusion, I told myself to give her the benefit of the doubt. Maybe she'd wanted to see me, but Danial had forbade it. She and the rest of the foxes seemed to do anything he asked them to with no protest. Or maybe she just didn't want to get in the middle of it. It had only been a few days now I'd been gone. She might think it was just a tiff, something we just needed to talk over. If only it had been…

No one had yet emerged from the truck. Ghost and Darkness were motionless, watching raptly, the latter growling softly. I began to get uneasy. Too much had happened to me since knowing Danial. A stranger in my driveway could be more than someone needing directions because they were lost; the person could be a killer looking for Danial.

I fingered the fox head on my choker. The collar and scars I wore labeled me as someone important to Danial. If the person—possibly persons—in the truck knew what the choker or the scars meant and were after Danial, they'd be after me, too. That Danial and I were taking some time apart wouldn't matter. A heavy weight settled on my heart, knowing I'd be wondering the same thing about every stranger for the rest of my days.

"Sarelle?"

I jumped, letting out a shriek, and stumbled over Darkness, who was trying to get to her feet along with Ghost. I fell but strong arms caught me, as looked up to see the grinning face of Terian.

Chapter Four

Both dogs barked, wagging their tails happily. I got my feet under me, as Terian released his hold.

"What are you doing here?" I said grumpily. "How'd you get from the truck to here without me seeing you?"

"I can move fast when I want to," he replied with a wide smile. "But what are you doing here all alone in the dark?"

"Being alone," I said with a sigh.

Terian's grin faded. "Sarelle, what's wrong?"

I tried to get a breath to tell him what had happened, but I didn't know where to start. "A lot."

"Is Danial here?"

"No. And he's not likely to be anytime soon," I said sadly, wiping away a tear.

"What did he do to you, Sar? Did he hurt you?" Terian was radiating heat now, some of the unearthly evil leaking out from him. Concern and worry was etched into his features. "Terian, it's okay." I took a deep breath. "Danial and I, we're just taking some time apart. We moved a little too fast. Some of that was my fault—"

"I'm sorry, Sar." Terian clasped me to his chest, hugging me.

I was uneasy, but his arms were comforting, so I hugged him back tentatively. By degrees, he grew cooler, as the dark feeling faded from around us.

"Terian, you can let me go now," I said finally. "I'm okay."

He opened his arms reluctantly, and let me go. "Sorry. Hope I didn't squeeze too hard."

"No. But what are you doing here?" I replied. "I thought you were going to leave for a few months? It's only been what, one month?"

"Should I not have come?" Terian said seriously. "I saw you here alone with no guards on the porch, so I thought it was okay to stop in."

If Danial had said that, I'd have known he was being sarcastic. Terian, however, actually seemed to wonder if I'd welcome him. Big surprise, after the way I'd treated him at the fabrication shop that night he'd stopped by work to see me. Back then, I'd been under pressure from Danial not to see him, and his taking me hostage had seemed the worst thing in the world. Now, I was grateful for the distraction of Terian's company, even if he was part demon.

I gave him a smile. "I'm happy to see you. Come on in, if you want?"

A smile broke out over his face. "Sure. That's why I came."

Terian turned off his truck's ignition, and we went inside. I gave the dogs Cheweez and they settled down happily to munching.

"So tell me why you're here and not wherever you were planning to go?" I asked, sitting on the couch.

Terian sat down on the other end. "I decided to put it off," he said. "I had to come and see you right away."

"What's wrong?" I said, sitting up in alarm.

"Sar, I'm sorry to tell you this, but from what I was able to tell, those potions I made for Danial…well…um…"

I decided to help Terian out, since I had an inkling of what he was going to say. "You're going to tell me that they were fertility potions for Danial. That he was planning to try to get me pregnant."

"Sar, I'm sorry. I didn't know that they could be used for that when I made them."

"Don't be sorry, Terian. It's not your fault. I'm the one who told you that it was okay. I'm the one who believed Danial." My words were flat and empty. I'd certainly cried enough tears over the past week to get them that way.

"Did they work?" Terian asked. "Did you, um, you know?"

"Yes," I said. "But I lost it."

"I'm so sorry," Terian said sadly. "I didn't want anything to happen to you, Sar. Not from something I created."

"Tell me the truth, Terian, if you know it. Would having Danial's baby have hurt me?"

Terian looked at me as if he was considering what to tell me.

"Terian, spit it out—"

"Sarelle, do you really want the truth? Once I tell you, you might regret knowing. It might be better to—"

"Tell me."

Terian took a deep breath. "So far as I can tell from what little I was able to find out, you would not have been hurt. The baby would have been born a normal child. Only later on would its dual nature present itself, when it went through adolescence possibly." Terian took my hand in his. "What happened to my mother would not have happened to you."

Relief washed over me. I sank back onto the couch limply. "Thank you for telling me that, Terian."

"Does it make you feel better, Sar? You could have had a child with Danial. It's possible that you still can."

"If it would have been so easy, why are you so relieved that I didn't? Why did you break your plans to come here and warn me?"

"Because I knew you didn't know what he was planning. If you had, you would have mentioned it when I asked you about the potions that night I came to you. It's one thing to make a child you want, and another to end up with one that you didn't plan on. Especially one that's half vampire."

"Why couldn't he have asked me, Terian?" I said loudly, my anger getting the better of me. "Why didn't he tell me?"

"What did he tell you?" Terian replied.

"He said that I only had so many years to have a child. That I might reconsider, and it might be too late. That if we didn't start trying now, there wouldn't be time enough later."

"I understand his fear," Terian said softly. "Years pass by so fast—"

"Are you taking his side?" I asked Terian incredulously.

"Sar, I'm on your side, always," Terian assured. He gave my hand a squeeze. I hadn't realized he was still holding it. "But I'm immortal, too. I can't have children without risking the mother's life. I know I'd have given a lot, if my brother had had a child." He paused. "I miss him a lot. He was my only living relative. I'm lonely now like I wasn't before."

I clasped his hand and said nothing.

"Have you had dinner?" Terian asked suddenly.

"Not yet," I replied.

"Want to go out with me and get some?" Terian asked.

I started to say no, and then thought, what the hell. "Sure, let me get my coat."

31

I grabbed my coat, and locked up. As we walked to Terian's truck, I stated, "I'm paying my way."

"Okay."

He clicked open the doors with his keychain, and we got in. I remembered that he'd been driving a small Chevy when I'd seen him last. This was a full size Chevy, with four-wheel drive.

"This is a nice truck, Terian," I said, running my hand over the dash appreciatively.

"I know you're wondering how I can afford it, Sarelle. You can say it."

He smiled at me, looking out of the corner of his eyes as he drove off. I laughed, and felt better for the first time in a week.

"So tell me, Terian. How did you afford this?"

"I've suddenly been made a moderately rich man."

"Really! That's great! How did you manage that?" I asked.

Terian looked at me out of the corner of his eye. "Danial paid me three quarters of a million dollars for those two potions. That was my cut for making them. The other alchemists got a quarter million, to split."

I was shocked into silence. We rode that way for a while.

Finally, I managed to say, "Why would he have spent so much money on potions that he wasn't sure would work for a baby I might never agree to have?"

Terian was silent so long I thought he wasn't going to answer. When we pulled up to the restaurant, Terian shut off the truck, but didn't get out.

"Sarelle, he did it because he loved you. The money was nothing to him compared to what he might gain. It was a risk he was willing to pay dearly to take. That much should be obvious."

Terian got out of the truck without saying another word and I followed him silently, thinking over his words.

As he held the door, the name on it registered with me. He'd brought me to a restaurant that I had come to a lot with my late husband. I paused there on the threshold, uneasy.

"Is this okay?" Terian asked, looking at me quizzically. "We could go somewhere else."

I hadn't been back since Brennan had died. But the food had always been good, and Brennan and I, we'd had a lot of good times here together.

"It will be fine," I said with a smile, crossing the threshold. "Come on."

Dinner was nice. It was ordinary fun, just two normal people out for an evening. We had a large pizza and salads, with some soft drinks on the side, seasoned with some casual conversation, and some that was non-casual. Terian wanted to know how I'd been. I related the tale of the party, about being cursed, and Stephen taking them off me.

"—compliments of Dr. Stephen," I finished. "He's a good doctor."

"They actually call him Dr. Camlyn. Stephen is his first name."

"I know that," I said crossly, irritated at my mistake, then did a double take. "You know him?" I said, surprised.

"Sure," Terian said. "He is the best doctor for paranormal beings around. After Danial and I fought, I made an appointment to get checked out, to make sure I really was part demon. Tests that Stephen ran confirmed it. He is the one who hooked me up with the optometrist who fitted me with the contacts."

I looked into his eyes of cherry wood. "He made a good choice. Very complimentary."

Terian actually blushed, which I found endearing. "Thanks."

"Tell me about yourself, Terian. Except for what you had to go through with Danial and Alexa, I don't know anything about you. You have an online shop?"

"Yes." He told me some of the weird things that he got requests for, explaining more about what he did for a living. Terian's shop was an online order business, specializing in hard to manufacture potions. He catered primarily to a very rich clientele for its bread and butter, as they were the ones that could afford the more expensive spells.

"You don't sell potions that poison or kill though, right?" I said uneasily. "Curses?"

"No, Sar," Terian said seriously. "I do get requests for them, sure. If I agreed to make all the ones I get requests for, I'd easily have double the money Danial gave me. I try to sell only spells that are used to help, like luck potions, or are basic enough to be non-threatening. I also demand the name of the buyer, and check them out before I agree to make what they want. Sometimes a potion that is seemingly innocent can be used to hurt someone else. Most of the time though, my clients want something to impress their spouse or their friends for a party. Temporary magic, with an expiration date. They want to grow wings, have red skin, levitate, or create fire from their fingertips. Stuff like that."

"Halloween must be your big time."

"You'd think so, but I get a lot of these requests other times of the year. The summer is actually a hot time for my business, and Christmas."

That was surprising, but there were a lot of bored rich people. Curiosity probably motivated a lot of purchases also. I wanted to know what it would be like to sprout wings myself.

I ate a last bite of pizza, and the waitress came with the bill. Terian grabbed it, and handed her some money despite my protests.

"Hey," I said, frowning. "I was paying my half."

"You can treat next time, Sar." Terian grinned at me. "Are you busy tomorrow night?"

Tomorrow was New Year's Eve. I found myself grinning back. "You're on."

Later that night, I questioned if seeing Terian tomorrow was the right thing to do. I rationalized that I really needed casual conversation with a friend who knew about everything I was going through with Danial. I didn't have to pretend with him. Not having to cook was also a big plus.

* * * *

Terian showed up at my door at about seven p.m., this time with some Chinese takeout for both of us. I paid him for the food, despite his protesting. We ate, as he related a funny story about some people he'd heard from today online who'd wanted rush orders for tonight.

"I told them becoming a lion wasn't possible, not on such short notice. So they asked what they could get and I told them that the best I could do was a sheep."

"Did they take it?"

"No," he laughed. "They settled for a much less expensive spell to grow claws. I hope they look at the container. It takes several hours to wear off."

"It's going to be hard to hold things," I replied. "I can't imagine just having normal long nails."

Terian moved closer to me and handed me a small vial with some dark liquid in it. I looked for a label, but the vial was blank. He had made me one of his potions.

"What's this do?" I asked.

"You wanted to know about my spell casting, so I made this for you," he said easily, giving me a smile. "You need some cheering up."

"What do I do, just drink it?" I said dubiously.

"Yes," he said, looking me over. "But you should take off your sweater before you do. Just leave on the tank top you're wearing."

Did I trust him enough to swallow whatever was in there, and to take off my clothes? I looked at him with raised eyebrows.

"Go ahead," he said. "Trust me."

I downed the contents of the glass, and then quickly took off my sweater. "I don't feel any differently. What's supposed to happen?"

Terian grinned from ear to ear at me. "Look over your shoulder, Sar."

I turned, watching in disbelief as a pair of bat-like wings sprouted from my back. They quickly grew to about seven feet long. This was why Terian had warned me before we started. I would have burst my sweater open.

"Can I fly?" I said excitedly.

"Sorry, Sarelle, these are just for show. But you can move them."

"How?" I said, trying and failing.

"Think about moving one, in the way you'd move your hand."

I concentrated and my right wing flapped. Wow, this was great! I laughed and he laughed with me.

"Now the other," Terian instructed.

I got the left one to flap too. "This is incredible!"

"Now do both together. Wait! We'd better go outside. The wind you create will knock over lamps and things."

We went out on the deck, carefully maneuvering me through the door. I flapped with all my might and rose off the ground. I did it a few more times, and then Terian cautioned me to stop.

"You don't have real wings, Sar. Exercising them will not make them get stronger."

As I stood there, the wings faded away. I almost fell over from the loss of weight affecting my balance. Terian caught me, quickly steadying me.

"I'm tired," I said yawning. "But that was great."

Terian nodded. "It's the spell. It takes a lot of your energy to move big wings. You'll be fine, but you should sit down for a while."

We walked inside, and I shut off the outdoor lights. I yawned again.

"Sorry, Sar. I should have warned you not to use them that much.

Those were really just for show, like a costume."

I turned to him. "Can you make real ones? Not for me, though it was fun, but flying is such a common dream. I imagine you get requests for some?"

"Yes. Real wings have enough strength to really lift you in the air. So it's creating both the wings and the muscles to move them. Old magic, Sar. Expensive stuff."

I assumed in the way he'd said it that the cost was close to what Danial had paid for his potions. I didn't want to think about Danial. My brief joy faded.

As we moved past the front yard window, Terian stopped.

"What is it?" I asked him.

"Someone is out there," he said angrily. "Someone is out there watching us."

Blackness coiled out from him as he stood there. I looked out the window, and noticed a figure standing outside, just at the edge of the barn. I knew that familiar silhouette: Theo.

I debated going out to talk with him, but he knew where I was. He could come to the door if he wanted to talk to me; I was not going to walk all the way to the barn to find out what he wanted.

Terian watched for a moment, then headed for the door with a purpose.

"What are you going to do?" I asked.

"I'm going to go and see what he wants," said Terian, his words hot with anger.

I watched as Terian walked all the way to the barn, but by then he was too far way to see clearly, especially in the poor light with the corral in the way. I busied myself building up the fire tossing out Terian's empty containers, and putting away my uneaten Chinese food while I waited for him to return.

Ten minutes later, there was a thump as the door opened. Terian came in, knocking a little snow off his boots.

"Well?" I said.

"He was there," Terian said. "But he took off by the time I arrived at the place he had been."

"He's probably watching me for Danial. I don't think he believes I'm coming back, even though we're oathed."

He looked at me for a long moment, then turned and went to the door. "I'd better be going," he said, putting on his coat. "Thanks for tonight."

"Terian," I said, confused. "You don't have to leave—"

"Sar, I don't want to get you in trouble. Theo's clearly watching you for Danial. And you just told me that you are oathed. So I'm better off leaving now." Terian went out the door.

I followed him. "What's wrong?"

"Nothing's wrong," he said, stepping fast to his truck.

"Something is wrong, Terian," I said, exasperated. "Tell me why you have to leave?"

Terian turned suddenly, and pulled me into his arms. I looked up at him with wide eyes.

"This is why."

He brought his mouth down on mine, his hands tangling in my hair. His kiss was not soft; it was full of need and longing. In shock, I stood there and let him kiss me, one moment stretching into the next with exquisite slowness.

Terian had been warm to start with, but by the time he was finished, he was almost too hot to touch. He looked into my eyes for a long moment afterward, and I saw what he wanted me to see there. There was more than friendly affection in his eyes; there was desire.

"Sar, I like you. A lot, actually. I wanted to be with you. But now that you're taken, there is no way it will ever happen. Danial will never release you from your oath—"

"What?" I gasped. "I thought there was no breaking it, ever."

"He can release you, Sar. It's true that it's almost never done. Vampires, like others, rarely want to relinquish what is theirs. I wouldn't release you either, if you were mine."

That last Terian whispered in my ear, his radiant heat bathing me in warmth. He drew back, looking at me hopefully. "Do you feel the same for me, Sar? Could you ever look at me and see a man and not a friend?"

I cared enough about him not to lie to him. "No," I whispered, my answer seeming very loud in the night air. "I'm sorry, Terian. I don't think of you as more than a friend. I don't think I ever will."

He held me close, hugging me. "Thank you for telling me the truth." Terian pulled back from me and met my gaze. His eyes were sad and resigned. "Do you understand now why I have to leave?"

I understood Terian's point all too well. He needed to be away from me so he could love someone else. I wasn't available, and even if I was, I wasn't in love with him; I was in love with Danial. "Yes," I said, nodding. "Please take care of yourself, Terian."

Terian kissed me gently on the forehead. Then he stepped away from me, and got back in the truck. "Good-bye, Sarelle."

I waved to him as he left, and then turned around and walked back to the house, where my dogs welcomed me back inside. I gave them another treat. What the hell, it was New Year's, someone might as well be happy.

I got a bottle of Black Opal shiraz, and opened it. After poured myself a large glass, I settled down to watch an old episode of FX's Damages. I was through almost all of both when the doorbell rang.

Chapter Five

Shit. I knew who that was. I went to the door, and sure enough, there was Theo.

"Please come in," I said sarcastically. "You've been waiting long enough outside."

He said nothing as he pushed past me. I took his coat, and hung it up on an empty peg near the door. Then I went back into the living room, grabbed up my wine glass, and sat back on the couch. Theo took up a stance directly in front of me, his hands folded over his chest, a cold look in his icy blue eyes. He was clearly in one of his moods, spoiling for a fight.

Great. After Terian's big revelation, this was just what I needed. "Want some wine?" I asked finally.

"No, Sar," he said, glaring at me. "I'm here to bring you back to Danial."

I looked at him for a long moment. "I'm not going," I replied, taking a sip of my wine.

"You'll go if I have to drag you," Theo growled at me.

"You're angry," I said conversationally. "Why?"

"You're oathed," he spat back at me.

Here we go again. "Theo, if you spent a little more time talking and a little less spying, you might know what the hell you're talking about some of the time," I said nastily.

"Fine, Sar, then why were you kissing another man? It's been less than a week since you gave Danial your oath." Theo wasn't angry, he was utterly furious.

"If you were really watching, you'd know I didn't kiss him, dumbass. He kissed me. He told me he cared for me. I told him I was oathed, that I didn't love him, and that I was sorry. He said he was leaving and he left. End of story."

Okay, it hadn't happened exactly like that, but that was the gist. I was the one who'd been too dumb to see Terian liked me.

"You don't care for him?" Theo accused, eyes narrowed. "You don't desire him?"

"I care for him the way I care for you, Theo. He's a friend. I'm not in love with him. Why don't you sit the hell down and stop overreacting?"

Theo was taken aback. I snorted, then went and refilled my glass.

"Sar, please pour me a glass too," Theo said after a moment, his shoulders relaxing.

I got down another glass from the cupboard, and poured him one. "I hope you like dry reds," I warned as I handed it to him.

"It doesn't matter," Theo replied letting out a breath. "I'm not picky. I need a drink."

We sat down on the couch, he at one end and I at the other. I put my feet up.

"So what's up your ass tonight?" I said conversationally. "You come in here full of accusations based on what? One kiss?"

"I'm sorry, Sarelle. From my vantage point, it did look like what you described happened. But when I saw you kiss him back, I thought that it might be more than that."

"Theo, if I wanted Terian I would never have oathed to Danial. I don't fall in and out of love so quickly. Do you know how long I agonized over oathing to Danial? How many times I went back over the pros and cons, how many times I wanted to say yes before I finally said it? Terian deserved a kiss from me, just for telling me tonight that Danial could remove me from my oath. That is yet another thing Danial neglected to tell me." I fixed him with my eyes. "Something you neglected to tell me, too, by the way."

Theo opened his mouth. I held up my hand, stopping him.

"I don't want that. But Danial told me that the oath was forever, that once given it couldn't be broken by anyone. It's another truth he distorted."

Theo was silent. I sipped my wine until I couldn't stand his silence any longer.

"Why are you out here spying on me anyway, Theo? Are you really here to drag me back to Danial? To punish me for misconduct? What?" I said wearily.

"I'm here because you punched Devlin," Theo said.

I raised my eyebrows, but said nothing. "And that means what?"

"You hit him for Cia. I think of the werefoxes as my family, but I could never take action against Devlin, not without getting killed in retaliation. Danial possibly could have, but he never did, except for when Devlin went after you. But you didn't care about any of the rules or risks, you hit him anyway. That matters to me. So I came to ask you to come back home with me, tonight. Because sooner or later, Danial will send me to come and bring you back to him, and I don't want to have to do that to you."

Theo sipped his wine, as I considered his words.

"I can't go back with you," I said finally. "Not yet, Theo. I'm still trying to decide what to do."

"What can you do, Sar? You are his. I told you that. He won't release you, not ever."

I hoped he was not remembering Neoline, a past love of his who had oathed to an evil vampire called Gareth, only to beg for the release of death when she found out what a bastard he was.

"I meant I have choices to make. Do I tell Danial it's okay, that we can try to have a child? Do I tell him he has to wear protection from now on or have tests? Or do I say no way, I came close enough to dying already? I made an appointment with a doctor for next week, to find out if what happened was because there is something wrong with me. It may be me who can't have a child."

Theo was silent, watching me.

"And then there's the deeper issue: that he tells me whatever best suits him for whatever plans he decides are best. I don't know if I can live with that, no matter how much I love him. I can't go back until I decide."

Theo's glass was empty, so I poured us both another half glass.

Theo rolled his eyes. "Sar, I have to drive, you know."

"I have a spare bedroom below if you need it, drunkard. By the way, where is Suri?"

"I saw you leave, Sar. When I came in, Danial was on the couch. He wouldn't say anything, except that you needed some time to be alone. So I stopped Suri before she left, and told her you were coming here to do some mental recovery, and needed to be alone."

"You had to phrase it like that." I rolled my eyes, then remembered something else I needed to say to Theo that was overdue. "By the way, I've been meaning to tell you, Theo, that I'm pissed off about your bullshit non-warning the night of the Hallow's party. Remember how you told me about how I might need to perform as a hostess? You clearly knew what was going to happen. Why didn't you warn me I'd get bit?"

"If I had told you, you wouldn't have done it, and Danial needed you there beside him. The same way he needs you now. You need him, too. Come back with me."

"Theo, if you're so sure we're right for each other, why did you say to Danial in the car that night that we would not end well?"

I had never asked him before; I'd been too afraid to. Was he drunk enough to tell me now?

"I told you, Sarelle. Danial can't change who he is. He needs sometimes to take without asking, to possess something utterly. I could see from the first that you were a woman who needs to be asked. It was easy to see there were going to be problems."

We were on a roll. I might as well keep asking questions, as long as he was talking. "When did Danial start planning to get me pregnant?"

"I can't answer that. He talked about you that first night after you saved him. We were all worried, especially when we hadn't heard from him for almost three days. We tried calling his cell, but it was out of service. We found it later, destroyed. When he finally called in and told us the story—what you'd done for him—it seemed ludicrous. What woman would do that for a stranger…um, no offense, Sar—"

I was offended, but I had done the ludicrous, so it was my own fault. "It's okay. Go on."

"When he couldn't feed off of you metaphysically, he was really intrigued. Right afterwards, he had the choker made and he began talking of you as being more than someone he was grateful to. He was so happy he'd met you, that you knew what he was and you accepted it—"

That was enough. I didn't want to hear about Danial falling in love with me. It just made me want to be with him more, to be back in his arms.

"Why don't my dogs like you the way they like the foxes?" I interrupted. "They would never have gone after Cia, not even if I asked them to. Even now, they are watching you uneasily."

"They sense the cat in me. It's not like the cat they know, and it's strange enough that it makes them nervous. Foxes are members of the canine family, they are closer kin. Or I don't know, maybe they just don't like me?"

Theo finished off his wine. I poured him a little more, and also some for myself, finishing the bottle. I checked the clock. It was about eleven thirty. New Year's would be here soon.

"I saw you with the wings, Sar," Theo said quietly. "What was it like?"

I smiled, remembering moving them. How to describe it? "It was wonderful, probably like what you feel when you change—"

"I get no pleasure from changing, Sar. I hate it," Theo said abruptly.

I remembered Cia's words, about how Theo tried not to change form at all. Shit. I'd put my foot in it again. Why hadn't I remembered? I wanted to know suddenly why he didn't like changing, when all the foxes I talked to embraced it fully. They all seemed to revel in it, enjoy it. Why didn't he?

"Why don't you like yourself?" I asked bluntly.

"Because I'm alone. Because I'm hunted if anyone sees me. If I were a fox, I could blend in a little. People might notice, but they wouldn't go for their guns, or alert the media—"

"Why not leave the area? Go to Europe, and be with Tawny?" The words just came out. I held my breath, waiting to hear his answer.

"I'm bound to Danial, Sar. I may not be oathed like you, but I like my job. I like the foxes. This is my home. I have a sort of peace."

He didn't sound very peaceful to me. Maybe I was being too judgmental.

"But to change into a mountain lion," I said softly. "It must be so exhilarating—"

"Don't compare yourself to me, Sar," Theo growled. "You have no idea what I feel, what I care about, what I want out of life—"

"I'm not, Theo. I like myself," I spat back to him. "I don't pretend to be what I'm not!"

"You want to see, Sar? See what I become?" Theo stood up in a violent motion, knocking over the table and the glasses that had been on it. I lunged to stop them spilling, and he grabbed me roughly, pushing me against the wall. I hit the wall with an "Oof!" A picture to the left of me fell off the wall, clattering to the floor.

43

"Theo!" I yelled. "What the hell are you doing?"

Both dogs were growling low, snarling at him.

"Look at me," Theo whispered.

His eyes turned light yellow, the pupils reforming to sharp ended ovals. Theo snarled at me, showing long fangs, longer than Danial's. His nails were reforming into claws, growing and curling, digging into my forearms.

"Ow!" I yelled.

"I want you to see!" he snarled.

His body was jerking underneath his shirt, every inch moving unnaturally. I was in deep shit now.

"Theo, stop!" I screamed.

He threw his head back and roared. The sound was wild, sending chills down my body.

My dogs were growling and snapping, but they didn't dare get too close.

I did the only thing I could think of. I reached my hands into his hair, and pulled his mouth down on mine. I kissed him as hard as I could, willing it to break the change and stop what he was becoming.

He went still for a second, and then pushed me against the wall with enough force to crack it. Dust landed on my shoulders. He kissed me back, his arms tightening around me. His fangs grazed my mouth, but I ignored the pain and kept kissing. He kissed me like a drowning man drinks in that first real gasp of air, and I responded to him, kissing him back that way. He pressed me to the wall with his body, and I felt him against me, hard and ready. In that moment, I knew I wanted him.

Stop, Sar. It doesn't matter what you feel this is wrong! You can't do this. Not to Danial and not to Theo.

"Theo," I said breathily, breaking the kiss. "Stop, please. Please!"

We were both breathing heavily. But his eyes were back to blue, his hands normal again.

"Theo, you aren't a monster. And you aren't alone," I said between breaths. "You are the one I depend on, the one who always tells me the truth, no matter how much I hate to hear it. When I thought I was dying, you held me. Your calmness, your strength got me through it. You are the only one who never wanted anything from me, never asked me for anything. I'm not afraid of you. I trust you, Theo. I trust you with my life. Don't hurt me now."

Theo had been silent through all this, watching me. His eyes were guarded, the same way they'd been when I'd asked him to turn me. There was only one key difference; tonight they were dark with lust, like a thundercloud.

As we stared at each other, the grandfather clock struck twelve and began to chime.

"Happy New Year, Theo," I said softly, trying to lighten the moment. "Why don't we call it a night and—"

Theo kissed me again, cutting off my words and slamming me back up against the wall. Another picture fell off, this one breaking its glass. More dust rained down on me. He no longer had fangs, but his kisses were so rough they almost hurt. His tongue darted into my mouth suddenly, and I gasped. He liked that, letting out a groan and again pressing himself to me, grinding his hips against mine as he kissed me. His arms were on either side of me, trapping me, holding me against the wall.

"Sar," he groaned between kisses. "Oh, Sar."

I could hear how much he wanted me. In that moment, I wanted to give in to him more than anything. He felt so good…

No, I could not, would not, do this. "Theo, stop!" I yelled, breaking my mouth away from his.

He finally stopped kissing me.

"We cannot do this. I gave my word." I was starting to shake a little. "I'm oathed!"

Theo lowered his head, breathing hard. A tremor went through him. He made a sound—almost a growl—that rode the edge of pleasure and pain.

"You kissed me, Sar," Theo said, letting out a breath. "I felt your desire—"

"To stop you from changing. To let you know that I care about you and I don't want you to hate yourself. I didn't know what else to do to make you listen!"

"I felt heat in your kiss, Sar," Theo growled, looking into my eyes with his blue ones. "I felt you wanting me."

I closed my eyes so I wouldn't have to see him. Yet his body was still pressed against mine, his heartbeat pounding fast, as fast as mine was pounding. I felt him raise one hand. I opened my eyes when his fingers dug into my face.

"Look at me, Sar," Theo snarled, "and tell me you don't want me. Because I want you."

I met his eyes and had tremors of my own. I wanted him more than anything. Some of it was the wine, some of it was all that I'd gone through with Danial this week and now Terian tonight. Some of me just wanted to know what Tawny had meant when she said "the best night ever." And some part of me loved him; loved his sense of humor, how he'd been there when I needed him, how he'd never let me down. But all of that together didn't make this right.

"Sar—" Theo growled.

"Okay, I want you! I do! But what about after it's over, when we're sitting here naked and wondering what to tell Danial? You're his most trusted friend. I'm promised to him. What are we going to tell him, Theo? That we wanted one another? That that was the reason we trashed three lives? This is wrong, and you know it!"

Theo abruptly let me go. He turned from me, picked up the wineglasses, stuck them on the kitchen counter, and left the room. I righted the table, then followed him.

He went to the door, and opened it.

"Theo—"

"Sar, do not say one word. Not one. All I can think about is how your body felt against mine. I hear your voice one more time, so help me God, I will have you right here on the floor and everything and everyone else can go to Hell."

I abruptly shut up. He left, slamming the door behind him.

I was shaking badly now. Unsteadily, I went to the nearest chair, and sank down.

Chapter Six

God, that had been close. I had wanted him so badly. What the hell had gotten into me?

The main thing was we'd stopped in time. We hadn't done anything that we'd regret in the morning. Yet the feel of him, his hard body against mine, his mouth against mine…

Stop, Sar. It's late. Go clean up the mess and think about this later.

I let out a deep breath, then went in to survey the living room. I quickly cleaned up where a little wine had spilled on the couch and the rug. Deciding the rest would have to wait until morning, I let the dogs out and went to bed.

The phone rang about five minutes after I fell asleep.

I picked it up. "Hello?"

It was Theo, sounding contrite. "Sar, I'm sorry for what happened. What I said and did."

"It was my fault, Theo. I gave you the wine—"

"I didn't do and say what I did and said because of a little wine, Sar," he said gruffly.

Oh…yow. I mentally wiped that thought off my tongue before it spilled out. "Nothing happened, Theo. No one needs to know. I told you I trusted you and I do."

"Something did happen, Sar. Danial needs to know about it, and that it was you, not me, who stopped it. He trusts me and maybe he shouldn't. Maybe you shouldn't."

"Are you going to do it again?" I asked him hesitantly.

He knew what I meant. "No. I won't let myself get out of hand again with you. If I hadn't started to change, you would never have kissed me. I never would have kissed you if you hadn't kissed me first."

"Look, Theo, Danial is going to be mad enough hearing from you about Terian kissing me, and that was innocent. He is going to be furious about this, especially if you tell him I wanted you, you wanted me back, and we nearly did something we'd both regret. You are his good friend, his best friend. We have enough problems. Don't say anything."

Theo sighed. "I'll think about it, Sar, but it's not in my nature to lie."

"I know," I said, sighing myself "That's what I find so attractive about you."

"That's it?" he said with innuendo.

I laughed, then fell silent, a hot blush staining my cheeks.

"Good-bye, Sar," he said softly, and hung up.

I replaced the receiver, crawled back in bed, and fell asleep.

* * * *

That night I dreamed of Theo, of our scene at the door. Instead of keeping quiet, this time I spoke.

"Theo," I said softly. "Don't go."

He went still, the open door in his hand. He turned in a lunge and was holding me before I knew he'd moved, pushing me to the floor as we fumbled with our clothes. He kissed me roughly, as he threw off his jacket and tore off his shirt. His chest was covered in soft golden hair, and I ran my fingers through it, splaying them across his skin. He groaned at my touch, and shuddered. He rolled off me to take off his pants, and I shed mine too, pulling my tank top and sport bra over my head. He was on me again in a few second, kissing me, touching my breasts. He was hard all over, coiled muscle and warm skin. I felt the weight of him on me lessen as he pushed up from me, felt his fingers sliding into me, moving inside me. I thrust up, meeting his eyes. I'd never seen them so dark, like the sky at twilight. I put my arms around his neck, and pulled him down to kiss me deeply. I opened my mouth to him, licking him eagerly. He almost crushed me then, his arms on either side of me, his body fully atop mine.

I felt him against my leg, nudging me, and I opened my legs so he could slide between them. He wasn't gentle. He thrust himself into me hard, and I cried out. He found his rhythm quickly, hammering himself into me as his mouth devoured mine. In a few seconds, it was over as he roared out his pleasure, his straining body suddenly going limp on mine.

I drew a shaky breath. Theo rolled over on his back, holding me tightly. His chest rose and fell beneath me. I felt his heartbeat again with my fingertips, strong and fast. Then the magnitude of what I'd done hit me, and I began to cry.

"Sar, please don't cry," Theo said gently.

I cried harder.

He picked me up, brought me into my bedroom, and laid me beneath the covers. He got in beside me and held me. I got myself under control in a few moments.

"Sar, was I that bad?" Theo said, humor in his eyes.

"Theo, *how* can you joke now of all times, after we just—" I started.

Theo rolled me over, laying his form atop mine again. He stayed there, motionless, then moved his hips once, suggestively rubbing. He kissed me roughly, and I let myself melt against the heat of him, parting my thighs. He slid inside me at once, and I let out a whimper. He stopped abruptly, his eyes staring into mine.

"Sar, do you know how long I've wanted to be with you like this, just like this? To feel you under me, surrounding me? I was able to deny it, knowing you didn't love me, that you would never touch me in any way that might be other than friendly. That you would reject me, and be shocked if I told you how I felt. But when you kissed me, I couldn't stand it any longer, to have you so close and not to touch you. It was so hard for me, seeing you every day, and knowing you were Danial's. That there would never come a time when we would be like this."

"When you were bleeding, and you asked me to change you, to make you like I was…I was going to do it, Sar. If Dr. Camlyn hadn't come in, I was going to do it, even though Danial would have been cnraged. Because once it was done, it couldn't be undone. Because if you were werecougar like me, then Danial would probably release you from your oath. He hates the taste of were blood. There are no other werecougars in the Northeast, Sar, none. Even if you felt nothing for me when you were human, once I'd changed you, your new nature would draw you to me, want me as male to your female. Then, even if you didn't love me, I could be with you." His eyes looked down into mine, and he said softly, "I'm in love with you, Sar."

I was crying again, this time for him. Because he was right; I wanted him, wanted him badly, but I didn't love him.

He kissed my tears away. Then he kissed me, and began moving inside me gently, insistently. He brought me, slowly building up the feeling until it washed over me, the wave of pleasure breaking over me so that I cried out, and into him as he covered my mouth with his. As my orgasm ebbed, he withdrew from me.

"You didn't—" I began.

"I will, don't worry," Theo said with a grin, though his eyes and tone were serious. "I just want you to know, I'll bear the brunt of the blame for this. For what has happened between us. And for what is going to happen between us again very soon."

"It was as much my fault as it was yours," I said, letting out a deep breath. "He'll—"

"Stop, Sar," he said, kissing me. "I'm not going to waste a moment of this night thinking about anything other than pleasing you and me. At dawn we'll deal with everything else."

I protested, but he kissed me into submission. Theo made love to me the rest of that night, stopping only for brief periods to rest and cuddle. Dawn came too quickly as we lay together holding each other. I was exhausted and sore. My body was mortal; it couldn't keep up with his.

"Sar?" a male voice called. "Are you home?"

Danial's voice.

Theo and I looked at each other, horrified that he should find us this way, naked, the smell of sex heavy in the air. My bedroom door started to open.

I shrieked loudly, falling out of my bed to land on the floor hard. I blinked awake to discover I was dressed in pajamas, alone. Dawn had come some hours ago, by the clock. Light was streaming in my bedroom windows.

I was alone.

"Thank you, thank you, thank you, God!" I panted, trying to control my breathing. My bed was a tangle; I'd been thrashing around all over last night. The pillows were everywhere, one somehow over by the far wall. I smelled of sexual excitement. Hell, I reeked of it.

I took a shower immediately, washing myself thoroughly. Getting out of the shower, I wrapped a robe around me. Quickly, I grabbed all of the bed linens, put them in the washing machine, and started it. Last, I sprayed some room fresher around my bedroom, and the smell dissipated.

It had just been a dream. What a relief.

I went out to see to the dogs, tensing up at the sight of Theo's jacket still hanging there by my door. I remembered how he'd felt against me last night in the flesh, sequences of my dream rising unbidden of his body against mine, sliding into me so deftly. The smell of his skin; slightly musky, mixed with the scents of earth and trees and wide blue skies.

Transfixed, I went over and smelled the jacket. It smelled of blue skies, earth, and prairie. The same scent he'd had in the dream. The exact same scent.

I backed away, telling myself it was nothing. Then I put Theo out of my mind, reminding myself forcefully that I had work to do.

I took care of the dogs and cats first. Then I picked up the fallen pictures, wrapped the broken glass up, and threw it away. I'd have to replace the frame for one of them; its wood was cracked, too. The other picture was fine. I hung it back up. The wall also needed repair; it had a big crack in it, I assumed where my shoulders had hit it. Now it made sense why my upper back was stiff…

I put down my broom and dustpan, worriedly going to the bathroom. I eased off my robe and looked into the mirror.

Shit with a capital S. I had bruises all over me, the darkest on my back from hitting the wall several times. On my shoulders, there were lighter ones from Theo's arms, when he had held me so tightly. I had light bruises on my face and neck, where he had forced me to look at him. I had one much smaller and lighter by my top lip, from where he had kissed me so hard. There were also bruises on my legs, but those weren't unusual; I'd made them myself, carrying and stacking wood.

I hoped no one would be coming to see me anytime soon. I needed to heal these, primarily the ones on my neck that were clearly from someone's hand holding my face.

I got dressed, and went about my day. What else could I do? I had to work tomorrow, and the house was not going to heat itself. Besides, I had a huge crack to patch and repaint.

* * * *

I heard nothing from Theo, Danial or anyone else that week. At work, I got caught up with a few things I'd been letting slide when I was considering quitting, putting in an extra two days. My boss said he was glad I was putting in so much time, but I could see he knew that I wasn't doing it because my life was going well.

The only day I didn't work, I went to the doctor's. Dr. Fremen was no Dr. Camlyn. He gave me a thorough checkup, and said I was completely okay, in terms of how everything looked. He saw the signs of my recent pregnancy, though, so I had to tell him that I'd miscarried, and had an emergency D &C under another doctor's care. He tested me as I requested for fertility, saying he'd let me know in a couple of months.

"I don't think that's a problem, Ms. McGarran. You got pregnant once after only a few months of intercourse, so your fertility should be fine."

"Is there any reason you know of why I might have miscarried?"

"There are a lot of possibilities: cells not dividing right, abnormal cells in the egg or sperm, stress, a uterine problem, etc. Sometimes it happens, and there doesn't seem to be any reason. A woman can have a miscarriage, and then pregnant again, and the next time everything is fine."

"What should I do?" I said. "I don't want to miscarry again."

"The only way to be sure that never happens is to not try to have a child," he said. "There is a chance every time of miscarriage. You have to decide if the risks are worth the possible gain."

That helped a lot. Not. "Dr. Fremen, what are the odds I'll miscarry if I get pregnant again? Give me some numbers." I wanted to yell, but I was being polite.

"Ms. McGarran, if you get pregnant again, you have no increased odds of miscarrying. From what you've told me, you were only pregnant a few weeks, maybe a month. We checked you out, and everything looks fine. I hate to say this, but it is most likely there was something wrong genetically with the baby. It had nothing to do with you, or the father." Dr. Fremen said this gently, but it still hurt me to hear it.

I got dressed and left, telling him I would call for the results. I was glad he hadn't noticed my bruises, but I'd covered the ones I couldn't hide with makeup. They had faded a bit, but the one on my back was still there, just as Theo's jacket was still hanging by my door.

* * * *

Friday night. It had been two weeks now since I had last seen Danial, a week since Theo and Terian had stopped by. I was adjusting back into my old routines; tending the fire, gathering wood, being up in the daylight and asleep all night. It was strange to me how fast my life could change. How fast I could adapt, even when my heart was still back in the life I'd had so briefly.

I was in bed reading, the dogs in their beds twitching and dreaming. Sometimes Ghost or Darkness would let out a little "woof…woof" as they barked in their dreams. It never failed to make me smile. Casting a look at the time, I chastised myself about how I should be sleeping, and not trying to finish my book. But even when I was exhausted and my eyes wouldn't stay open, I'd shut off the light, and instead of sleep, I'd start thinking about what a mess my life had become.

I was no closer to any decision about Danial. The incident with Theo had thrown a wrench into my careful columns of pros and cons. Now that I knew he desired me, how could I go back to viewing him as a simple friend and guard? A line had been drawn, and I didn't know how to erase it and go back to where we'd once been.

The phone rang.

It was after eleven. That meant the call probably was Danial and I'd be better off not answering. But I wasn't going to be afraid to answer my phone in my own home. There was always the possibility it was an emergency with a friend or family member.

The phone rang again. I got up and checked called ID. The number wasn't one I recognized. If it was a wrong number, whoever was on the other end was going to get a loud correction.

"Hello?" I said in my normal voice.

"Sarelle." It was Danial. If I didn't know better, I'd say he was drunk. Perhaps he was, if a vampire could be drunk on blood.

"Danial." I'd meant to be smart and sassy, yet I sounded anything but.

"I wanted to call you." He spoke quickly, too quickly.

This was going to be bad. I should have let the phone call ring through unanswered. "About what?"

"Can't you guess?" he said seriously.

I didn't know how much Theo had told him, but even if he only knew about Terian kissing me, it would be enough to make him furious. If he wasn't going to yell at me, he was going to do something worse. "No."

"Sar, I want you to know something. I am spending tonight with Erica. She's a beautiful twenty-year old woman. A law student even! She has the most beautiful dark hair, and eyes like the night sky. I wanted you to know that tonight I'm going to make love to her for hours—"

Danial went on, but I had stopped listening, though I didn't slam down the phone.

This was petty, mean, and such an obvious in your face slap that I should have gotten angry. But what he said cut me deeply. I didn't want to think of him with someone else. I could picture him with another woman easily. All he'd have to do was walk into a bar, and there'd be more than a couple women to pick from. Fuck, he didn't even have to leave his house. Angelica made house calls, and he could have her anytime he wanted her. All he'd have to do is ask her.

He was still talking, going on about the things he was going to do to her. I caught a bit of it, and was disgusted at his behavior. And this woman, wasn't she appalled too? I wouldn't have wanted to be used this way, to be just someone to have sex with to get back at someone else. That realization gave me the calmness to answer him.

"Sar, are you listening?" Danial said angrily.

Ah, there the anger was. "Danial, I have just one question. When you're done having sex, and you're about to take a nice long bath together, will she notice any tiny flecks floating in the water? And if she does, will she reach out to save the tiny life struggling to live? Or will she just remove it from her sight, and leave it to die alone by inches, because it's just a spider?" My voice sounded tired, but I took pleasure at the vengeful note in it. "You know she wouldn't save a helpless spider. And you know she wouldn't have saved you either, if she had found you hurt and helpless."

There was utter silence from the telephone.

"It doesn't matter what you do with her, to her, or how many women you seduce. It will never be as good as what we had together," I said to him softly. "What we could have had. Never. Did you get all that?"

There was silence, and I heard Erica say, "I can't wait any longer, Danial! Are you done with your phone call?"

The phone clicked, the dial tone suddenly loud. Danial had hung up.

I hung up the phone. I felt better than I had, but there were still tears in my eyes. Still, I hadn't gone to pieces, and that counted for something.

I worried that he would call back, but the rest of the night passed uneventfully.

Chapter Seven

Saturday came and went. It was a miserable day, rainy with thunderstorms. Global warming was certainly making its presence known this year. Worse storms were forecast for tonight. I had been painting the inside of the living room, after laying down some new vinyl floor tile. It was inexpensive, but it really made the house look a lot different.

I needed my home to be different. Too much had happened in this room. I'd had to paint over the cracked wall anyway, so I'd figured it would be easier to do the whole thing. I'd fixed it with joint compound, and it looked as good as new.

I wasn't as good as new, but I was well on my way. My lighter bruises had all healed up, except for the one on my back. It was some mix of brown and yellow now, but hopefully in a few more days it would be gone. The cut Theo had made on my mouth with his fangs had healed. The bruise by my mouth was also taking it's time going away. But now it was so faint, it was easily passed off as something I'd done to myself. I was trying very hard not to think of Theo, or the dream I'd had of him and me. It was working for me most of the time, and I hadn't dreamed of him again, so I was making some progress.

Sometimes I wanted to move away, but love of my land made me dismiss that for the idiocy it was. I couldn't run away. I just needed to make some new memories to ease the pain of the old ones. Besides, there was no point in moving, as Theo had once told me. Danial would find me wherever I went.

I had just finished up painting the hallway. It was about eight, and I was overdue for dinner. I put away my painting gear, made myself some quick soup and toast, and then settled down to watch TV.

There was a knock at the door. The dogs were instantly barking, but their tails were wagging, too.

Terian wouldn't show up this late without calling. And if it had been Theo, the dogs would have been growling. There was only one person this could be. Sigh.

I got up, and walked to the front door. Someone was standing there in the dim light from the motion sensor beside the door. I opened the door to find Danial, looking bedraggled. The harder rain forecast for tonight had started, and he was standing in a downpour.

"Did you need me to hide you again?" I said sarcastically.

He just stared at me, soaked to the skin. The wind was picking up, and some of the rain began landing on me. My bare arms were already damp from just a few seconds worth. I pulled him inside, and shut the door. I made a point not to stare at Theo's jacket as I hung up Danial's next to it. The wood stove was going, so it should be dry soon.

"Sar, I'm so sorry," he said brokenly.

I thought he might have been crying, but he was so wet I couldn't be sure. Ignoring his words, I pushed him into the laundry room.

"Danial, you're not only wet through, you're dirty. What have you been doing?" I said incredulously. Despite living with him for two months, this was the only time I'd ever seen him dirty, except...

My eyes shut as I remembered finding him, covered in dust. When he'd needed my help, and I'd needed him...I took a deep breath and let it out, forcing my eyes open.

Danial hadn't answered me. He just stood there forlornly, dripping on my rug.

"Get undressed, and put your clothes in the washer," I said. "Now."

He pulled his T-shirt over his head, and I stepped outside quickly, closing the laundry room door between us.

"I'll bring you some of your clothes," I said to him through the door. He didn't reply.

I went to my room, to the drawer where I'd put the few clothes Danial had left behind at my house. I'd meant to toss them out, but still couldn't bring myself to do it. I grabbed some underwear, a clean shirt, and some jeans. A quick search didn't reveal any socks. Oh well, he could get along without them.

I went back to the laundry room, knocked once, and handed them to Danial through the door. He made no jokes, overtures, or comments. I was surprised, having never seen this side of him before.

"I'm done, Sarelle," he said finally, opening the door.

He looked good, as always. I was suddenly conscious of the fact that I was in my paint clothes, and my hair was tightly pinned back, probably flecked with paint. He'd never seen me like this before, except in passing as I got ready for him after coming home from work.

I resisted the urge to make myself more attractive, instead plopping back on the sofa to resume eating. Danial stood there, watching me.

"Sit down already," I said finally. "I don't know why you're acting so oddly tonight."

I finished my meal, then took my dish to the sink.

Danial followed me. "Sar," he said hesitantly.

I turned reluctantly to face him. "Danial, say whatever you have to say and get out," I said wearily. "I'm exhausted."

"I love you," he said, his eyes tearing.

"I know you do," I said evenly, meeting his gaze with my own, before turning from him to start washing the dishes.

I felt him behind me in an instant, and put down the dish I'd been holding before I dropped it. His hands rested on my shoulders, and then slid down my arms, enfolding me as he pulled me close. His hands were cool, as they had been in the beginning.

How many nights had I longed to be back in his arms? How many nights had I wished he would come to me like this, and tell me he loved me? Almost every night since we parted. But it didn't change anything between us.

"I was wrong, Sar. I was wrong to do what I did." He leaned his head on my shoulder, holding me. "I want you to know, I didn't have sex with her. I left her, after talking to you. Please forgive me, for the things I said to you that night," he whispered into my ear. "Please forgive me, my Oathed One."

I didn't answer him, but neither did I move away from him. He seemed to be content with that, and continued to hold me close.

"Sar, will you forgive me?" he murmured again.

"I forgave you already, Danial," I said carefully. "It's part of loving you to forgive you."

"Do you still love me?" he said hopefully.

"You know I do," I said, turning to rub my cheek against his cool one.

"Then please come back to me, Sar. Come home. I don't want to be without you."

"That's exactly why I can't. At least, not yet," I said, regretfully.

"I don't understand," he said, with a trace of anger.

"Danial, I have to come to terms with something else, besides what happened between us. You are going to get older, but you'll look just as you do now. You don't age. I do. I will get older and older. I have to come to terms with that before I come back to you. The things you said to me that night we fought...I think about them a lot..." I trailed off.

"I can't change what I am, Sarelle. And you knew what I was from the first."

"I'm not saying that you should." I was fighting tears again. "I need time so I can change enough to accept it. This is my problem to deal with. It's not your fault at all."

Danial was silent for a while, still holding me. Then he spoke.

"If you don't want to be with me for your lifetime, then be with me while you are young. If I've learned anything over the centuries, it is that nothing stays the same. People change, places change. You can plan for years and have those plans destroyed in a matter of minutes when tragedy strikes—"

"Don't you think I know that, after everything I went through with Brennan?"

"I'm just saying don't be alone because you think in ten years you'll feel like leaving. Or that you'll begin to think I'll want you to leave. You don't know what will happen," Danial was murmuring, but his conviction was cutting through my well-formulated logic.

I moved away from Danial and he let me go. Leaning back on the counter, I faced him.

"I am going to go shower. You can make yourself at home."

I went to my bedroom and showered, washing the paint out of my hair that I could. After, I put on some leggings and a long sweater, along with new undergarments. I took time to condition my hair, wondering irrationally if Danial might have left while I was gone. But when I returned to the living room, he was there waiting for me. I moved past him to the counter, and got myself a wineglass.

Danial took a deep breath. "Sarelle, if you don't want to have a child with me, then don't. But come back to me. Come back with me tonight. We'll be happy, I promise you."

"I can't, Danial. Not yet," I said softly. "I need more time."

He didn't ask if there was anyone else. Theo or someone else reported to him regularly on my movements, most likely, so he knew I spent my nights alone. Except Theo must have edited out most of New Year's…

"You know I could make you come back with me tonight. You gave me your oath, Sar. It's within my rights." Danial was edgy, just this side of daring.

I was suddenly furiously angry, angrier than I'd been the night we broke up. "Yeah, you could. Or you could release me from my oath instead."

He didn't reply, but the depth of the sorrow that came off him at my words made me regret what I'd said. I changed topics, as I poured myself a little wine from the tap of boxed Banrock Station Shiraz on the counter. "Where were you tonight, that you were so dirty?"

"Don't ask me that."

"What happened, Danial? Or is this something else you want to keep from me?" I said sarcastically.

Danial stared at me, and then seemed to decide something. "I fought with Theo." He turned away from me abruptly, and headed back to the living room.

I was uneasy at mention of Theo, so much so that I followed him. "What about?"

"About you. Theo said if I had any brains I'd come up here and say whatever you wanted, anything, in order to win you back. I refused, and told him it was none of his business. He hit me. We fought, though not for long," he finished bitterly.

"So you're here…because of Theo?"

"He said that if he had someone to love like you, who would look at him the way you used to look at me, he wouldn't let anything stand in the way of being with them."

I drank most of the wine quickly, savoring the bitter taste. I'd have maybe expected this from Cia, but not Theo. Not after how he had kissed me, and told me he wanted me himself. Maybe this was Theo's way of making things right with Danial without telling him what had happened New Year's Eve. His loyalty to Danial had always been strong.

I finished my wine, and put the empty glass on the counter, trying to find something appropriate to utter.

"What do I need to say, Sar? Tell me and I'll say it," Danial said, coming to stand in front of me.

I closed my eyes, but even then, I could still feel him there, so close to me I could touch him. My words seemed too loud when I finally spoke. "Tell me that it doesn't matter to you if I have your child."

"It doesn't, Sar. Not after—"

"Tell me that you won't lie to me again about anything."

"I swear it, I won't—"

"Tell me that it's enough that I gave you my word I'd come back to you. That I can stay here as long as it takes to come to terms with what happened, and with your non-aging. That you can wait for me to do that. That you are willing to do that, because that is what I need."

Danial looked at me, a battle going on inside him. His jaw worked, but he kept silent. Finally, he looked away.

"Would it be enough, to hear me say that? Would that make the difference to you, that action that would bring you back to me?"

"Yes," I said, staring into his eyes. "I would probably come back to you, in time."

Instead of kindled hope, Danial's eyes held anger. "What about you, Sarelle? Would you love me, want me, if I told you I was yours, and then the next night left you, and refused to come back when you asked me to? How would you feel?"

"It's not the same," I said with a sigh.

"It is to me," Danial said.

I smiled sadly, and reached up to touch his face. He caught my hand easily in his, and kissed it. I was slightly drunk by this time, which was no excuse, but I couldn't stand the tension, to stand there arguing about my love for him after all that I'd gone though to be with him. After I'd told Terian that I couldn't love him, because I loved Danial. After I'd stopped Theo from making love to me, because of my oath to Danial. I should have told Danial to stop, but I didn't, and he took my silence for acquiescence. He moved closer, and then he was holding me. I melted into his embrace, and he began kissing my neck gently, his fangs brushing me.

"Please leave, Danial," I whispered.

"No, Sar," he said, lifting my chin to look into my eyes. "Not tonight. Tonight, I'm staying."

He kissed me passionately. His lips were soft, and cool against my warm mouth, and I drank in the sensation, remembering the way we used to be before everything had happened. When we'd first dated, and started sharing ourselves with each other. I put my arms around him, and kissed him back, my body responding to him. He reached up into my hair, and pulled me against him tightly, and I felt at once how aroused I still could make him.

"Danial," I said breathily.

"I never meant to hurt you, Sar," he said, still kissing me. "Tell me you know that. That the things I kept from you weren't because I didn't want you to know, but because I was afraid if you knew, you wouldn't love me, or want to be with me. I was afraid."

"I know it," I murmured back. "I never wanted to hurt you either. But I'm still afraid, and until I get past my fear, we can't be together."

He put his hands on my waist and lifted me so that I was sitting on the counter. He spread my knees, and slid between them, pulling me tight against him. Danial put both hands into my hair on either side of my head, and held my face inches from his. The look on his face was of deep and complete loss.

"Danial, why are you so sad—?"

"You know the reason," he said, resigned. "I can't change how I feel, or what I am. You can't come to terms with that. Time is not going to help, Sar. So it's better if we end this before we hurt each other any worse."

I couldn't say anything, choking on my sadness, and my hopelessness.

"I won't wait for you, because there is no point," he said with a note of finality. "So I'll let you go." Danial kissed me again, as tears ran down my face. "After tonight, I'll let you go."

I bared my neck to him. "You have my permission, if you—"

"No, Sar," Danial said achingly. "Not yet."

He suddenly lifted me in his arms while still kissing, and carried me into my bedroom. He laid me down on the bed, and took off my clothes, kissing me all over, until I was burning up. He moved away from me to take off his clothes, but if this was going to be our last time together, I wanted something else. I stopped him, and he looked at me questioningly. I eased off his shirt, kissing him, his chest, his neck. He hadn't been wearing his shoes, so he stood there in only his jeans. I unbuttoned them, sliding them down his hips so he could step out of them. He was naked beneath the jeans, no underwear. I was slightly shocked. What had he done with the pair I handed to him?

"You're making things easy for me," I said teasingly.

I held his eyes as I went to my knees in front of him. The incomprehension in his eyes changed to sudden dawning, his eyes widened, and he opened his mouth.

I held my finger to my lips, and said "Shh." Then I put my hands on his hips, bowed my head, and began to kiss him as I never had before. He arched against me, and his hands went into my hair. I rubbed him along his length with my tongue, and sucked the tip of him. I bit him gently, rubbed my face against him, and then put just the head of him in my mouth, kissing him again. He let out a moan then, and pushed my head down so that I took him all in. I massaged him gently with my mouth, making swallowing motions. He began to move against me, thrusting lightly, letting out soft cries as we moved together.

It became apparent to me at once that I was out of practice. I began to ache with the strain, but kept going. If this was going to be our last night together, I wanted it to be one he'd remember.

His thrusting became harder, faster. Suddenly, he stopped and gently pulled me away from him, laying me on the bed. Then he was inside me, thrusting hard and fast, kissing me, touching me. I was slick from what I had done to him, from feeling his body respond to my touch. He came quickly, spilling himself inside me. He was breathing hard, but so was I, my breaths gasps.

"I'm sorry," he said with shame. "I couldn't wait."

I laughed, despite the sadness that hung over us. "It's okay, Danial. I was hoping for that, actually. I wanted you to lose control."

"It's been a long time since someone did that to me," Danial said softly. "I'd forgotten how good it could feel."

"I'm glad I could help you remember," I said, kissing him.

He pulled me to him. "What can I do for you, Sar?" he said silkily. He touched me intimately with his fingers, opening me, to finally slide inside me. I moved against him, letting out little gasps.

"Tell me, my Darling—"

"Make love to me again, Danial. Please," I said, reaching for him and stroking gently.

He kissed me deeply, his tongue thrusting into me as his penis filled out and lengthened under my hand. Then he was easing inside me, touching me all over, and I lost myself in him. He made love to me then as he had that last night in Switzerland. When I came for him, tears ran down my face from how loved he had made me feel. For a long time after, we held each other, taking comfort in each other's closeness. He made love to me again near dawn, and this time, he drank from me, making the noises I loved to hear him make for me. But he took only a little of my blood before he healed me. Then we slept briefly, and a few moments before the sun rose, Danial went to leave.

"You don't have to go downstairs," I said, holding onto his hand. "Stay with me."

"The sunlight—" he began wearily.

"Remember the blackout curtains?" I said, interrupting. "I moved in with you, so we never used them, but I had put them up, in preparation for next summer..." I trailed off. It was too painful.

Danial looked at me, then at the curtains, and eased back down next to me. "Yes, Sarelle. Come here."

I awoke sometime later. I immediately felt Danial beside me, and rolled over to look at him, remembering the past night. For a while, I just watched him sleep. Then I heard the grandfather clock chime four times.

Fuck, it was late afternoon and I'd forgotten the dogs.

I leaped out of bed, and went to check. The cats were fine, but I'd left the dogs too long, and there was a mess to clean up. I let them out and fed everyone, apologizing to the dogs for not letting them out when I should have. Alter cleaning up the excrement, I threw Danial's wet clothes into the dryer and then had some breakfast, or what I was calling breakfast. I guess it was more like late lunch. As I ate, I thought about last night.

Why couldn't I just go back with him tonight? What was I afraid of?

I was afraid he wouldn't want me when I was older, when I was Mary's age. I was afraid that someday I'd look into his eyes, and see that he regretted asking me to share his life. I was afraid that he would ask me to go then, push me from him with distaste, but even more afraid that he would try to honor his promise to me, to take care of me. That he would tell me I was still welcome in his life, but he couldn't bear to touch me any longer, or have me share his bed. And I'd live to see another woman take my place as his lover...

I couldn't bear even thinking about it, much less the possibility of it really happening. I was making the right decision. Last night had been wonderful, and I loved Danial as much as I ever had. But nothing had changed for either of us. I still needed time, and he still didn't want to grant me any.

I got the clothes out of the dryer, folded them, and went back into my bedroom. I wanted to spend these last few hours with him, before he left. I lay back down next to him, and cuddled up against him.

"Sar," Danial said, opening his eyes. He pulled me to him. "Is this paint in your hair?" he said teasingly.

"Yes, I tried to get it all out, but some of it might have to grow out." I grimaced.

He smiled and kissed me. I wished for him to take me in his arms, but he moved past me, and got out of bed. He stepped into his jeans, quickly pulling them up.

"I promised myself I wouldn't say it again, but I'm going to anyway."

He buttoned his jeans, grabbed his shirt, and put it on. I also put on my clothes quickly, knowing what was coming. I turned to him, dressed, his clean clothes in my hands.

"Sar, I love you. Share however many years you have left with me. Have my child if you want to, or don't. But be with me. Come home with me tonight."

"I can't, Danial, not yet. I need more time."

Danial smiled sadly, and kissed me. He nodded once. "I said I'd let you go, and I will," he said, taking a deep breath. "I release you from your oath, Sarelle McGarran."

I felt the tears start to come. Just like that, he'd dissolved us. He paused, and looked at me one last time. Tears were on his face, too.

"Good-bye, Sar," he said softly. "Take care of yourself."

He grabbed the clean clothes from my hands and left, the door closing behind him. I heard him grabbing his jacket, and the front door shutting behind him as he left. The sound had all the finality of a gunshot. My legs buckled, and I sank to the floor. My dogs whined, licking my tears as I began to cry.

Chapter Eight

I don't know how long I stayed there, sobbing on the floor. It was long enough to feel like I couldn't get up.

Finally, some time later, I climbed to my feet. I felt better, but all the crying had left me feeling empty, closed off. I felt only fear now, fear I'd made a mistake in letting him go, fear that I'd never feel again what I felt with him.

As I went into my room, I caught sight of myself in the mirror. I looked awful; damp, red and swollen-faced. But I saw the choker still around my neck, the fox eyes winking at me, and felt a rush of hope.

There was still time. I could go to him now, tonight, and tell him I'd changed my mind, that nothing else mattered but being with him for as long as I could.

But I would be lying then. Because I still had reservations and they weren't insignificant. Besides, I had only told Danial the truth. And he hadn't heard it, as he was too afraid of my rejection of him.

I looked at myself in the mirror again, and made a decision. Then I went and got a pair of sharp scissors. I put my hair into a long braid, and tied both ends of it. Then I sawed through the braid. I put it aside to send to Locks of Love, as I'd planned to all those months ago. I undid my bobtail; it was too short to be a ponytail now. It hung to just below my shoulders, curling softly. I cut a few shorter pieces in front for shape, and pushed it back. It had a lot more bounce and curl now. The best thing was it would be much easier to take care of.

Later that night, when I was a good deal calmer, something occurred to me that boosted my spirit: Danial had not removed my choker, asked for his ring back, or healed the scars at my throat. He took the oath seriously, which is why he'd said the words he had when he left, like a formal breakup. But the facts were that according to vampire law, we were still oathed. The choker or ring might not have meant much by themselves, but the scars did. That vampire in Switzerland had known what the marks represented, that I was very important to someone of his race. Danial hadn't healed the marks, or even mentioned them.

Danial had bluffed by giving that speech about releasing me. Maybe he'd hoped to get me to agree to come back with him tonight. When I'd called his bluff, his pride hadn't allowed him to do anything but leave. What he had done was like telling a spouse you were divorced, but not filing any papers; emotional words that created no real lasting change. Afraid as it made me to consider, I concluded that if I went and saw Devlin, telling him Danial was still oathed to me, he would have no choice but to believe me.

Danial wasn't an irrational man who made slip ups like this, not with all I knew of him. He was a one-woman man, passionate, yes, but tightly controlled when it came to his actions. He would never have left me marked as his unless he wanted me to remain his. He would have politely asked me to come to his house to remove the scars, or done it right then. Moreover, he had hated me pretending I was his when I wasn't yet, even with me wearing all the trappings. If we weren't together, he wouldn't have wanted me wearing his symbol and giving other vampires reason to think we were. Logic told me that he would have removed the choker and asked for his ring back if he was really ready to call our relationship quits.

The more I thought about it, the surer I got that Danial had planned the entire thing to get me back, that nothing had changed between us. He said he hadn't loved anyone for decades; he wasn't going to let our love go so easily. He hadn't healed the marks on purpose; to let me know that he loved me, that it was okay to take my time in coming back to him. That gave me hope.

* * * *

The next few days passed slowly and quietly for me. I finally broke down and called my mom, and told her that the marriage was off, that I'd broken up with my fiancé. She said a lot of disparaging things about Danial, trying to make me feel better, but it didn't help. Kat was the same, when I spoke to her. I promised my mom a visit and Kat a lunch date in the next week.

The doctor called a few days after I'd met with Kat, saying my fertility levels were normal. He didn't advise me trying to get pregnant though for at least another month, maybe two. I scheduled a final checkup for two months out, the end of March. Whatever happened with Danial, I decided I needed to know for myself.

I had heard nothing from Theo, or from the foxes. It hurt to think I mattered so little to the latter that they couldn't be bothered to come see me. They knew I obviously couldn't come to see them. Or perhaps I did matter, and they were just angry with me. Either way, my reasoning made me feel bad.

Two weeks after seeing Danial, to the day, two huge sturdy boxes arrived for me with a note. It said:

Sarelle,

I thought you might need these, so I'm sending them to you.

Danial

One box held all my winter clothes, and the other had some of my cookbooks, and cooking paraphernalia in it. I was glad to have them back, especially the clothes. I would have had to go buy some soon, as I'd taken only a week's worth of outfits with me for winter. Oddly, I noticed that none of the sexy clothes Danial had bought for me were there. Again, it gave me hope that he'd kept them for me at his place, for when I returned to him. He was right in thinking I wouldn't be likely to wear them here by myself.

In February, I built up my resolve, and put an ad in the paper for Brennan's car. I had been looking at getting a new SUV, as mine was getting very old, and I'd put a lot of miles on it commuting from Danial's home to work those few months. With my SUV as a trade in, and the money from the Forrester, I thought I could swing it, maybe not for an SUV, but something smaller.

I'd gotten used to seeing it in the garage, and it hurt me to part with it, to envision coming home and having Brennan's SUV not there, to have an empty space there instead. Yet I reasoned that holding onto it was another way of me not letting go of the past. If I did go back to Danial, or eventually love someone else, I'd need space for his car or truck. Leaving my former husband's car here was another obstacle I was leaving for my future relationship. Instead of being forced to confront it then, it was better to deal with it myself now, in my own time.

A few people called in the following week and finally an older couple came out to look at it. They made me a reasonable offer, which I accepted, even though it was a little low for what I was asking. But they paid me in cash the next day, as I'd requested, which made up for the deficit. As I watched them drive away, I felt lighter. As I closed the door on my car, and the empty space beside it, for the first time I felt encouraged and hopeful, instead of sad.

* * * *

Weeks passed, and winter wore on. Valentine's Day came and went. I saw all the hearts, flowers, and cards, couples embracing together everywhere I went. It ate at me for most of February, knowing I wasn't part of a couple anymore.

I'd felt the same last year, but it was worse this year, as I'd gotten my hopes up, imagining that Danial might send me some flowers. I gritted my teeth, and told myself I was okay without a visit from the florist. I'd plant some flowers for myself in spring.

It was late February soon, and the cold of winter was finally easing up. There were still too many days below zero for me. I hated this time of year, the world locked in ice and snow, the spring so far off. Sometimes I felt as though I'd been frozen, too, with so many gray cloudy days that blurred together. Still I hoped that with the spring would come a thawing eventually, both for the world and for me.

I thought a lot in those weeks, about what my future held if I stayed here, and what it would hold if I were with Danial. Finally, I decided that if I couldn't make a decision by the end of April, I'd go back to Danial. I wouldn't oath to him again, but I'd go back to live with him. I knew he loved me. That would have to be enough for now, both for him and me. I'd tell him about what the doctor had said and maybe we could try for a baby, if he still wanted that with me, that is.

* * * *

That last night in February, there was a knock at the door. The dogs were barking, but their tails were wagging.

I opened the door to find Danial on the doorstep. This time he'd had the foresight to bring the right gear. He was dressed in a western duster and a broad brimmed hat. The rain was sheeting over him, but he looked pretty dry. He looked great, actually.

"Been out west?" I said finally.

"Yes," he said. "I did one of those spiritual journeys where you go off and find yourself."

He flashed a tentative smile.

"Did it work?" I asked, smiling faintly.

"I'm kidding, Sar. I knew it was going to rain, and I didn't want to be a mess by the time I made it to your door, like last time."

We stood there for a minute in silence, standing in the light of the door, rain splashing us both. Darkness came from behind me, and stuck her head through the opening. Danial stroked her head, and she grinned for him. Ghost was not too far behind, and he petted him, too.

"Why did you come?" I asked Danial abruptly.

"I came to remove the choker. I promised you I'd remove it if you asked. I am here to honor that promise."

"You're a little late," I retorted, arching my eyebrows. "It's been two months."

"Was Terian able to remove it for you?" Danial said, letting out a deep breath.

My hand went to my turtleneck. I pulled it down to reveal the choker. The motion set the pendant to swinging, the fox's jewel eyes winking in the light.

"Terian called me," Danial said, confused. "He said that he thought he might be able to remove it for you, but that it would be better if I did it. That's why I came."

"Terian could have removed it," I said lovingly. "If I'd wanted it gone."

His eyes widened with hope as he understood. "You mean—"

"Come on in," I said, moving aside to let him pass.

Instead of coming inside, he pulled me into the rain. I was soaked in an instant, but I didn't care. Danial was kissing me as if he would never let me go. And I never wanted him to, never again.

I held on to him and whispered to him between kisses, "I'm yours, Danial Racklan. For tonight and the rest of my life, I, Sarelle McGarran, promise myself to you—"

I abruptly woke up. I began crying, just as I had since my first dream of Danial returning to me. I'd had variations on that dream all month long since Valentine's Day. I was beginning to wonder if Danial had cursed me with a longing spell of some kind. But it was far more likely I was just grieving for what I was missing.

Having the dream so much did remind me though of one fact; my choker wasn't coming off except by either magical or vampiric means. Terian had said once he might be able to remove it. I decided I needed to know if that had been sheer bragging, or just a statement of fact.

On March 1, I called Terian. He had sent me a letter from Denver, Colorado, saying he was enjoying the west and hoped to be back in a few months. He had given me his address and the number where he was staying in the letter. I waited until ten, thinking with the time difference, it should be seven there. The phone rang eight times, and then a woman picked up.

"Yes?" she said.

This was unexpected. He hadn't mentioned a roommate, romantic or otherwise. "Hi, I'm Sarelle, a friend of Terian's. I wanted to talk to him, if he's around."

"He's in the shower," she said easily.

I wondered if she was about to join him. Sooo none of my business. "Can you take a message, please?"

"I'll have him call you back. Does he have the number?"

I thought he did, but I gave it to her anyway, and hung up. Ten minutes later, Terian called back.

"Sar, is everything okay?" he said with concern.

"Everything sounds great with you," I smiled into the phone. "I hope she's good to you."

Terian stammered, then got out, "Yes."

Trying not to smile too much at his discomfort, I moved the topic to my work. After a few seconds of small talk, he said abruptly, "Sar, what is it?"

Surprised as his directness, I said, "You told me a few months ago that you could take the collar off. Can you stop in next time you are in town and do that for me?"

He was silent so long I thought he'd hung up. "Terian? Are you there?"

"Sarelle, I can remove your choker. But I'm not going to."

"Why not?" I asked, shocked.

"Because you need to ask Danial to do it. He's the one who put it on you. If this is really the end of the two of you, he should remove it. He's going to have to remove those scars of yours anyway, unless you want to keep them as some kind of reminder of how much you loved him in the beginning—"

"Terian—"

"No, Sarelle. That's my final word on the subject."

70

"What is this? I thought you were my friend. How can you—"

"How can you, Sarelle?" he said angrily. "You shot me in the back to save Danial. You told me repeatedly how much you loved him. Now you are breaking up over a little fight?"

"Terian, it was not a little fight. He tried to get me pregnant without my consent, without telling me he could—"

I heard another extension pick up. I stopped in mid-sentence.

The same woman's voice said, "Terian, this woman shot you and you still talk to her?"

Whomever she was, she had a little of my spirit, if not my way with words. "Who is this?"

"Rhinestone, get off the phone," Terian said angrily. "This is a private conversation."

I heard a click, and some yelling. I welcomed it, as it gave me time to regain my composure. A door slammed, and then silence.

Terian picked the phone back up. "Sorry about that."

"Rhinestone?" I said curiously, succeeding in not snickering.

"I met her a few days ago. She's a stripper in a local bar."

"Listen, Terian, that's your business, not mine. If it makes you happy, go for it."

"I'm not looking for love. I'm looking for female companionship. I spent the better part of my life alone, and now that I can control my temperature, and hide my eyes, I'm making up for lost time—"

TMI. "You don't have to explain to me, Terian," I said again. "It's not my business—"

"I clearly do, because you aren't getting it, Sar." He said bitterly. "I don't have what you had with Danial with her. I may never have it, even if I live another century."

"What are you saying?"

"I'm very bluntly telling you to get your ass back to Danial as soon as you can, and tell him you love him. Tell him you'll stay with him as long as he'll have you. Tell him you need him. Tell him you aren't going to leave him."

"You tell me this now, after all your words to the contrary, all the times you thought he was going to hurt me—"

"I was wrong, Sar. Do you hear me; I was wrong!" Terian yelled.

"I hear you. You don't have to scream at me."

"You told me back then that everyone lies. Maybe they do, and maybe I have. But I'm not lying to you about this, Sar."

I didn't remember saying that at all. Had I? "Terian, I didn't mean—"

"You figured that something would come along to ruin your relationship with Danial, and a lot of things did: Me, Devlin, Maximillian, Ryan, the lies you told one another. But you made it past all that. Then when it got calm and you moved in, and everything sort of fell in place, you were happy with Danial. So happy, you gave him your oath. But as soon as he made one mistake, you latched onto it, and decided to get away. Was it a mistake? Yes. Did he deserve all the misery you put him though over it? No."

I wanted to hang up, but it was like I'd opened the floodgates. "I needed time—"

"You've had two months and a half now. Have you come to any conclusions yet?"

No, to my embarrassment. "I want to make sure I'm making the right decision."

"Is it? Or are you just afraid to let yourself depend on someone again? It was only when Danial offered you a real life that you started wanting out. And why? Because you'd been there before. You thought that it couldn't last, that one day he'd look at you, and see the lines on your face, your body growing older, and he wouldn't want you anymore. You didn't have to face that fear with your husband, he died too young. But Danial isn't going to die anytime soon."

"Terian, ease off me right now—"

"No, Sar, not this time. Danial loves you. He knows you're going to age, knows that you won't always look like you do now. He **doesn't** care!"

"I care!" I screamed into the phone. "This is easy for you to say, you who doesn't age. You can't know what it's like—"

"I do know what it's like," Terian said roughly. "I saw my brother age before me, year by year! I knew that I was going to outlive him. And he knew it too! I didn't love him any less!"

"That's different! You don't know how Danial would feel, when twenty years had passed. From how he acted, neither does he, not really. This is the real world, Terian. And in the real world, men like their women to look beautiful and young."

"I know because I wouldn't care, Sar! If it were you and I, it wouldn't matter to me that you were getting older. It would be enough that you were with me, that you cared about me."

I felt a rush of unease, and covered it up with quick words. "For how long, Terian? Until I got to be fifty? Sixty? How long would it be until I saw in your eyes how much my aging body was affecting your love for me?"

"Don't give me that. You might be vain, but not that vain."

"I am that vain and so are most women."

"It's okay if you're vain," he said softly. "You're beautiful, Sar. But that beauty is inside you, too, it's not just on the surface. Your personality, your kindness, that isn't ever going to change, no matter how many years passed." He paused. "It wouldn't ever matter how many years had passed, Sar. Not to me."

I couldn't form a reply. I was too uncomfortable, hearing that from him. Terian had fallen silent, also. I decided at that moment that he had at least one point I should listen to: this was between Danial and I. I had to try to work this out for myself, without Terian's help. Involving him when he still clearly had feelings for me would be a big mistake.

"Look, you're right, I do still love him. If I can come to terms with what I need to, I'll go back to him. I shouldn't have asked you to remove the choker. You're right, he can remove it then if he doesn't want me, or I'll keep wearing it if he does. If it's too late for us to be together, that is something I'll have to accept. But again, you're right, you shouldn't interfere."

Terian was still silent. Maybe he had hung up? "Terian?" I said questioningly. "Are you still there?"

"Sarelle, I'm sorry for what I said," Terian said quietly. "Danial and you are none of my business. You should do what you think is right for you, and no one else."

"Apology accepted, Terian," I told him. "That's what I've been trying to do, by the way."

"I should go," he replied. "I need to see if Rhinestone is downstairs waiting for me, or if she left for work without the ride I promised her. She'll be late if we don't leave soon—"

"Terian, I need to ask you something," I said urgently. I'd had more than one reason for calling him. I hadn't been thinking only of Danial these past two months.

"Ask away." He was hurried, wanting me to get off the phone.

"Terian, tell me the truth. Was there anything in the potion for my wings that was something you added extra?"

The silence stretched.

Uh oh. "What was in it, Terian?" I said icily. "Tell me the truth."

"Sar—" He was hesitant, and very, very guilty.

Son of a bitch! "Tell me!" I yelled into the phone. "What the fuck did you give me? A magical aphrodisiac?"

"I added a little something to get you to reveal what you really felt about me. A kiss activates it. I kissed you, and shared it with you from your lips. Neither one of us could hide our feelings. We bared what was in our hearts, all of it. I told you I cared about you and you told me you didn't love me. There was nothing to incite passion, the spell just let out what was already there."

I couldn't breathe.

"Sar, I'm sorry, I just wanted to know how you really felt about me, and to have the courage to finally tell you how I felt. It was harmless. The spell only lasts a short time."

I let out a deep breath. "You're saying there wasn't anything in it to provoke, say lust?" My voice wavered. "I had a dream, a very realistic dream. It lasted all night."

"No, I wouldn't do that to you. It did nothing to heighten emotion, it just made sure any emotion would not, could not be denied. I—" Terian cut off abruptly. "Did you dream of me?" he said longingly.

"No. But the dream was so real—"

"Sarelle, what did you dream?" His voice was edged with razors, dangerous.

I couldn't tell him. I couldn't begin to tell him. "Something I should not have, not without some help from a potion of some kind. That's why I thought magic had to be involved."

"Tell me. This is important!"

"Why is it important?"

"There was something about dreams that you have when you use this particular spell. I can't remember, but they warned about it in the book I got it from. There was a separate paragraph under the spell with a warning, which is never in a spell book unless there's serious danger—"

"Well, look the spell up, and tell me what it said!" I yelled.

"I can't, the book wasn't mine; it was a colleague's!" he yelled back.

"Terian, you've got to find out what it said about dreams. Please, if

74

you care about me at all, find out, and let me know as soon as you can."

"Okay." Terian hung up without saying good-bye.

I had a sinking feeling in my chest. I went over to my bed, sat down, and picked up Theo's jacket, smelling it deeply. I'd taken the jacket down from its hook a few days ago, and brought it into my bedroom. I slept with it now each night, hoping to dream of Theo again, to find comfort in his arms. But I had not dreamed of him since that night. Not once.

* * * *

An early thaw hit in the first week of March, melting the snow, and bringing me some much needed relief. I was regaining my strength rapidly after two months of taking care of myself again. I was happy to discover I still had what it took to handle things on my own. Coupled with that was the deep disappointment that I hadn't made that choice, it had been made for me.

It was getting harder every day to think that Danial still cared about me. I'd been so sure in the beginning, that day after he left. Now, I waited each day to get some message that he'd arranged for an appointment with Dr, Camlyn for my scars to be healed, or to ask for his choker back. That didn't make sense to me logically, but neither did his complete silence, not after how he'd said he loved me so much.

It had taken me until now to figure out that I wanted to try with Danial again. Terian's arguments had been sound ones. The only problems now were working up my courage to go see Danial, and getting ready some ideas to make our relationship go smoother this time around. The former was easy; it was the latter I was having trouble with.

I'd spent more than a few nights contemplating how quickly and easily I'd lost my identity, how close I'd come to giving up who I thought I was. Really, I'd done it because I'd wanted a new life with Danial. I'd wanted to be someone new, to leave the lonely, melancholy widow behind in the past. I'd changed too fast, mostly because he'd moved so fast and I'd gone along for the ride. Initially, I told myself I'd been dumb for that. But the more I thought, I'd decided I hadn't been dumb; I'd gone where my heart led me. Yes, Danial had broken it. Yes. It had hurt. But I was proud of myself that I'd taken that chance.

I wanted to take that leap again, and make sure this time I landed safely. That meant I had to have some plans for how I was going to handle my concerns, both about his immortality and my own sense of self. I was also going to have to resolve how to act around Theo, once Terian told me what sort of danger I'd exposed him and myself to through the spell. Once I had that info, I figured that it wouldn't take long for me to work out a plan, maybe a week at best.

* * * *

I'd settled in to read more of my book that night when Darkness let out a sharp bark, then a long low growl. Ghost went immediately to the window and looked out, also growling.

Shit. I got up, and went to the window. Taillights were heading down past the barn. They winked out of sight, then came into view again, heading down to the far end of the cornfield. There they abruptly winked out.

I let the curtain fall back. The dogs looked for a moment more, then satisfied there was nothing still moving, settled back down to the floor.

I bit my lip, wishing that I could do that, too. But I couldn't now; I'd seen the lights.

I looked back outside, scanning the darkness for a flashlight gleam. There was nothing. I listened for a moment, but didn't hear any gunshots.

Déjà vu came over me, as I debated what to do. There was no way I wanted to involve myself in anyone else's problems, even if the probability was low that there was another vampire in need of rescue out there. But I didn't like being afraid to go outside as I'd always done, to stand up for myself. That made me angry. It also made me angry to think of people trespassing blatantly, as whoever was in that vehicle had driven right down my driveway in clear view.

I wondered briefly if it could be the farmer who'd sublet the field from me. He did keep cows as well, so it was possible he was hunting coyotes. In that case, he'd park by the gate—it being locked now—and walk out onto his field. In that scenario, what I'd seen made perfect sense.

Logic told me to call him, to ask him if it was a friend of his. But I looked at the phone and didn't lift it, because I knew deep down it wasn't him out there. He would never have driven onto my property at night without calling first to make sure it was okay. I'd never told him I'd moved in with Danial.

My bad feeling got worse. I'd been gone two months at Danial's house. There had been lights on in my house here, sure, but I wasn't sure if Suri had made her presence known. No one had ever told me of any problems with hunters this past deer season. I almost always had at least one per year. Maybe word had gotten out that the bitch who lived here had lost the taste for using her guns. Maybe word had gotten out that no one lived here now at all.

A deafening gunshot rocked my thoughts, making me jump.

"Son of a bitch," I swore and went quickly to dress. My dogs clustered around me, eager at the possibility of a walk, their ears down from nervousness at the loud noise.

"You have to stay here," I said firmly. "Guard the house."

I strapped on my exploding bullets gun, just in case I was wildly off in my vampire probability reasoning, and went outside. The air was very cold, with a pure hard feel to it that made my throat dry almost at once. The night sky was clear, the moon a thin sliver.

Another gunshot sounded. This time I saw a flash of light near the trees.

I walked fast, making sure my gun had its safety off. In the unlikely event they made a run for it up the driveway, I wanted to be able to shoot out their tires.

I rounded the barn in a few minutes. The night was now still and quiet, the clouds coming in, slowly obscuring the crescent moon's weak light, making the night darker.

I cursed myself for not bringing a flashlight.

A few minutes later, I arrived at the truck. Its lights were off. The keys were in the ignition. I debated taking them, just in case they tried to make a run for it, then told myself I was being crazy. I wasn't a policeman, just a citizen entitled to a good night's sleep. Accordingly, I did write down the license plate number.

I looked at the footprint trail in the snow. The prints, three sets, led into the woods. Surprise of surprises, they did not lead into the farmer's field; they led into a neighbor's.

I stood there, smelling the night air. The faint scent of burnt gunpowder came to me on a little breeze.

I followed the footprints. It took some time, as the snow was not fresh, and there were many animal prints around, plus my own from walks with my dogs. Soon enough, the three sets of prints broke off and went off solitarily into the woods.

I kept following it. Ten minutes later, I came to a large bloody spot in the snow. Intestines were in a pile, still steaming slightly in the cool air. Large intestines.

"Son of a bitch," I swore softly. "I should have guessed it was deer they were after."

I looked around. There was no sign of the deer being dragged through the snow. There was some disturbed snow that looked muddy or dirty, I couldn't tell which. Then I came across another set of prints, two different kinds.

I followed them. Oddly, they looked like they were running. Had they heard me? No, more likely they'd hit two deer. The first had fallen, and the second had gotten a flesh wound, and ran. Likely, one had cleaned the fallen deer and the other was running after the wounded one. A deer carcass left in winter woods overnight would be partly gone by morning.

I followed them uneasily. I was now off my land and trespassing myself, something I tried never to do, even though these neighbors were my friends. I decided to go a little further, and then turn back. This had gone way beyond a little talking to, and it was now almost eleven. Besides that, a light snow had begun to fall, making the light very poor and obscuring the footprints.

Suddenly, I smelled something burning. I walked after it, but found nothing, only some more of that muddy dirty snow.

Enough was enough. I was not following any more of the footprints, even though I could see that there was more up ahead.

I retraced my steps, being careful not to get lost. The moon was obscured completely now, and the light was very bad. The snow had thickened, and was now falling in big clumps.

I came back to where the intestines had been, but they were gone. Fresh coyote tracks lead to where they had been, then off into the woods south.

At least they'd gotten something to eat. The night wasn't a total waste of time for someone. I gave a halfhearted smile and followed the tracks dejectedly backwards.

As I expected, when I got back to the truck, it was gone. I did find a few droplets of blood that proved my case in the snow near where it had been parked.

"At least I got the number," I whispered to myself.

I began to walk back. I was glad I turned back. The night was thick with snow now, and the barn light was very comforting to me.

Just as I drew even with the woodshed, the barn light winked out.

I stopped abruptly, freezing still. There was no way in hell that light sensor had failed, not when I'd replaced it with a new one just this past summer…

"Sar," a voice called softly.

I didn't recognize it. I didn't answer, sliding myself close to the shed.

There was a pause. I was afraid to move, and was desperately trying to listen for the approach of any footsteps. I looked behind me, then all around, and saw nothing but blackness.

"Come out."

I didn't reply, trying to think if I should shoot at the voice. What if the bullet exploded the metal of the barn? Would it send shrapnel my way?

"I know you're there. I can smell you."

My heart was pounding wildly. I tried to breathe as quietly as I could.

A truck came slowly up the street, its headlights washing the road in light. I breathed a sigh of relief and then a gloved hand clamped down on my mouth.

I struggled, tried to bite, and got a mouthful of wool.

"Stop," a voice said. It was neither high nor low, but the complete surety within it made me freeze.

A hand groped my pocket, and then quickly removed the paper with the license number on it.

"I'll let go," the voice said softly. "You stay put. Don't turn." It was muffled, I finally understood. Whoever held me was wearing a ski mask. My fear rose a notch.

"You go inside now. Don't report this." The man loosened his grip on me.

"Damn you, I'm going to report this," I grated out, trying to sound brave.

"I work for Danial," the voice said, amused.

Anger shocked me, then worry. Danial had told me it was over. Why was anyone guarding me? But the man in the ski mask had said he could smell me. Reasoning said this had to be a werefox. I wanted to turn, but was too afraid to.

"Did you make them leave?"

"They won't be back."

"How do you know?"

"Those weren't deer intestines. Go inside. Now."

I ran for the door, slipping and sliding in the snow. I got inside and collapsed, slamming it behind me and locking it. I looked out just in time to see taillights going down my driveway.

Fuck, I'd missed the license number.

I sat there, petting my dogs and trying to think of what to do. Danial had made me complicit in a murder. He'd crossed a line.

I bit my lip, my thoughts turning darker. What if this was just some trick? Here I was worried there had been a crime, and what evidence did I have? That a strange man who'd scared me had told me there was? He'd used Danial's name, but word likely had gotten around town that I was dating again. If he'd really worked for Danial, why had the man been wearing a mask? I hadn't recognized his voice, either...

Then it hit me. No drag marks. No one had killed three men in my woods tonight. There had been no signs of struggle, no bodies. I hadn't found any guns, or even heard one more shot. This had been a trick to scare me. Those had probably been pig intestines. Or they had jacked a deer and carried it off with them.

I sat and fumed the more I thought that had to be it. Bastards. They'd got the deer, and then ran off with it. Once they'd led me far enough away, they'd taken it to the truck, and lain in wait for me, to scare me and make sure I didn't report them.

Tears of frustration leaked from my eyes. I tried to remember the license, but got only the first two letters, BN. There had been a 3 in there too, somewhere.

I had a glass of wine to settle my nerves. Tomorrow, I'd block the road to the field near the barn. That would stop this from happening again. The snow would help, too. There was at least two inches out there and it was still coming down hard.

Mollified but determined, I let the dogs out and went to bed.

* * * *

The next morning, my mother called just as I was having breakfast.

"Sar, did you hear about those men killed on the train tracks?"

I woke up instantly. "What?"

"A group of men were out driving and drinking. They drove onto the tracks and turned down them, where they cross the road. A train clipped them as it went by and they blew up."

"They're dead?" I was relieved, and then very guilty.

"Dead. Alcohol was involved, it says. They also had guns and a flashlight, one of those big ones like a spotlight. The paper doesn't say this, but I bet they were out jacking deer. Your stepfather thinks so, too."

"I had some people here last night hunting," I said without thinking. "That sounds like them."

"Did you have any trouble?" my mom said angrily. "You didn't call us."

"They left before I could talk to them," I said, wincing at the slight lie. "They might have gotten one of my deer, I'm not sure. Was there any deer meat found in the wreckage?"

My mother ignored my question, intent on being protective. "Be careful. Don't be going out and confronting strange men at night alone."

"I'm going to block the road today," I assured her. "Don't worry."

An hour later, I did exactly that. As I moved the old fallen log into position across the access road with the front-end loader, relief washed over me. There would be no more uninvited late night visitors.

The question of how the barn light had been switched off was also on my mind. I looked carefully around the barn, but saw no signs that anyone had broken in. All the locks and doors were intact, as was the light bulb that had gone off. Closer inspection revealed the truth; the electrical box on the pole outside the barn had been opened, the tiny padlock forced. Inside, the breaker had been turned off. I flipped it back on, making a mental note to check that the barn light came on once full dark descended tonight.

I thought about calling Danial to tell him what had happened. He would be able to answer my question of whether the man who'd grabbed me had been legit or not. After weighing the pros and cons, I decided against calling him. I was 99% sure by this time that the man was already dead, killed in that car crash with his buddies. Besides, I wanted to call Danial when I was ready to talk about us. Calling him with this weird story sounded too much like me looking for an excuse to contact him.

I walked down later with the dogs to the gate, trying to retrace my steps from the night before. But snow and wind had covered over all of the tracks, leaving vast unbroken whiteness. I shrugged, and decided to let it go. The situation had been handled for now, if not permanently.

* * * *

March flowed past. Every day I hoped to get a call from Terian, but there was none. Nor was there any word from Danial, Theo, or any of the foxes. Happily, no one unwelcome bothered me, either. My nights were quiet, devoid of gunshots. Still, I looked outside every night before going to bed for any lights and the next morning for tire tracks on the access road, just in case. There were never any, save those made by myself.

* * * *

By late March, the weather had warmed up some. There were still nights in the negative numbers, and my wood supply was dwindling fast now, but spring was close enough I wasn't worried. I'd made it through the winter, more or less, and I felt a lot better about my decision to be on my own for a while. I'd remembered who I was in the process; a strong woman who didn't have to capitulate to anyone else to be happy.

Not that I was blaming Danial for how I'd felt. He'd overwhelmed me during our romance, swiftly taking control of our relationship, but he hadn't done it in an urge to control me. It was just his nature was to be protective, bold, and decisive. However, I was just as bold and decisive as he was. If I was a little firmer about my needs and wants, we'd be fine.

I went back to the doctor, and he told me that I was cleared, everything looked good, and to come back pregnant if I wanted to. I gave him a smile, and told him I'd do my best.

Looking at the calendar, I decided to call Danial this coming Friday and ask about seeing him Saturday, if he was free. I'd leave a message if he wasn't home. We could go from there.

* * * *

Early on the morning of March 21st, the phone rang. The caller ID said it was Flora.

Surprised she was calling me so early, I picked up the phone. "Hello?"

"Um, Sarelle, it's Ken, Flora's grandson. Flora died the night before last."

I sat down quickly, tears sliding down my cheeks. "What happened?"

"She died in her sleep. She was fine last night when I talked to her. But she'd been feeling weak lately. I figured I'd better call, as you don't get the paper."

"I'd stopped by a few weeks ago to see her," I said sadly. "She told me she felt tired then. I told her I'd come back and visit another day, but I hadn't had a chance to—"

"You were a good friend to her, Sar. The wake is tomorrow, at ten a.m.," Ken said tonelessly. "It'll be held at her house. The funeral is going to be at one, just a simple ceremony in the cemetery. She had told me what she wanted years before, when my grandfather died." He let out a sad laugh. "She had everything arranged to a T, as usual."

"I'm so sorry," I said gently. "I'll be there. Thank you for letting me know."

After hanging up, I called my boss to arrange the coming Friday off. Then I took the rest of the day to mourn a woman who had been a very good friend.

Chapter Nine

The morning of Flora's funeral was rainy and gray. I stood by the casket, glad it was closed. I wanted to remember her vibrant and alive, not in a box with makeup on her face.

"Thank you for coming," Ken said emptily. His eyes were swollen and red.

I hugged him tightly. "I'm sorry."

I let him go, and moved on, as he began greeting the others behind me in line who had come to pay their respects. Ken would be okay. He had other family members here from out of town that were helping him get through this, so he could honor Flora, and her life.

When I'd seen Flora two weeks ago, I'd known then that she'd been near the end of her time. She'd been so thin, and frail. Yet her eyes had sparkled as they always had, and she'd laughed easily when I'd told her some jokes. I'd stayed until she had said she was tired, then I'd hugged her one last time and told her I'd loved her, that I was grateful she was my friend. I'd known when I left, that it might well be the last time I'd see her.

I looked down at the casket, and silently said good-bye one last time. It was then I remembered her words to me, that day back in September:

People come in and out of your life. It's the time you have with them that matters, not that they might not be around forever.

God, I'd been an idiot.

A day would come when I'd be in a box like this one. My life was finite, and one day, it would be over. I had someone who loved me, wanted to take care of me. Someone I loved. Someone I was letting slip away from me, because I was thinking of my own vanity, instead of believing in his love for me.

I told Flora silently that she'd been a wonderful friend, and that I hoped she was at peace now. Then I added on a heartfelt thank you, and excused myself.

I wasn't going to wait and call this weekend, leave messages, and be polite. I was going to go to Danial tonight, and tell him I'd been wrong to leave, that he'd been right. Then I was going to tell him I loved him, and I wanted to be with him, if he still wanted me.

* * * *

As I drove to Danial's later that night, thoughts went through my mind about what to say. I'm sorry; forgive me? I love you and I'm back? It took me three months, but I realized I was wrong?

I still hadn't decided on what to say as I drove up to his door. My stomach was a tight hard knot, and I was shaking. Why was I so scared? The worst thing he could do was remove the choker and scars, and tell me it was too late.

I took a deep breath, and walked up the front stairs. The porch light was on. I rang the doorbell, and knocked, too. I heard someone coming to answer and smiled, hoping it was Cia.

It wasn't. To my horror and chagrin, I discovered there was something worse than having Danial tell me it was too late for us.

The door opened to reveal Angelica. She stood there holding a bit of gauze to her neck per usual. Her attire was anything but.

I took a long shuddering breath. She had on no shoes, and her usual low cut dress was absent. She was wearing my black velvet robe. A silver choker was around her neck. From it dangled a silver fox head.

"Hello, Sarelle," she purred, obviously enjoying herself. "Have you come to feed Danial? Sorry, but I believe I've already taken care of his needs tonight. All of them."

I held it together. I was going to go to pieces as soon as I was alone, but here, in front of her, I would hold it together if it killed me. "Hi, Angelica. I need to talk to Danial. Can you tell me if he's here?"

"He's away on business for the night, but he should be back by dawn," she said, yawning. "He told me not to wait up. Want to leave a message?"

There was no way she was going to tell him I had been here, and no way I was going to ask her to. "Thanks. Have a good night," I said, turning around and forcing myself to walk to my car.

I got in my SUV, and backed out, trying to simultaneously drive and process that this was really happening. I passed Ivan coming in, swinging out of his way just in time.

He stopped the car and rolled down the window. "Sarelle! How are you? Have you come back to stay?" He was smiling at me hopefully.

My throat worked, but nothing came out.

Ivan saw my anguished expression. "Please come back, Sar. Danial might be with her—"

His words were like a hammer hitting me.

"—but he doesn't love her, he loves you. She's nothing to him."

That wasn't true. I'd seen the choker, something he'd had made for her...

"Sarelle?" Ivan said worriedly. "Are you okay?"

"Ivan," I said, my voice like sandpaper. "Give this to Danial for me, please." I slid my diamond ring off my finger, and gave it to him. "Sarelle, that's your ring from Danial. You shouldn't be giving it to me—"

"Ivan, I'm sorry, but I've got to go." I stepped on the gas and pealed out down the driveway. I made it to the road before I was crying so hard I couldn't see. I didn't want to sit there and sob, so I drove to the Chinese Eatery in Alan's Creek. At least there, I knew I wasn't going to run into Danial.

I parked in the corner of the parking lot, and let loose. How could he pick her of all people to share his bed? How could he let her wear my clothes? This was like a nightmare I couldn't wake up from.

The parking lot was busy, people coming and going with food. Unwilling to cry in front of strangers, I started the car and headed home.

The events of the night kept replaying in my mind, torturing me. I had told myself that if Danial didn't wait for me, if he didn't want me, I'd let him go. Down deep, I realized I'd never admitted the possibility to myself. I'd never really thought I'd be too late. But he'd meant what he said. Now he was with Angelica and it was serious enough that he'd given her a choker...

Thinking of what I'd given up made me start sobbing again. Rather than risking a collision, I pulled off the road into the nearest parking lot. I shut off the SUV, sat there and let loose again.

A slight pattering of rain on the windshield startled me. As I lifted my head to look, the pattering became a deluge, pounding the car. A boom of thunder shook the air, lightning illuminating the darkness for a split second.

I looked up, trying to see where I was through the smeared windshield and my teary eyes. There was a red-lighted sign on the front of the building, but it was behind the large truck in front of me. The parking lot was mostly empty, with only a few trucks parked near mine. There was no outdoor light, leaving the parking lot murkily lit.

"The Tavern," I made out finally, speaking the words aloud. "It must be a bar."

I sat there and thought seriously about going in. I'd never gone to a bar alone before. Even when I'd gone to bars with girlfriends in college, it had been just once or twice. But I was feeling reckless and vengeful enough to do it.

I told myself I was being stupid, that going in wouldn't help my problems, or ease my broken heart. The only thing it would do would make things worse. Danial wouldn't care in any case. I'd be the one who'd care and regret if I did something foolish tonight.

Still, all the crying had made me thirsty, and I had no tissues left in the car. I needed some water and some paper towels would be a godsend. The question was how willing was I to be ogled when I went in looking like a mess?

While I was sitting there debating that, a sudden urge to use the restroom took hold of me. I wasn't going to be sick, but I also wasn't going to make it home in time either. This wasn't a choice; it was necessity.

I swore, and then opened the SUV door. I was soaked the instant I got out, the rain pelting me hard. I dashed for the door, grabbing the heavy handle with both hands and throwing it open.

I made for the bathroom quickly, trying not to run, feeling eyes watching me. I cast a quick glance at the bar, my eyes finding only three men sitting there, all with their backs to me.

I used the facilities with relief, and then drank some water with cupped hands from the faucet. I took my time cleaning my face up, using several wetted paper towels to blow my nose. After splashing water on my skin, the redness of my face eased somewhat, though my eyes were still bright watery green.

Looking at my reflection, I was disgusted. What was I looking for here anyway, a cheap thrill? I was better than this, I deserved better. It

87

was past time to go home.

I walked out, making a beeline for the door.

"Miss?" the bartender called. "Hey, Miss!"

I turned, hoping he wasn't going to tell me that only customers could use the bathroom. "Yes?"

"One of the gentlemen wants to buy you a drink. What'll you have?"

I blushed, my eyes looking at the men at the bar. There were only two there now, both strangely not looking at me at all. The one who'd been by himself at the end was gone.

"Nothing, thanks," I said awkwardly. "I just needed your restroom. Sorry."

"No problem," the bartender said, nodding. "We get that a lot, being way out here. You sure you won't have that drink?"

"Yes," I said quickly. "I've got to go home. But please thank the gentleman for me for offering."

"You can thank him yourself," the bartender said, winking. "He'll be right back. He just stepped away for a moment."

I looked nervously toward the restrooms, then toward the parking lot. I didn't want to meet an admirer alone in a dimly lit parking lot. But if he was in the bathroom, making a dash for the SUV was the best thing to do...

"He liked your long brown hair," the bartender added, taking my apprehensive thoughtfulness for indecision. "He's just in the bathroom, he'll be back—"

"I'm blonde," I said apologetically. "It's just wet. Sorry." I ran out before he could reply, jumping into my car and starting it quickly. I gunned the engine, tearing back onto the road in a clatter of gravel.

Driving down the road towards home, I heaved a sigh of relief.

* * * *

There was a message from Terian on my machine. "Sar, call me immediately. I have that information you wanted."

I changed out of my damp clothes, put on a bathrobe, wound a towel around my wet hair, and then called him.

He picked up on the first ring. "Sar?"

"Terian, what did you find out?"

"I'm sorry it took so long to get back to you, but the book had been loaned to someone else, and then—"

"Terian, what about the dreams?"

"Sar, you aren't going to like this."

I took a deep breath. Screaming at him was not going to help. "Tell me already."

"Like I said, the potion brings out your deepest feelings. It reveals them, no matter how well they are hidden. You have to kiss someone to activate it. Then both persons are affected by it—"

"The dreams, Terian, what about the dreams?"

"If you kiss someone and they share your emotions—your love, lust, rage, fear, etc.—then, in rare cases, you can dream of them. It feels real, much more real than a normal dream. And they dream of you. You share the dream. It's powerful stuff, supposedly very real, and—"

I closed my eyes and felt nothing, heard nothing for a few moments. Now I knew why I hadn't heard from Theo, why he'd never come for his jacket. He couldn't face me for the same reason I hadn't called him.

"Who did you kiss and dream of? I know it wasn't me." Terian said hesitantly. "At least, not from the descriptions in the book of how the dream should feel."

I didn't answer him.

"Sar, I'm sorry. I made this quickly and didn't read carefully enough. I didn't know this spell had this side effect when I gave it to you."

My mind was reeling. Carefully, I formed a reply. "Terian, thank you for telling me this. It explains a lot."

"Sarelle, are you okay?"

I couldn't tell him about the dream. Instead, I took a deep breath and told him about Angelica opening the door to me tonight at Danial's.

"Sarelle, I'm sorry," Terian said again sadly. "Do you want to talk about it?"

I didn't. I wanted to get off the phone and think about Theo. "No, thanks. I should go—"

"Do you need me?" Terian said seriously. "I'm worried about you. You shouldn't be alone tonight after going through what you have. You should talk to someone—"

I closed my eyes, willing myself to focus. I didn't want to tell him anything about my romantic life, not knowing how he liked me. Yet just hanging up was rude, especially as his concern was real. I settled for bait and switch.

"Terian, please tell me about what's going on with you. I can't think about my life right now. Go ahead, it will cheer me up."

Terian told me that everything was going well for him. He was with a new girl called Peaches now. I laughed, and told him to find out their real names, not their stage names.

He was learning more advanced magic from that half demon who had told him what he was. "He's great, Sar. He has a few friends who do magic, too. That's whose spell book I borrowed last year…" He trailed off, then cleared his throat. "It's nice, being with people who understand me."

"I'm happy for you," I replied. "Please take care of yourself. I'm going to go to bed."

"You sure you'll be okay?" Terian said querulously. "You'll call if you need someone to talk to, or anything?"

"Yes," I assured him. "I'll call you in a few days, okay?"

"Good," Terian said, satisfied. "Goodnight."

"Goodnight."

I hung up the phone and sat down, trying hard to work up my courage. There was no way I was going to bed without calling Theo, to tell him what had happened to us. That would have been really easy if I still had the cell phone Danial had given me. But I'd left it at Danial's the night I left him. My regular phone was old enough that it predated call logs, so that was no help. I had my older cell phone, but it only had Danial's number on it. There was no way I was calling the main house. Hearing Angelica's voice a second time tonight was not an option.

Finally, I went to my phone list and checked to see if Cia's number was listed there. I'd exchanged numbers with her back in the fall, the day we'd baked together. Luckily, I'd written it down. Uneasiness suddenly filled me; she was mated now to Aran. If this was her regular phone, maybe the number had changed. I cringed a little, remembering how I'd missed her wedding months ago.

Calling her suddenly after months of silence would be nearly as bad as talking to Angelica. What if Cia hung up on me? Or maybe she'd be cold to me, for what I'd done to Danial.

Screw it. I had to talk to Theo to tell him what I knew. I had to risk it.

I dialed the number. The phone rang and rang. I hung up when it went to voice mail. That was a relief, as the message said this was Cia's phone, which likely meant it was her personal cell phone. I tried again.

Again, the phone rang many times and then went to voice mail.

I'd try once more, then leave a message. I dialed, and again the phone rang many times unanswered. I was just ready to give up when an annoyed guy answered the phone.

"Yes?" he said haughtily.

"Aran?"

"Who is this?" There was no recognition in his tone.

My heart sank a little. "It's Sarelle."

"Sar! How have you been? Are you okay?"

The sudden joy in his voice moved me to tears. "I'm fine, Aran. How is married life? How's Cia?"

"She's great, Sar. We're trying for a..." He trailed off.

I knew he was remembering my miscarriage. Likely, everyone there knew all about it. "Aran, I'm happy for you and Cia. Name one girl after me?"

He laughed. "Cia already suggested that. She wanted to come and see you, but Danial said no one was to visit you, that you needed time to yourself, to be completely alone—"

Anger rose up in me. He hadn't done that out of caring, but out of prickliness. "I'd welcome a visit by both of you. Just call before you come." I wanted to add on that everyone was welcome except Danial, then told myself being spiteful wouldn't heal my heart. "But I really called to speak to Theo. I don't have his number. Is he around?"

"Are you okay?"

"I'm okay, but I have information for him." Please let him not be out of the country, or on a plane somewhere.

"Is it urgent?"

"Critical," I said honestly.

"He's here, most likely in his room. He spends a lot of time there now. He says he's sleeping, but none of us believe him. No one could sleep that much, I mean really—"

I closed my eyes. I understood why Theo was sleeping so much. He was trying to dream of me again, just as I had been trying to dream of him. "Please, give me his direct number, or take this phone to him."

"I have orders not to disturb him unless we're attacked, or Danial asks for him," Aran said apologetically. "If you give me a message, I'll tell him as soon as he comes out."

"When will that be?"

"Probably daybreak," Aran replied.

I couldn't wait that long. I had to get him to wake Theo. My mind seized on my intruder weeks ago. "A little while ago, a truck came onto my land. I went to investigate, and there were three sets of tracks. I followed them into the woods, and found some innards—"

"Probably men illegally shooting deer," Aran said. "Did you report it?"

"No. When I went back out of the woods, the truck was gone. I got the license number, but—"

"Just poachers," Aran interrupted. "Suri had to ask a few to leave when she was there, and so did Cia. They had no trouble, really. We sometimes get hunters and poachers here, too, because they think Danial's land is vacant. Just call the police and give them the license number—"

"Aran," I said forcefully. "I didn't report it because when I got back near the house a man grabbed me. He told me he smelled me—"

"What?" Aran said, concerned. "What did he look like?"

"He was wearing a ski mask, dressed in dark clothes. I didn't get more than that; he grabbed me from behind. He took the number from my pocket, and told me to go inside. He told me he'd killed the men in the woods. He said that he worked for Danial."

There was silence, then Aran said worriedly, "We have no one there watching you, Sar. No one has been there since you went back there to live. Whoever he was, he didn't work for Danial."

I needed to hurry this up. "I thought I saw the same truck tonight," I lied. "I saw headlights, anyway. I'm worried that maybe the man came back—"

"You stay in the house, and lock the door," Aran said firmly. "I'll take the phone to Theo, right now. He should hear this from you." There were sounds of Aran opening a door, and walking around. He opened and closed a few more doors, then said, "Keep holding on, Sar. I've checked the common room and kitchen, and hallway, and he's not there. He's got to be in his room."

My luck being what it was, he was probably out for a walk. "I'm holding."

Aran banged on a door, hard. There was some swearing, then the sound of a door being opened, and finally Theo's voice, weary and angry.

"Haven't I told everyone that when I'm in here you are not to disturb me, unless it's an emergency? I was trying to sleep!"

"It is an emergency, Theo. It's Sar. She says she needs to talk to you," Aran said.

"About what?" Theo said angrily. "It couldn't wait a few hours?"

"An intruder on her property. She was scared by a man a few nights ago. She thought it was a prank. But now she thinks he's back—"

There was noise of the phone being transferred, then the sound of a door shutting.

"Sarelle?" Theo said. His voice was so guarded it didn't sound like his voice at all. "What did he look like?"

"Theo," I breathed. "Hi."

"I said, what did he look like?"

"I didn't see him."

"Is the truck still there?"

"It's not here anymore," I admitted. "But I had to talk to you—"

"About what?" he snapped. "What's your crisis today?"

"I need to know something." God, how to say it?

"Be specific, Sarelle. You want to know who is parading around in your clothes? Who—"

"I already know about her, Theo. I was there earlier tonight."

"I'm sorry you had to find out that way," Theo said much more kindly. "She hates you. She's a total bitch, that one. Danial's an idiot for letting her get her way—"

The passion in his voice hit a cord in me, despite his harsh words. I remembered what he'd said to me in the dream, how he'd touched me so tenderly. How he'd told me he loved me. I couldn't seem to get out any words, and the silence stretched out for thirty seconds

"Sar, say what you have to say, already," Theo said, again angry and impatient. "I have a lot to do, like get some sleep before my shift starts tomorrow."

I forced out the words. "I need to know if you dreamed of me, Theo, the night after you left. I dreamed of you that night."

Silence. It stretched out longer and longer. I was shaking, and he hadn't even replied yet.

I gathered my courage. "Theo?"

"I'll be there in forty-five minutes, Sar." Click.

Chapter Ten

I put down the phone, and sat motionless. Theo was coming here tonight, right now.

I trembled, afraid of myself, of what he would do when he got here. Of facing him, now that he knew I had been there with him when he bared his heart to me.

Full of restless energy, I went out and took the dogs for a walk. It was almost ten p.m. by now, but there was no way I could sit there and wait for him. I had to move.

The night was cool, but not cold. Spring was finally in the air, along with the faint scent of rain. Ghost and Darkness frolicked in the damp air, chasing each other. I walked fast, a sense of urgency making me hurry, checking my watch every few minutes. When it got close to ten twenty, I turned for home, my steps quickening.

Theo drove up as we were just coming up from the field to the house, to my surprise. He'd made the trip in a little less than forty minutes. He must have gone through every stop sign and light between here and there.

He got out and slammed the SUV's door, walking fast towards the house.

"Theo, I'm down here with the dogs!"

Theo stopped and turned in a smooth motion, striding towards us. We met next to the porch. The dogs growled at him, showing their teeth.

"Shh. Be nice," I said to the dogs, then turned to him. "You're early," I said, giving him a smile as I looked him up and down. "You said forty-five minutes—"

Theo grabbed hold of me, cutting my words short with rough kisses. His skin was warm; his fingers insistent as they pulled me close. He embraced me as he had in the dream, lifting me off my feet. I kissed him back, wrapping my legs around him so he could carry me into the house. My dogs followed us cautiously.

Theo opened the door with his hand, his fingers fumbling with the knob. The dogs darted in quickly, then Theo entered with me, kicking the door shut behind us. He moved to the wall, pressing his body into mine as he ground against me, still kissing me hungrily.

I struggled in his embrace. He instantly let go of me, his blue eyes dark, his face flushed.

"In case," I said carefully as I locked the door, drawing the dead bolt so it couldn't be opened by a key.

He nodded once. I went back to him, tilting my head up to kiss him. He kissed me fiercely, then grabbed me up in his arms again. Quickly, he took me into the bedroom, and put me on the bed gently, still kissing me. We never stopped touching as I pulled off my clothes, and he pulled off his. He was in real life as he'd looked in the dream, all hard muscle. I lay back on the bed, and beckoned to him to come to me. He leaned down, and crawled up my body, kissing me as he went, bringing soft moans from my parted lips. Then I was in his arms and it was just like the dream had been, only better.

I pushed him away gently. He drew back from me, his blue gray eyes dark as thunderclouds.

"Don't you want to know what happened to us, Theo?" I reached out and caressed his face, sliding my hand to tangle in his hair. "Why we dreamed together?"

He kissed my neck, even my scars. "Not now, Sar. I just want to be here with you." His voice was soft, softer than I'd ever heard it, even in the dream.

He kissed me one final time, and rolled to lie at my side, reaching for his jeans. A few seconds later, he moved atop me wearing a condom.

I was surprised and also touched that I hadn't needed to ask him about protection. "Thank you."

"I can get you pregnant, Sar," he said softly. "I don't want you to worry."

He kissed me, then lowered his body down on mine, quickly easing himself inside me.

I groaned, remembering him like this. "You feel the same," I sighed, moving gently against him, running my hands over him.

"So do you," he sighed.

Theo began thrusting himself in as far as he could, his body contracting on mine. I cried out in pleasure, and he muffled my groans, his tongue licking me. Excitement flooded me, and I licked him back, trying to devour him. He renewed his efforts, his body straining, his breaths coming fast.

I expected him to come, but suddenly he stopped still and rolled over, so I was on top, straddling him. I looked into his eyes, dark with desire.

"Come for me," he said commandingly.

He crushed me to him, and thrust into me for all he was worth. Waves of pleasure hit me, as I moaned, rocking on him, his strong hands guiding my movements. I came screaming a moment later, and he came right behind me, letting loose a roar that arched his back, pushing him even deeper inside me.

I lay there on him, gasping. Embarrassingly, he wasn't breathing near as hard as I was. He gently moved me off him, then removed and threw away the condom. He lay back down, pulling me close as he caressed me gently, rubbing my skin with his deft hands.

He kissed my shoulder delicately, then my throat. "Now," he said into my ear, "Tell me what happened to us, how we were able to dream together that night."

I explained everything: how Terian had dosed me, how my kiss had passed on the potion to him when we had kissed, and how the shared dream was a rare side effect. "I called you as soon as I knew," I finished. "I'm sorry it wasn't sooner."

"It blew my mind," Theo said, still stroking my body gently. "I couldn't believe the dream at first. It was like I was able to go back and replay the night, making whatever I wanted happen. And you wanted me, Sar, that was the best part." He sighed contentedly.

"I'm surprised then you didn't just take me on the floor when you brought me in tonight," I replied, laughing.

Theo rolled over on me in a smooth motion, pinning me to the bed. "Did you want me to?" He was smiling, but there was something serious in his tone, as if he wasn't sure that he'd given me what I wanted of him. "It can be arranged."

Again, I was touched by that, that he wanted to make sure I was completely satisfied. "I'm happier to have you here in bed with me," I said reassuringly, stroking his face. "I missed you."

"I'm happy to be here," he said, kissing me long and slow. "I missed you, too."

We lay back down, holding each other. A few minutes passed.

Theo suddenly shifted, kissing my ear. "Sar, um, I'd like to…um…"

"Again?"

"Yes," he said, blushing slightly.

"Theo, you can have me as many times as you want," I said with a smile, kissing him again. "I was hoping for a repeat performance."

Theo laughed, then reached over the side of the bed. "You got it. Give me one second."

Theo took me up on my offer. As the night wore on, I became very glad he'd thought ahead, and brought a jumbo box of prophylactics with him. By dawn, I was as sore as I'd been in the dream. We passed out holding each other; my head nestled in his throat.

My alarm went off at six. My forgetting to turn it off was actually as Godsend, as I remembered my pets just as I hit the off button.

Theo woke when I moved to get up. He sighed happily to see me, smiled, then asked "Where are you going?"

"I have to feed the dogs and cats, and let them out," I said, pulling on a bathrobe. "And I have to start a fire. I'll be back afterwards."

"Do you want me to help you?" he said, offering me another smile. "I think I remember how to work your wood stove, even though it's been a while."

I went completely still, his words shocking me. Then it hit me why they were such a surprise: I'd never heard them before from anyone but my husband.

For all that Danial said he wanted to be with me, what he'd really wanted was for me to be with him. He'd always made sure I was taken care of, but he'd very rarely helped me do some chore, or even cook. I'd thought the latter was because he didn't eat. But whether that was true or not, the facts came down to these: he'd never once asked me if I wanted him to help me with anything. He'd bought me everything I'd asked for and more besides, and had people tend to my every whim. But he had never said those words to me once in the months we'd been together. Theo had been with me for about ten hours, and he'd both said them and meant them.

"Sar?" Theo said worriedly. "What is it? Are you worried I'll cause

97

a fire?"

I went back and kissed him, tears in my eyes. "I'll take care of it today," I said haltingly. "It means a lot to me that you offered to help."

Theo looked mystified, but let me go. I took care of everyone, then got the fire going. Taking off my robe, I crawled back in beside him. He pulled me close, and we slept again.

We got up about noon, and shared the guest shower. Mine was too small in the master bath, as I'd sacrificed all the space to the Jacuzzi tub. I liked watching the water roll off him. His body was very muscular, but still lean. Powerful was the best word that came to mind. I spent so much time watching him that soon I got shampoo in my eyes. The stinging quickly helped me to get my focus back. Finishing hurriedly, we both got out and dried off.

I handed him an extra robe to wear. "Do you want me to wash your clothes?" I said, as we went back into my bedroom.

"No, I'll need to wear them back when I leave," he replied. "Can I borrow some sweats though, and a T-shirt? If you have loose ones they should fit me, even if they're too short."

I gave them to him, and he put them on. I watched him, blushing when I realized he wasn't putting on underwear. I was thinking naughtily that that wasn't a problem for me when Theo noticed his jacket on my bedpost. He grabbed it and turned to me with it in his hands.

"I—" I tried to speak, but I couldn't get the words out.

Theo was before me in a second, holding me against his strong body tightly, as if he would never let me go. I stopped trying to talk and just held him, loving the feel of having him really here with me in the flesh.

"You don't have to say it," he said softly. "I tried every time I slept to dream of you again, too. Every night I hoped for it. But I never did."

We said nothing for some moments, and just stood there holding each other.

"Do you want me to make you breakfast?" I said finally, looking up at him and giving him a smile.

"Sure," he smiled down me, reaching out again to caress my arm gently. "If you want to."

"What do you want? Eggs? Bacon? Toast? Pancakes? Sausage?"

"All of that sounds good, Sar. Whatever you want to make is fine."

I made him a huge breakfast. He ate it all, which astounded me, until I remembered that night last fall he'd eaten half a pie in one sitting. I had some bacon, eggs, and toast, rationalizing that I'd been burning a lot of calories myself. When we were done, I stuck the dishes in the dishwasher, and turned it on.

Theo hugged me again. "We should probably talk now," he said softly.

I nodded, suddenly shy. I led him to the sofa, and we sat down.

"Okay," I said, resisting the urge to hug him or initiate sex. "You start."

"Sar, I want to be with you like we were last night, but more if you want to give it. Is that what you want?"

"Yes," I said, realizing in that moment that I meant it.

Before I could think on that, Theo continued. "Why now? You refused me before, that night I told you how I felt."

"Because I want to, and now I'm free to be with you. Danial released me from my oath months ago. I admit, I thought he didn't mean it at the time, but now it appears he did. I didn't trust Angelica, so I gave my diamond ring to Ivan to give back to Danial. He'll do it." I took a deep breath, and looked away from Theo, feeling guilty for my omission. I had to tell him the truth, that last night I'd been ready to take Danial back. But how?

"No, Sar. Look at me," Theo said, that note of command in his voice again. By his expression, he was bracing himself for what I might say. "Tell me everything."

"All right. I had planned to go back to Danial last night, to tell him that I'd have a child with him if he wanted to. I was going to tell him I wouldn't oath to him again, but that I'd stay with him if he wanted me."

The words hit Theo as hard as I thought they would, and he dropped his eyes. Finally, he said with effort, "Are you still going to?"

I reached out for him, but he held up his hands to stop me, waiting for my answer.

"No," I said, drawing my hand back. "If I were, I would never have let last night happen. I couldn't be with you like that casually, or pretend it doesn't mean anything. I had the dream with you, remember? We shared the feelings that made it possible, or we wouldn't have been able to dream together. What is between us is real."

"What about Danial? You still love him. You're still wearing your collar."

"He's got someone else wearing my clothes in his bed," I said angrily. "He's with Angelica now, Theo. He doesn't want me. Despite all his talk about me being the first woman he loved in decades, he couldn't wait three months for me. He rescinded the oath, rather than give me the time I asked for. I feel stupid for caring about him at all, after how he's acted."

"I hope you mean everything you've told me," Theo said grimly. "Because we are going to have to tell Danial about us."

Apprehension engulfed me. "Why, Theo? It's none of his business—"

"As long as you wear that collar and his marks, it is his business, and he's still your master. He should have taken off the collar, and healed the marks when he released you from your oath," he replied angrily. "That he didn't worries me. I thought he had."

"Won't he have to bite me, and then give me his blood to heal them?"

"Yes." Now Theo was positively snarling.

"I don't want him to do it," I said, looking away uneasily. "There'll be pain, and—"

"And I don't want him to see you or touch you or even talk to you, but I'm a reasonable man," Theo said firmly. "He has to do this. You can't be with me and with him at the same time." He cleared his throat. "That's the only thing I care about, Sar, my only condition. That if you are with me, it's just me. I don't want to share you with Danial, or anyone else."

"I'm not asking you to. But understand I'm worried about you and me, about how Danial's going to react—"

"I'll handle it, Sar. Don't worry."

"Did you tell him what almost happened between us back on New Years?"

"No. I decided you were right on the way home. He was furious when I told him about Terian, that he had kissed you. I knew he'd be uncontrollable if I told him what I'd nearly done with you. I was afraid for you, that he might tell Devlin you had left him, and you were alone here, without any guards—"

My apprehension became real fear at remembering Devlin, the heat in his golden eyes. "Maybe we should say nothing—" I began.

"He's my friend, Sar, my best friend," Theo interrupted. "I know what he's done to you, but I wouldn't hide this from him if I could. I

100

respect us all too much to even try that."

I felt ashamed then that I'd suggested it. I was the one who preached about honesty all the time. "You're right. We should go to him together. Tonight," I said wearily. "If we wait, and he finds out before we tell him, like the dream—"

"—it will be that much worse," he finished. "You're right. I have to go back there tonight anyway. I'm on duty, it being Saturday night."

"What will you do if he fires you?" I said reflexively.

"Make him buy me out. I own a lot of stock in his company, I helped him build it, helped him choose the location, when he relocated here from Colorado—" Theo stopped suddenly and shot me a look. "Sar, don't worry, I can—"

"Theo, I am going to ruin your friendship. I just don't want to ruin your life too," I said quickly. "That's all I meant."

"It's my life, and I choose to be with you. How is that ruining it?"

"I asked you before why you didn't just leave, and you always said you loved your job—"

"Of course I loved my job then. I didn't have someone to love, someone who loved me."

This was getting dangerous. What if he asked me if I loved him? What could I say, a little bit?

To head that off, I asked a more pressing question. After all, I wasn't the only one who'd been with someone else. "What about Tawny? Do you still care for her?"

"Yes, I care for her. But I won't be intimate with her again, now that I'm with you." Theo paused. "We haven't been together since that trip to Switzerland."

"Do you love her?"

"There was a time when I did, yes. But not now. For years I asked her to come here, to be with me. She refused. She'd be with me whenever I went to Europe and cry when I left. But she'd never come and live with me here. I invited her each time, even the last time I saw her—"

"Did she say why?" I interjected.

"There were always reasons, but they changed over the years. I don't know what her real reason was. She told me she loved me lots of times. Maybe she just didn't love me enough."

We lapsed into silence. I checked the clock, and it was now about three.

"We have about two hours until dark. When do you need to be back?" I asked.

"I need to be there at nightfall or before," Theo replied. "My shift is until dawn."

"So we have one hour," I said. "I need to go walk the dogs before we leave."

I got up, and he did, too. "I'll come with you," he said, reaching for my hand.

Chapter Eleven

March sunlight was weak, but it was a nice day. There was nothing green yet, but most of the snow had melted and we could walk more easily. The dogs cavorted looking for mice nests revealed by the melting snow. There was nothing in them, of course; natural foxes and coyotes having removed the contents long since. But they had fun shaking them, and throwing them up in the air, the dried grass scattering everywhere.

We walked for a while, not saying anything. I hadn't walked with Theo in daylight since the day he'd helped me with wood. It was good to see the sun on his hair and the way it shone, to feel the sun on my face. When he smiled at me and took my hand in his, it seemed the most natural thing in the world to let him.

On our way back, I finally asked him what I'd been thinking for most of the walk. "Theo, how did it happen that Danial met up with you?"

He looked at me out of the corner of his eye, and kept walking. "What you're really asking, Sar, is if I was born this way, or became werecougar, right?"

"Always cutting to the chase," I said, giving him a soft smile. "But yes."

"I was hiking with my parents in the Appalachian mountains. We were attacked. They got killed. I lived, but I was changed. I discovered it the first time I got really angry, when I grew fangs and claws."

His voice was bitter. I kept silent.

"I was nineteen when it happened. When I found out what I was, I went back into the mountains looking for the animal that had attacked us. I found him, after a week. He was overjoyed to have someone like him. He said he'd been attacking people for years, and I was the first one to change. Turns out he had been scratching them when he needed to bite them. The wound had to be mortal, or serious enough to shock the victim's immune system long enough for the werecougar virus to infect their cells. Then the virus needs to replicate enough so the DNA is altered, or the person just dies." He let out a sigh. "I killed him, Sar. I'd brought a shotgun loaded for bear, and I blew his heart to pieces. He died almost immediately."

I had tears on my face, but I needed to hear this. I needed to know where he came from. "Please go on."

"I couldn't go back to being a college student, or studying art. I went back to a favorite place I had near the mountains, and stayed there as a cougar. But I was new to changing, and not careful enough. A few people saw me as the days stretched into months, and soon I was being hunted. Danial found me there six months later. I've been with him ever since."

I wiped my tears away, then put my arms around him and hugged him to me. "I'm sorry, Theo, I'm so sorry."

His arms went around me, holding me so tightly I worried he might be bruising me again. Then he drew back, and looked at me emotionally for a moment. "You're only the second person I told," he said quietly. "Danial being the first. I don't like to talk about it." He embraced me again. "But I wanted you to know."

"I'm glad you felt you could tell me; that you wanted to," I said, squeezing him tightly. "You can tell me anything."

"I'm glad to hear it. Come on," he said, grabbing my hand again. "Let's go back."

We made it back to the house with fifteen minutes to spare. Theo picked me up, and carried me into the bedroom.

"What are you doing?" I said, as he deposited me on the bed.

"You said as many times as I want." He grinned at me, and raised his eyebrows.

I had said it, hadn't I? But that was before I was so sore. Still, we were heading into the vampire's lair, and we might not be coming out, at least not unscathed. No matter how I tried to look at it, tonight was going to be tragic.

Screw it. I pulled off my sweater, and Theo's hopeful look became one of desire.

"And I meant what I said," I smiled at him, beckoning him to me.

"Come here."

* * * *

Somehow, we managed to get going on time. Theo drove, at his insistence. He had put back on his clothes from last night, and his jacket. I had changed as well, putting on jeans, a wool sweater and sneakers.

"Tell me, what's your plan?" I knew he had one, or at least the beginnings of one.

"We park the car. I gather up some essentials from my room. We get anything you left behind, and put it in my truck. I rarely drive it—I drive so much for Danial—so it's in the garage. We park it near the house's front door. Then we go in, and ask Danial to remove your scars, and the choker. I admit to him I've fallen for you, and we're lovers. He and I may fight. I'm stronger and faster than he is though, so I'll most likely win. Then he hopefully does what we ask him to and we leave." He glanced at me. "I will most likely need to stay with you for a few days. Danial's reasonable, but he isn't a saint. He'll need time to come to terms with us. I hope that's okay."

I touched his hand. "That's fine. I'll feel safer with you near me."

"That's the good scenario," he said, grimacing.

"And the bad, as in worse case scenario?"

"If Aran told him you called me last night, that it was an emergency, he'd have sent someone to your house to check on us, when I didn't return, call him, or answer my phone. They would have seen my car there all night, maybe even seen me kissing you or heard us together having sex if they were near the house. He'd know before we told him, and he'd be waiting with a gun loaded with explosive bullets for me, and maybe some chains for you."

I felt like I was going to throw up. "That can't be possible."

"You asked, Sar. That's the truth, and you need to be prepared. But I'm fairly sure the worst thing you'll see is a few punches thrown and taken."

I closed my eyes. How did it come to this?

"Now, if he shoots me—" Theo started.

My eyes snapped open. "Theo, let's not do this."

"—if that happens, I have my gun on my back, the explosive bullets one. Draw it, and shoot him, enough so that we can get away. Aim for his torso, not his heart, just enough to slow him down. Don't kill him—"

"You want me to shoot him?" I was incredulous. "You're telling me

105

we might have to shoot him to get away, and you somehow still think this is a good idea?"

"I want us to give him a chance to accept us—"

"I know he won't. You know it, too."

"—but I don't intend to die now." He squeezed my hand. "Not when I have you. Really, don't worry. I've known Danial for ten years. He's never been anything but rational and reasonable. He'll be upset, but he'll be happy for me, too. He's told me often enough that he wanted me to find someone to mate to—"

My uneasiness spiked instantly. "We need to talk about something else, too," I said hastily.

"What, Sar?" he said, his eyes on the road.

"We need to cover children," I said heavily. "I didn't cover it last time with Danial, and look how well that turned out."

Theo swerved, and just missed the ditch, overcorrecting.

"Nervous?" I laughed brittlely.

"I didn't think we were there quite yet," he said nervously. "Are we?"

"We had sex—"

"Protected sex," he countered.

"Accidents happen, Theo. I'm a walking billboard for it. And I should have discussed it earlier with you, back when we talked."

"Why?" Theo said, casting his eyes to the road, then back to me. "Do you want some soon? Or do you not want to have any at all?"

I took a breath. "I need to know what you would want me to do, or might insist that I do, Theo. What you think you might want of me in the future, if you know."

Theo was staring at the road, lost in thought. Then he said "There is a much better than even chance that my werenature would be passed onto any child I had. I never planned on having children, so I can't answer to that. But if it happened to us in the next few months, accidentally? It's your choice. I wouldn't stop wanting to be with you if you decided you couldn't handle having my child. But if you wanted it, and it happened, I'd be there for you. I tell you this, never having been in the position I'm talking about. But that is what I'd expect to do and feel."

He glanced at me. "Sar, please answer my question. Did you ever want children? Did you and your husband ever try? What did the doctor say? You said you were going to go to one, to get checked out."

"No, we decided not to have any, and so we never tried. My doctor gave me a clean bill of health, though, and said it shouldn't be difficult, if I wanted to try having one."

Theo lapsed into silence.

"How old are you, Theo?" I asked.

"How old are you, Sar?" he countered, eyeing me speculatively.

"I'll be thirty-one next July."

"I'm thirty-five," Theo said.

I was shocked, and tried not to show it. "You look only about twenty-five," I said finally.

Theo laughed. "Thanks. Some of that is exercise, and some of it is my were-genes. I will age a little slower than normal humans, but not by much."

That was a relief. "Theo, when did you realize you liked me?"

I thought he might need a minute, but he answered right away.

"I always liked you," he said, giving my hand a squeeze. "But I didn't understand you. You'd act rational, and then you'd do the opposite of what you should, like the time you walked in on Danial and Angel—"

"Don't say her name," I said wearily.

"—on Danial feeding. When Lander came on to you and I felt jealous, I knew that I had feelings for you that were more than friendly. So I stayed away from you, hoping they'd go away. I knew you and Danial were in love, that you didn't love me. He's my friend, and he'd been alone so long. I knew what that was like, to be alone, and I was happy for him, even in my jealousy." He paused. "I guess the night I really knew it was love was the night you miscarried. You were bleeding, I was sure you were dying, and I was going to change you to save you. Part of me wanted to do it for selfish reasons, so you'd be mine. I knew then that I wanted you for myself."

Theo glanced at me. "Sar, you told me on New Years that you thought of me as a friend, that you didn't love me. But when you kissed me, and I kissed you, something seemed to break loose. I could feel your desire for me, that you felt something for me besides friendship. Was that when you realized you liked me as more than a friend?"

I HAD to get this conversation back to lighter topics. I didn't want him to ask me if I loved him. "Yes," I said. "When you kissed me, I wanted you to. Even though I had to repair my wall afterwards—"

"I'm sorry about that. I didn't mean to break anything—"

"Don't be, I enjoyed it. And I fixed the wall. You saw the new paint, right?"

"Yes, I was wondering if you painted it that color on purpose, or if your paint was tinted the wrong color—"

"Always a smart ass." I rolled my eyes. I was relieved though that he was joking again.

"You like it," he said, grinning.

He was right; I did like it, and him. "So you were always so harsh to me and brutal with the facts because you liked me?"

"I could handle it if you were with Danial. I knew he loved you, and would take care of you. I wanted him to be happy. I wanted you to be happy."

"But Terian angers you, because he's in my life, though he's only a friend?"

"I was jealous, when I saw you kissing, though I put all my emotion into righteous anger for Danial's sake. There is something you need to know: it might be his demon nature, or something else, but I can't stand Terian, not any more than Danial can. And the feeling is mutual, Sar. But I know he's your friend. If he comes by some night and I'm with you, I'll leave until he's done visiting you."

"You aren't jealous of him anymore?"

"No. I'm the one in your life and in your bed, not him." He smiled at me.

I went to return the smile, then suddenly felt the SUV lurch, as our wheels switched from dirt and ice to clean blacktop. Turning, I saw the lights of Danial's house coming into view and my spirit sank. We were here.

Chapter Twelve

We pulled into the driveway and parked near the garage.

Theo turned to me. "Stay here until I come back, no matter how long it takes. It's going to take me a while to walk to the werecompound and back, but you'd be noticed for sure if I drove there first. I have to make sure someone is going to cover for me tonight, because if I fight with Danial, and leave, he'll need someone to guard him. I'll likely run into problems explaining where I spent the night, and why my cell phone was off." He squeezed my hand, and jumped out of the SUV. In a second, he had disappeared around the side of the garage.

I stayed there for what seemed like hours, though the dashboard clock said only minutes had passed. I was so anxious I started to hyperventilate. Realizing my panic, I took deep breaths to calm myself down.

Theo appeared suddenly out of the gloom, a couple super size gym bags with him stuffed to bursting. I wondered what was in them. I'd only ever seen him in jeans, denim or cotton shirts, T-shirts, and sweats, if you counted the ones I'd lent him briefly. That couldn't all be just clothes. Guns, maybe?

He threw the bags in the back. "Now for part B. Come on."

"Theo, I can't think of anything I want that I didn't take except my gold nugget earrings, and maybe that damned black velvet robe. I have no idea where they are. It's not worth it—"

"Come on, Sar," Theo said, and held out his hand. "We have to do this for more than just our stuff. Don't worry; I'll be right there by your side."

I took his hand, and reluctantly climbed out of the truck. We walked to the front door together. He dropped my hand, and tried the door. It was unlocked.

"Either someone knows we're coming, and has set the stage, or Angel there is pretty dumb," Theo said disgustedly. "Anyone could walk in here, it's wide open to attack. I've told her more than once to make sure this is locked at all times."

I nodded agreement, both worried for Danial and angry at Angelica. I'd always locked the door.

Theo walked inside. I went in after when he said it was clear. He checked the kitchen first. I found my favorite pair of measuring spoons, and my American Woman's Cookbook, which I slipped into an empty shoulder bag.

Next, we walked into the dining room, which was empty. My eyes caught the woodcarvings again. I'd walked past them a hundred times, and had always been meaning to ask Danial about them, and never had. Odds being what they were, I wouldn't be able to tonight.

I opened the door silently, and took one out. They were all woodland creatures: birds, trees, flowers, animals. There had to be twenty of them there on the shelves of varying sizes.

"Sar, we don't have time for this," Theo said impatiently. "Come on."

"Who made these, Theo? Someone Danial knew in another century? I never got to ask—"

"I made them for him. One for every year of the business, and a few more besides. I told you I studied art. Sculpture and woodcarving were my two passions. They still are."

"They are beautiful, I—"

"I promise I'll make you one if we get out of here. Now come on," he said urgently.

We walked into the great room. The Christmas tree I'd put up was long gone. I wondered what had happened to the decorations I'd made. I hoped they'd been put out for birds or deer to nibble on, not just trashed.

I steeled myself to open up the bedroom door.

Theo stopped me. "They're in there," he said quietly. "And they aren't sleeping either."

"Well, now what do we do?" I whispered, grimacing. "Wait?"

"Yes. They're almost done," he said grimly.

Danial let out a loud cry of release, and then a woman—I assumed Angelica—screamed. Hers was not only pleasure, there was pain mixed in that sound. He was biting her, maybe marking her.

I turned away, heading for the front door. Theo pulled me into his arms and held me, giving me a gentle kiss on the forehead. Then he called out loudly, "Danial."

There was a pause. "I'll be out shortly," Danial said through the door.

There was no noise for a few moments. Theo suddenly dropped his arms from me, and stepped a little behind and to the side of me. The door opened a second later, and Danial came out, wrapped in only a robe. He was shining with that luster that meant he'd fed, and fed well. He looked as graceful and as beautiful as he ever had. Seeing him like that, I remembered him touching me, caressing me, and wanted to be back in his arms. Instead, I steeled myself, and stayed where I was.

"Why is she here, Theo?" Danial said, eyeing me coldly.

"Why don't you ask her?" Theo replied evenly.

Danial narrowed his eyes at Theo, but then looked at me. "Sar, why are you here?"

"Did you get the ring I gave to Ivan?" I said.

"Yes, I gave it to Angelica. She seemed to like it." He smiled cruelly.

I ignored his barb and began what I'd rehearsed in the car while I was waiting for Theo. "I'm sorry, Danial. I should have given it back to you the night you released me from my oath, but I didn't think. It's yours; you have the right to give it to whomever you want."

"That is why you are here, Sar, to remind me of my rights?" he said bitingly.

"I'd like my black velvet robe and my gold nugget earrings, if you wouldn't mind," I said, trying not to sound haughty.

"Tell me why I should give them to you now, after you've been gone for months?"

I lost it a little. Well, more than a little. "Because the earrings remind me of better times with you. And the other I want because you gave it to that bitch, and if she wants a black velvet robe you can damn well afford to buy her one of her own."

Danial gave me a hint of a smile, and went back into the bedroom. He came out with the robe, and the earrings, still in the box I'd put them in on Christmas. He handed them to me, and I put them in my bag.

"That's all you wanted?" he said seductively, moving closer to me.

"No," I said.

I pulled out his shirt from my shoulder bag, the red one of heavy cotton. He looked at it, surprised.

"I took it with me by mistake. I know what it meant to you, so I brought it back to you."

I handed it to him, and a real smile etched his face as he looked at it, and then back at me. "Theo, leave us," he said, his eyes locked on mine.

"No," Theo said with a touch of a growl.

It took Danial a minute to register that Theo hadn't done what he'd asked. He turned in slow motion to Theo, his dark eyes questioning.

"I want him to stay, Danial," I said. "I need something else from you. I want you to remove the marks. We aren't oathed anymore, and you are with someone else. For all I know, she's given her oath to you, when you gave her that collar. So please remove them."

He nodded once, gesturing for me to lie back on the couch, which I did. He lay partially on me, and I was uncomfortably conscious of the fact that he had on nothing under his robe. He kissed me, and I responded. I hoped Theo could take this, because if I wasn't at least a little relaxed, it was going to hurt all the more. Danial kissed down my throat, and over to one of the scars. He kissed for a while, then suddenly bit down. I flinched, jerking a little. He began to swallow, drinking me down. That made me angry, as I hadn't agreed to feed him, and I knew he didn't need my blood. Yet I said nothing, because when he was done he would heal me, and it was worth it to be rid of the scars.

I opened my eyes and located Theo. He was watching, and the look on his face said this was one of the most difficult things he'd ever done. Danial stopped swallowing suddenly, and I felt him holding his mouth over the wound on my neck, healing me. Then, Danial kissed his way to the other side of my neck, and healed that scar as well. Again, he drank from me for a while before healing the wound. By the time he finished, I was lightheaded.

Danial moved off to sit beside me. "Are you okay?" His voice was heavy with arousal.

I sat up, blinking. "I'm okay. A little foggy, but I'll be fine. Thank you for removing them."

"Is this really what you wanted?" he said seductively, caressing my cheek. "To be free of me? Or did you just want to feel me inside you again?"

I reached up, took his hand, and gently removed it. Just that small act made him narrow his eyes.

"You think on it," he said seductively. "Think about me at night, when you're alone. Theo, show her out." He turned to go back inside the bedroom.

"Wait, Danial," I said quickly. "I need you to remove the choker, too."

My words seemed to echo in the room.

Danial turned back to me, instantly alert, his face wary. "Why, Sar?"

Danial's tone was normal, but there was steel within those two words. Looking into his dark eyes, I knew suddenly that this was the last straw, the request that would break everything wide open.

"You promised me that you would if I asked," I said simply. "I'm asking now."

"What is your reason?" Danial asked again. "Any vampire could claim you, if I take it off. Every vampire in New York knows your name by now, and what you were to me, if not where to find you. If I remove it, you might be vulnerable to—"

"Isn't it enough reason that I'm asking you to?"

"No," Danial answered. His eyes were glowing with red tints. "You have a reason, don't you? Terian. I heard from Theo that he came to visit you months ago, that you kissed him—"

"It's not Terian, Danial. He's gone. He left when I told him I didn't have feelings for him. He knows I was oathed to you, but not that we no longer are."

Danial's reddening eyes suddenly went back to brown, as surprise registered on his handsome features. "You promised to come back to me, when you'd had enough time to come to terms with everything. Have you decided you can accept my non-aging, as you called it?"

I took a deep breath, trying not to think of how much I'd hoped to hear him say those words last night. Only twenty-four hours had passed, but everything had changed.

Danial moved closer. "That's it, isn't it? This is a surprise, a very welcome one—"

I used my memory of Angelica in my robe to build my fury hot enough to get out my next words. "I came back to you last night, Danial," I said, cutting him off. "I got here at dusk. I came to the door, ready to tell you I'd had enough time away from you, that I was coming back to you, that I would live here with you, that I'd have your child if you wanted it. And what did I find? A Ho-Ho who was wearing not only the robe you had given to me but also a silver choker with your emblem. She asked if I was here to feed you, and told me you'd just slept together, so I left. To top things off, I got to listen to you having sex with her a few minutes ago!"

The last was probably unnecessary, but I wanted to feel the anger, to remember how upset I'd been. It helped me not think about being in Danial's arms again. Despite Theo standing just behind me and everything else that had happened, part of me still wanted to be.

"Sar, you were here last night? Ivan said you gave him the ring, but I assumed you came in the day, to avoid seeing me. Angelica said nothing," Danial said emotionally.

He was suddenly before me, embracing me before I could stop him. Theo moved closer to us, but I told him with my eyes to keep still, and he stopped.

"Sar, I'm so sorry for Angelica, for what you heard," Danial murmured into my ear. "She is no substitute for you. I will tell her to leave tonight, that she and I are done, and you'll never have to see her again. Please forgive me," he added regretfully.

"Aren't you oathed?" I said nastily, trying to push him away. "That was no mere necklace she was wearing yesterday—"

"No, of course not," Danial said, hugging me more tightly. "I've given her no promise. I'm so glad you have come back to me, my love. I missed you so much. I filled our bed with her because I was so lonely for you—"

"You had sex with her because you were lonely for me?" I said sarcastically.

"Sar, I didn't mean that, I—" Danial was backpedaling fast.

It didn't matter; it was too late. "Danial, I told you that I needed time months ago. You said you couldn't wait for me. I came back because I promised you I would, because I wanted to believe that you would wait. But you didn't. Please let me go."

I moved back from him, as he reluctantly let go of me. It was on his face now that he was finally getting it.

"I am not here to offer you another chance," I said tiredly. "I'm here to end what we had, end it completely. Take off the collar. Take it off me and let me go."

"I will not, Sar," Danial snarled, his eyes tinged red again. "You are mine. Mine! I want a life with you too much to give you up now, not when you've come back to me—"

"Did you hear what I said?" I shouted at him. "It's over! Do you think you can hold onto me by making me wear it? It's too late! You've lost me, Danial!"

Danial stood up in a quick motion, the redness in his eyes glowing lightly. "Who have I lost you to, Sar? I thought I smelled some other male's scent on your body, and in your hair. Whose is it?"

"Mine," Theo growled. "Because she's mine, Danial, not yours."

Chapter Thirteen

Danial turned in slow motion to look at Theo. As he turned, his dark eyes filled with anger and became solid red, bright as fresh blood. Theo glared back at him, his eyes gone yellow gold as the pupils elongated to vertical slits.

Danial's face contorted in fury. He turned swiftly and backhanded me across the face with enough force to split open my cheek. I fell hard against the couch, and onto the floor. Pain radiated from my face and I began to cry, wondering if the bone was broken.

"Damn you!" Theo growled.

Loud scuffling and snarling from Danial and Theo inundated the great room, punctuated by crashes as furniture was knocked over. Every crash jarred the floor, bringing fresh agony to my pounding head and aching face.

I had to get up. I had to; Theo might need me. After trying once and failing, I pulled myself up the couch, holding on to the arm for dear life. I stood there swaying, my face throbbing, watching through teary eyes.

Theo had Danial by the throat, his claws out, his fangs elongated. He was screaming like an animal, his cry that of an enraged cougar. Danial was snarling, and trying to reach Theo's throat with his fangs. Theo quickly sank his claws into Danial's throat, and ripped him open. Yet as I watched, Danial's skin knitted back together seamlessly. Between the blood he'd taken tonight from Angelica and me, he was powerful.

Theo smashed Danial back against the wall. Danial punched him, and Theo went down, pulling Danial with him. They rolled over and over. Danial sank his fangs into Theo's neck, and ripped, trying to tear out his throat. But Theo pried him off before he succeeded, holding

Danial by his hair. He held Danial with one hand, and drove his fist into his face with the other. Danial fell off Theo backward.

Theo climbed to his feet. "I didn't want it to be this way Danial. You are my friend—"

"You were my friend," Danial hissed at him from the floor. "How could you do it? You knew how much I loved her, how long it had been since I loved anyone! You've outdone Devlin in your capacity for betrayal!"

"—but I can't help what I feel for her. If you weren't such an arrogant jerk, she would never have turned to me."

"She loves me, not you," Danial sneered at him.

Theo looked down at him, his eyes back to blue, his claws and fangs gone. "That may be, Danial. But I love her," he said softly.

He offered a hand to Danial. Danial took it, climbing to his feet.

I wondered suddenly if Angelica was watching or hearing any of this. Casting an eye at the door revealed it to be still shut. Understandable; I wouldn't have come out if I were her. Actually, if I'd been her and heard all Danial had said earlier, I'd have been packing my things to leave permanently.

"Please remove her choker," Theo said reasonably. "I'll keep her safe, I promise."

"I will not," Danial said evenly. His eyes had gone back to being dark, but they were still angry, still hurt.

"Why not?" Theo countered. "You've already got a replacement, like Sar said. That's not love, it's just bullshit possessiveness. You were willing to remove her marks—"

"Our love is none of your business," Danial said coldly. "There is no room for you in her heart, and there never will be."

"She said she's done with you!" Theo growled, finally angry.

"I'm not done with her, Theo," Danial said darkly, making me shiver. He leaned close to Theo, and said arrogantly, "And I want to know every time you're with her, anytime you look at her, you remember that she is mine, not yours. That in a short time, she'll leave you and be back in my bed."

Theo looked at him for a split second, and then decked him with enough force to knock Danial back to the floor. Danial lay there, hate in his eyes, looking up at him. Theo glanced at him, and then came over to help me.

My cheek had swelled so my eye was partially closed, the pain steadily increasing. There was some blood in my mouth where my teeth had cut my cheek; I could taste it. Touching my face gently left blood smears on my fingers. What had split my cheek open?

Theo was also still bleeding from Danial's bite on his neck, but his wounds were slowly closing. He put an arm around me carefully, grabbing my shoulder bag with his other hand.

"Come on, Sar. You need a doctor."

I leaned into him, letting him guide me. He helped me walk out of the house and out to the SUV.

"Sar, I'll be as fast as I can," Theo said anxiously, as he settled me in the seat. "Just hold on and don't talk."

He got in, started the engine, and drove around the house and out on a service road until we got to the garages next to the werecompound, as he called it. Theo opened the middle garage door, and backed out a gleaming slate blue Chevy truck. He transferred his bags behind the seats, then helped me into the front seat of his truck, and shut the door. He quickly pulled the SUV inside the garage, and then tucked its keys under the visor. He jumped into the cab of his truck, and motioned me to come to him. I scooted over to him, and he wrapped one arm around me, and drove with the other.

We made it to Alan's Creek in a few minutes, pulling to the side of the road. My cheek was throbbing now. Tears were leaking out of my eyes, for me in my pain, for Theo, who'd lost a friend, and for Danial, who'd lost us both.

"Sar, let me see," Theo turned on the dome light, and angled my cheek up. I cried out.

"Christ, if he'd hit you any harder, he would have shattered your cheekbone." He was angry and also worried. "It was his ring that cut you, damn him. I'll call Dr. Camlyn, and we'll drive to him right now."

"No, home," I tried to say. I was in a lot of pain, and the words came out unintelligible.

Theo was immovable. "No, you have to see a doctor. I could be wrong. If something is broken, we'll need to set it as soon as possible."

He called Stephen, saying we'd be there in a little under a half hour, and began driving.

He broke all the speed limits by about twenty mph. About twenty-five minutes later, we were there. Stephen drove up a few minutes after we did. Theo helped me into the doctor's office, and got me on an examining table. I laid there while Stephen checked me over.

"I think she has a hairline fracture, Theo, plus some scrapes both inside and out from the force of the blow. Who did this?" Stephen asked.

"Danial," Theo said in disgust.

"He hit her?" Dr. Camlyn said, shocked.

"We told him about us," Theo said, holding my hand and squeezing.

Stephen looked from Theo to me, as comprehension dawned. "Ah," he said.

"What can you do for her?" Theo said urgently. "She's in a lot of pain, she can't talk—"

"The scrapes and fracture will heal up on their own. Put some cold compresses on it tonight and the swelling will go down. I'll give you a prescription for some pills for pain, Sarelle, but that's pretty much all I can do for you. You're lucky he used only a tiny fraction of his strength—"

"I'm sure she doesn't feel lucky," Theo said bitterly. "Though I do agree with your assessment. Please call in the prescription to the pharmacy in Alan's Creek. We'll stop by and get it on our way to Sar's."

I tried to talk, and found I could, though it hurt a lot and I had to take it very, very slowly. "I gave him my blood. He healed my scars with his blood. Does it matter?" I managed to say.

"Do you have those vitamins I gave you, Sar?"

"No, they're back at Danial's," I said with effort

"Have you given him blood in the past two weeks?"

"No, not in the last two months," Theo said for me, giving me a worried look.

Camlyn nodded. "You should be okay then, Sarelle, but don't—"

"She won't be giving him any of her blood again," Theo said firmly. "Is there anything else I can do for her?"

"Then you'll be fine, Sar. Theo, make sure she eats something substantial tonight."

Stephen went to one of the white cabinets in the room, and removed an instant ice pack. He cracked it, and wrapped it in a towel, and handed it to me. I applied it to my face. The pain eased somewhat.

Theo's wounds had completely healed by this time, so he didn't need any treatment. I was both amazed, and more than a little envious.

Stephen left the room, and Theo helped me down from the table. We were walking out when something occurred to me.

"Theo, should I pay him? I don't have insurance—"

"Sarelle, Danial can pay for this. He's the one who hurt you. He can damn well pay to heal you. If he doesn't, I will. Dr. Camlyn will get paid either way, so don't worry."

He helped me to the truck, settling me in the front seat carefully. We drove first to pick up the pills from the pharmacy in Alan's Creek, and then to my home. I took two of the pills as soon as they were in my hands, dry swallowing them. Hopefully, they'd kick in fast.

Theo pulled into the driveway, steering to park his truck where he had last night.

"Wait," I said with effort. "Pull into the garage, Theo."

"Isn't the garage already full, Sar?" Theo asked awkwardly.

He remembered my late husband's Forrester. Again, I was struck by Theo's undemanding acceptance of me. He was willing to do so much for me and not ask for anything in return, not even a parking spot for an expensive vehicle he clearly cherished.

"I sold it, Theo, back in February." I put my hand on his. "There's room for you here," I said meaningfully. "Despite what Danial said."

His expression softened. "Good," he replied, his eyes meeting mine. "It's good to hear you say that."

I got out gingerly, keyed open the garage door for him, and he drove in. I opened the passenger door, and handed him the other operator that I'd been keeping in my SUV.

He took it, clipped it to his driver's side visor, then turned to me. "I suppose I should ask you what the password is," he said lightly.

"The password is 'lions,'" I said slowly and carefully.

He nodded as he grabbed the bags, and followed me inside. The dogs growled at him, but for once, they limited themselves to one growl, and then went and lay down. It was a start.

It was late, after nine p.m. It seemed much later though, after all that had happened. Happily, the pain pills had kicked in, and the swelling on my face had gone down some. I was glad talking was easier anyway.

"Do you want me to make you something to eat?" I asked him.

Theo came behind me, and hugged me. "Are you up to it, Sar?" he asked.

"I'm not great, but I'm okay. Pasta?" I offered.

"That would be great," he said, kissing me on the forehead. "I'm going to shower, if you don't mind. I've got a lot of blood on me."

I nodded. "Sure."

He left, as I set the water to boil and put the timer on. I unpacked my shoulder bag, throwing my rescued measuring spoons in the sink, and storing my cookbook away with my others. When I opened the velvet box to put my nugget earrings into my jewelry box, I was surprised to find the fox head earrings in there with them. Casting my mind back, I remembered removing them the night of Christmas day, before showering. I'd meant to put them back on that night, but forgotten. Not surprising, there had been a lot going on that night. I tucked both pairs inside the jewelry box, not wanting to remember any more.

The black velvet robe I threw into the washer, after looking at it with distaste. I should probably burn it, but in a perverse way, I thought of it as a trophy. I'd paid a high enough price to get it back.

I scrutinized my clothes, remembering Theo's comment about blood. There was blood on mine, too, both from when Danial had bitten me and from when he'd hit me. Some I thought might even be Theo's. Making a face, I took them off and sprayed on some stain remover.

Theo had gone into shower by this time. I gathered up his discarded clothes, and put them with mine into the washer. I'd wait to start it until he was done. I needed a shower, too, but one of my own with no distractions. I could smell Danial's scent on me, that nutmeg and cedar I'd once found so appealing. Now the scent just made me sick.

I went into my bedroom and opened my closets. Was there room for Theo's stuff in here? Only a little bit, for maybe a few shirts. I tried the dresser drawers I had shared with Danial, but even though there was room, I didn't want to share those with Theo. There was not much in them of Danial's, just a few pairs of jeans, and a couple folded denim shirts. I took them out, and walked them down to the basement, storing them beneath the spare bed in a drawer. Then I walked back upstairs, and moved my fleece sweatshirts, turtlenecks and sweat pants from the top drawers they had been in down to the drawers Danial had used. I left the empty drawers that they had been in open, as an invitation to Theo.

The stove was beeping loudly by this time. I hurried back and threw in the pasta. Remembering Theo's appetite, I put in the whole box, hoping that would be enough.

The shower shut off abruptly, then noises of the curtain being pulled back. Knowing Theo would be looking for his clothes, I grabbed both of his bags and knocked at the door.

He opened the door, wrapped in a towel. My eyes lingered over him in an appreciative glance.

I handed him his bags, saying with a shrug, "I didn't know which one you needed."

"Both, actually," he said, smiling as took them. "Thanks."

I went back to the kitchen to heat up the pasta sauce. Once it was hot enough, I turned it off and covered it.

Theo came up behind me, and hugged me. "Do you want to shower?" he asked after a moment.

I knew by the way he said it that he smelled Danial on me. That made sense. I could still smell Danial on me, and Theo's sense of smell was much greater than mine.

"Yes," I replied. "Watch the pasta, it's almost done."

"How will I know when it's done?" Theo's expression was hesitant.

Surely he'd made pasta before? I thought back to his life, how he'd grown up. Maybe he hadn't. "Get a fork, scoop some out, and taste it, but don't burn yourself. You'll know if it's soft enough by tasting it."

I got into the shower and used up the rest of the hot water, scrubbing myself raw to get Danial's scent off me. Once I finished, I put on some pajamas, and fixed my hair with some conditioner. It had gotten longer since I cut it, but it still was fully above my breasts, even wet.

I padded out on bare feet to see how Theo was doing. He was just tasting the pasta mixed with sauce with the spoon. Everything nearby looked intact.

"It's ready, Sar."

I dished up two plates, giving him the much bigger share. We carried our plates to the couch, and I set up the TV trays. With food came cats. Cavity and Asher and Jessica sat at our feet, their tails twitching, looking for a bite of pasta sauce.

"I'm surprised they aren't scared of you," I said, eating a forkful of pasta.

"They are, Sar. This isn't all about food. They'll get used to me in time."

Cavity came to the edge of the couch, and said his usual "M'eh?"

I replied with my usual "Eh," the hoped for invitation. Cavity jumped up onto my lap, purring, and settling down to sleep. It made it harder to eat, but I needed him, wanted him near me. I remembered the two months I'd been without him and the other cats, and guiltily wondered how I'd been able to do it.

Theo had paused, watching the exchange curiously.

I felt like I should explain. "See, he does this every night, when he wants to go up on my lap. He asks, then waits until I say it back to him. I know it's weird—"

"It's not weird at all. He's saying literally 'Room on you?' and you are saying 'Yes, there is room'."

"You can understand him?" I said, awed.

Theo held his serious expression for another few seconds, and then cracked up laughing. I glared at him, and ate my pasta.

"Sorry, Sar, that was too much, I couldn't pass it up—"

"Jerk," I said, grinning despite my annoyance. "I believed you." I stopped quickly though, as moving my face at all made it hurt again.

"Seriously, he probably is saying something like that. But it's not just the words, it's body language, too. No, I can't understand him; no more that you can understand all human languages."

I ate a little more of my dinner, then said quietly, "I left some drawers open for you, if you want to unpack."

"Okay," he replied, his expression exuding happiness.

When we'd finished, I turned on the TV, checking the weather channel for any late winter storms. Happily, there were none. Better yet, next week was the first week of April, and warm weather was forecast. If we could just get past this week, flowers and grass would begin emerging.

"We should probably go to bed," Theo said, then blushed lightly. "I mean that because you need rest, not, um, because—"

I shut off the TV, and looked over at Theo. "It's Sunday tomorrow, so we can sleep in. But the next day, Monday, I have to work in the morning. I've gone back to working normal hours, so I have to be there at eight a.m. Is the alarm going to bother you?"

"No. While I'm staying here, I'll keep your hours so we can spend time together, at least until I know where everything stands with Danial."

What he also meant was until he and I figured where things were going with us, too. That was good; it made things easy. I nodded.

I put the dishes in the sink, let the dogs out, and got ready for bed. Theo met me in the bedroom not wearing any pajamas. I had a few lustful thoughts, but was too sore to act on them. Instead, we snuggled up together, and were soon asleep.

The next morning, I woke up before the alarm sounded and shut it off. All I could think from the moment I opened my eyes was that my face was killing me. I glanced over in bed, saw Theo was next to me, and remembered everything.

I touched him softly on his face. "Wake up, Theo."

He opened his eyes, then leaned over carefully and kissed me very lightly on my nose.

"What's wrong?" I said curiously.

"I'm afraid I'll hurt you," he said. "I think you should stay home from work tomorrow."

I got up and went into the bathroom to look. Shit with a capital S.

Chapter Fourteen

The whole side of my face where I'd been hit was purple and blue-violet. Likely, it was going to look worse before it got better. The only reason I wasn't in agony was those pain pills Stephen had prescribed for me. The cut on my face had scabbed over, though the one inside was still raw. If I wanted to go outside the house in the next week, I was going to have to hide this with makeup, a lot of makeup.

Theo came to stand behind me, his hands gently rubbing my arms. "I'm sorry for what he did to you. I never thought he'd hit you. This is my fault."

Danial had bruised me before, yet I'd passed it off as nothing. I'd had all the signs, and Terian had warned me, too. I just hadn't listened. "It's not your fault or mine," I said tiredly. "We did the right thing."

Maybe it had been worth it. For the first time in months, I had no scars, no marks of ownership. I finally felt free. Well, almost free. The choker still encircled my neck, the ruby eyes of the fox head winking at me.

"Theo, Terian can remove this," I said, touching it gently. "He told me he could."

"Will he though, Sar?" Theo answered.

"I don't know, but it's worth a shot. I'll call him tomorrow," I said. "Today I'll stay home. Hopefully by tomorrow, it'll look a little better."

Theo gave me a dubious look. "We'll see."

* * * *

The next morning, I was depressed to see my bruise looked worse, not better. At least the pain was the same.

"You should call in sick," Theo said from the bed. "Sleep like you did yesterday. I'll take care of you."

"No, I'm fine," I said, scrutinizing my reflection. "I was off Friday for a friend's funeral; I can't be off two days in a row. I've got to get moving, and cover up whatever I can of this."

"Do you want me to drive you to work?" he offered.

"Sure," I said, surprised. "I'll be a while though, hiding this—"

"I'll take care of the creatures then," he said, putting on his jeans and going out the door.

"Thanks." I began to apply makeup. When I was done, if someone looked carefully it was obvious that I had a bruise, but it looked nowhere as bad as it had. Glad I'd invested in top of the line makeup when I met Danial, I threw on some clothes and started the fire. Then I ate some cereal, and made myself a lunch. Theo had already fed the dogs, and taken care of the cats. I offered him cereal, but he declined.

"Are you sure you want to do this?" I said, putting my bowl in the sink. "You'll have to come and get me later."

"I want to do it. Danial and I will come to terms or we won't, but either way, I'll go back to work doing what I know. I've made a name for myself, it's not like he'd be the only one I could do this type of work for." He paused, looking at me. "Remember, I'm tenth now."

I still wasn't exactly sure what that meant, other than he had some sort of rank as a bodyguard from killing that man of Garret's a few months ago. "I remember."

"What I'm trying to say is that I won't always be able to offer, and right now, I can. So let's go."

I followed him out to his truck. "We'll need to go down the road, make a left, and—"

"Sar, I know the way," he interrupted. "I checked into how feasible it would be to have someone watch you while you were at work, when Danial and I were worried about Terian."

"Ah." I hadn't known that.

He dropped me off in the parking lot after I kissed him good-bye. I went inside and clocked in, finding a message taped to my keyboard. My boss was out at an auction for the day, but he'd left me some instructions for some calls he wanted me to make, in addition to my normal duties. That was good; I could both keep busy and stay here in my office, where no one was likely to notice my face.

Near the end of the day, as I was finishing up some filing, my coworker Mark came up to me. He stood there watching me, almost staring, which was very unlike him.

"What's up, Mark?" I said, still filing.

"The guys and me, we noticed your face, Sarelle. Someone hit you pretty hard," he said quietly. "You tell me what's up."

I thought about lying, but what was the point? "A guy hit me," I said, turning to face him. "But I'm okay. He's out of my life."

"It's not that guy who dropped you off? The one in the Chevy?" Mark asked gruffly.

"No," I replied, turning back to my filing.

"Sar, if he did it, tell me. I talked with the some of the guys, and we'll wait until he gets here to pick you up, and—"

"He didn't do it," I said, turning to look at him again. "He beat up the guy who did."

"Then he's a good man, and I want to meet him," said Mark evenly. "You leaving about four, like usual?"

"Probably," I said.

He nodded, then left without another word.

As I was waiting in the parking lot about four, Mark strolled up to me. We made small talk, and he'd thanked me again for a chocolate chip cookie recipe I'd given him. His wife had made it over the weekend, and his kids had loved it.

Theo arrived a few minutes later. The moment he saw us waiting together, he drove right up close and rolled down the window. There was a smile on his face, but his eyes were wary. "Hi. Are you ready, Sar?"

"Mark, this is my boyfriend, Theo. Theo, this is Mark, one of the guys I work with."

Something passed over Theo's face when I said "boyfriend." I'd nearly stumbled over it myself. But he was more than my lover, he was my friend. It was time to call a spade a spade.

"Nice meeting you, Theo," Mark said gruffly as they shook hands. "Thanks for decking the no-good motherfucker who hurt her. I'll see you Friday, Sarelle. Stay out of trouble."

He turned without another word, and went back inside. I got in the truck.

"What was that all about?" Theo said curiously, as he drove out of the parking lot.

127

I explained what Mark had said about noticing my face. "They were just concerned about me."

Theo nodded. "It's good to have coworkers that care."

We parked in the garage. Noticing the bird feeder was empty, I filled it while he got the dogs. After taking the dose of pain medication Theo brought me, we all went for a long walk.

When we got back, I showered and took off my makeup. The bruise looked better, in that it was uglier. I debated covering it back up so I looked normal, but thought it would heal better if I left it alone. I compromised by brushing some light powder over it to make it less ugly. Then I went out to ask Theo what thoughts he had about dinner.

"Sar, you don't have to cook for me. I can get by with just eating meat."

"You can do whatever you need to regarding meat, cooked or no," I replied. "But if I'm going to fix something to eat for myself, I'll be happy to fix extra for you."

"You don't have to," he said almost defensively.

"You are doing things for me. I like doing things for you too," I said, wondering what his problem was. "I'm not talking a four course meal here, just some hot dogs."

He kissed me then with passion. I inhaled sharply with pain.

He broke away. "I'm sorry—"

I took my face in his hands, and kissed him lightly. It hurt a tiny bit, but I could bear the pain, now I knew it was coming.

"We shouldn't, Sar," he said, drawing back. "You're hurt—"

"My face is hurt, Theo, not the rest of me," I said, giving him a suggestive smile. "There are other places you can kiss me. Just be gentle."

He picked me up without another word, and carried me into the bedroom.

* * * *

Later that night, I had some soup and toast, and he had the better part of a chicken, raw.

"I would rather eat alone," Theo said as he'd put the meat on a platter. "All right?"

I nodded, thanking him silently for that, and went into the other room to call Terian.

128

I got his latest woman, Delilah, who said he was out. I asked her to have him call me, and gave her my number. Then I called my mother, figuring it was time to break it to her that I was again living in sin. Though we talked for at least ten minutes, I delayed telling her about Theo living with me, waiting for the right moment. That never came. I just managed to tell her that I had some news for her before she said she had to go.

Hanging up, I turned to Theo, who had just come back in and was putting his plate in the dishwasher. My quip about parental units died on my lips, beholding him. Theo was completely revitalized, his step springy, his movements quick and graceful. He looked almost as if he'd gotten younger.

Eating raw meat wasn't just a getting by sort of thing. His system clearly needed meat the way Danial's needed blood. Perhaps the rawness wasn't absolutely necessary? I resolved to see what recipes I had that were primarily meat, like chili or roast beef.

"What do you want to do?" Theo said suggestively, turning to me. "We have the rest of the night."

Even if he was feeling randy, I was beat. Besides, I was curious what he would do the first time he heard me say no. "I need to catch up on my TiVo," I said coolly. "Is that okay?"

"Sure," Theo said, moving towards the couch. "Click away."

We watched about five minutes of a late night FX Channel show until he made me turn it off.

"How can you watch that, Sar? All those people being so nasty to one another, so much back stabbing, and so much violence?" Theo asked.

I was surprised to realize that he was right; I'd just never seen it before. "Well, before I met you and Danial, my life was pretty boring," I said. "Now I've had some real life violence, I'm a little less enamored of it."

"I'm sorry," Theo said in a low voice. "We can watch it if you want to."

"No," I said firmly, clicking decisively to erase it. I cancelled my future recordings of the show, then went ahead and cancelled my other supernatural shows I'd had set up to record. "You're right about what I was watching." I cracked a smile. "I'm not about to start watching Green

Acres, but I am ready to give horror and the supernatural a break for a while."

"Go to bed and get some rest," Theo encouraged, touching my face lightly. "I'm still worried about you. I'll take care of things out here and then be right in."

"You just want me for my body," I said partly teasing and partly meaning it.

Theo caught the serious tone underneath the teasing. "What are you saying?"

"I'm not sure," I said after a moment. "I guess I'm worried things are moving too fast for me. I know that sounds dumb after how I acted with you earlier, and now—"

"It's not dumb," Theo said abruptly. "But I need to know what you want from me, Sar. Say what you mean. Do you want me not to stay here after all?"

"No," I said quickly. "I guess I'm not sure what I want for us. And I'm worried that you know exactly what you want."

"I do, I want you," Theo said, sliding closer to me and putting his arm around my shoulders. "But I don't expect you to just suddenly forget Danial because we're lovers now. I don't expect you to roll over on your back every time we go to bed—"

I made a face at his graphicness.

"—I do want you to tell me what you feel, always, and when you aren't in the mood. I'm a man, not an animal."

"That brings up something I was going to ask you about," I said awkwardly. "Do you need to change form?"

"I'll let you know when the time comes," Theo replied coolly. "But we were talking about you."

"I'm exhausted," I said. "I'd like to go to bed and sleep."

"Do you want me in bed with you?" Theo said bluntly.

"Yes," I said softly. "I like sleeping with you next to me."

"Go in to bed then," Theo said, giving me a chaste kiss. "I'll be in shortly, as soon as I tend to the fire and pets."

I went to my bedroom and got ready for bed, trying to think about my emotions. What was wrong with me? Why couldn't I just enjoy him taking care of me, and take the future as it came?

Because he seemed too good, I concluded finally, as I climbed into bed. He was everything Danial hadn't been, with all of Danial's good points. I was waiting for the cracks to appear, revealing what he was hiding. No man was perfect, especially not one who appeared to be. I'd learned that lesson a few days ago. Yet Theo appeared to be the exact kind of man I'd been hoping to find. The ease with which he'd become part of my life that had me worried. I'd just had my heart put through the ringer; I wasn't looking for another heartbreak.

I lay down in bed and was almost instantly asleep.

* * * *

That week passed quickly. My bruise healed up slowly, as all bruises eventually did. Even though my cheek looked nasty, I had no pain, thanks to the pills. Other than covering it up when I had to go off my land, I didn't think about it at all.

I was enjoying waking up with Theo, going to bed with him, falling asleep in his arms, eating with him, and doing things together. We went to a few movies during the week, mostly action ones, and threw popcorn at each other, and made out during the non-action scenes. We also watched the movie "The Ghost and the Darkness," as he had never seen it.

I abruptly shut it off before the lions got killed, right about when there are only three men left fighting them. "That's the end, according to me," I said, getting up from the couch. "The men give up and leave, and the lions live out their days. When they die of old age, the men come back, and start building again."

"What are you doing?" Theo asked in shock, giving me a look that said I'd gone crazy. "That's not the end. The men win, don't they?"

"Yes, the lions get killed in the end," I said sadly. "I don't like to see them get killed."

"You are rooting for them? They killed a lot of people, Sar," Theo said incredulously.

"They didn't ask to have someone build a railroad through their home," I answered. "They didn't ask to have a bunch of people drive away their natural food supply with noise, or to be hunted so someone could make necklaces from their claws and teeth to show how brave they are."

"You are one of the strangest women I've ever met," Theo said. He rose up and hugged me. "You never stop surprising me."

He kissed me chastely.

"I have a surprise for you, if you want it."

131

Theo smiled. "I think I know what the surprise is. You're sure?"

I nodded. "I'm not in pain anymore."

"Then I want it now," Theo, his hands sliding down to cup my rear. "Come over here on the couch—"

"No," I teased, sliding out of his grasp, as I began undoing my shirt. "You'll have to catch me."

Theo lunged for me, and I darted away toward the bedroom, him hot on my heels.

* * * *

With every day that went by, it was more and more obvious that Theo liked living with me, and that I liked having him there. What had begun as a few days had turned into something that was looking more permanent the more time we spent together.

We went to visit my parents that Thursday night, where I broke it to them that we were living together. As much as I was an adult, I thought it was best that they knew now, rather than finding out by accident.

My stepfather knew what was coming, and discreetly dragged away Theo to talk about possible fishing trips over scotch, before my mother let loose.

"Sar, you were engaged to someone else three months ago!" she shouted. "What are you doing? Where is your brain?"

"Mom, I broke up with Danial. He cheated on me," I admitted reluctantly, sneaking a peek into a nearby mirror to reassure myself that the remnants of my bruise were covered. I hadn't told her that he'd hit me. She'd have been after him with her .357 if she'd known of that.

"You know he cheated on you?" she said furiously. "How?"

"I walked in on them. Look, it's not important. It's been over for a while. I'm moving on. Please just be happy for me, okay?"

"Sar, I just want you to be happy—"

"Mom, I am happy—"

"Are you sure Theo's the right one this time?" she finished.

No, how could I be, really? I was just hopeful. Still, I wasn't admitting any of that to her.

"Yes, I am, Mom. I met him almost six months ago, and I've gotten to know him. I trust him completely. He feels right to me, he's a good man. I'm sure we'll argue our fair share—"

"You know I'm always on your side. I just want to know you're okay. Don't fall off the side of the earth again and not call me for weeks.

And since you're so sure he's the one, we are all going to go out to dinner together next week."

I smiled at her. This time, we could. "That would be fine. But we should be going, it's late."

I collected Theo who looked perfectly fine, despite overindulging. Though Danial had accepted one scotch when he'd visited, he'd refused any more politely. Theo, trying to be friendly, had said he'd try whatever my stepfather wanted him to try. In total, he'd had six different scotches in the space of an hour. My stepfather was a big believer in participation.

"Are you okay?" I said, as I drove us home.

"My body can handle it fine," he said grinning widely. "I can feel it though. This is the first time I've ever had more than two."

When we got home, he went straight to bed while I let the dogs out. When I came in to bed, he was fast asleep. I curled up next to him, liking the warmth of his body next to mine.

I hadn't expected things to work out this well with him, yet they had. How had such a bad situation resulted in such a good relationship? I had gotten a thaw in my own personal winter, just in time for spring. I heaved a sigh of satisfaction, closing my eyes.

The phone rang, just as I was drifting off. I got up to answer it.

It was Terian. "Hi, Sar, I got your message. Sorry it's been a while getting back to you."

"That's okay, Terian. When are you coming back in to town? Or are you going to stay out there?" I asked.

"Sar, if this is about the collar, I already gave you my answer," Terian said coldly.

A flicker of irritation entered my voice. "Terian, I went to Danial about a week ago. I gave him back his ring, told him it was over, and asked him to take off the collar. He removed the scars, but refused to remove the collar."

"I was afraid of this," Terian said with a sigh. "He thinks he owns you—"

"That's not all," I said angrily. "He hit me—"

"He hit you?" I couldn't feel the blackness across the phone lines, but it was thick in his voice, along with rage.

"Yes, my face is one big bruise. I'll be okay; I was checked by Dr. Camlyn. But I want the collar off, please. You're the only other one I know that can do it."

133

"I'm coming into town soon. I'll be there a week from tomorrow, maybe earlier. I've got some things to finish up here, but I am going to be moving back to the northeast. I've learned all I can out here." He paused. "I'll remove it for you then, okay?"

"That would be great, Terian," I said, relieved. "Call when you're coming in and I'll come pick you up, if you're flying in, that is."

"That's nice, but not necessary. I'll have my own truck, once I get it out of storage." Terian cleared his throat. "If you don't mind my asking, what happened with the guy you kissed? Did you ever tell him?"

Jealousy was in his casual words. Theo was right; it was better keeping them apart for now. Instinct told me that Terian wouldn't like me being with Theo anymore than he'd liked me with Danial.

"He dreamed of me Terian, like I dreamed of him," I said carefully. "I told him the same night you told me." I looked over at Theo, sleeping there in my bed—now our bed—and sighed.

"Sar, I'm so sorry, I—"

"Don't be sorry. You remember when I saved you? When you said you owed me one?"

"Yes," he said slowly, not understanding.

"This evens us," I said. "What you did saved me, saved me completely, no matter what you meant to do. And I'll be grateful to you for the rest of my life."

"What happened?" Terian said incredulously. "You've got to tell me."

"I've got to go, Terian, I've got work tomorrow," I said quickly. "Good-bye."

"Good-bye, Sar," he said, awed yet very curious.

I hung up the phone, crawled back into bed, and took Theo in my arms contentedly.

Chapter Fifteen

Theo took me to work again on Friday. After he picked me up, we both showered, and then met my parents for dinner.

Overall, the evening was good. There were just a few tense moments.

One was when my parents asked Theo what he did for a living. He explained honestly that he was between jobs, which made my parents share a meaningful look.

I hastened to explain. "Theo used to be Danial's partner in his business," I said carefully. "Danial knows I'm with Theo now, and he's angry about it. He and Theo are trying to work out an arrangement."

"He cheated on Sar with another woman and she caught them together," my mom said right there at the dinner table. "How does he think it's any of his business what she does?"

"Doesn't matter, he still thinks he has a claim to her," Theo said delicately. "So I'm taking a break from him for a while to let him get it straight how things are. When he does, he'll call me and we'll decide where to go from here."

"So you think he'll come around?" said my stepfather.

"He can't do without a partner for very long," Theo said with a shrug. "I'm betting he calls me by the end of next week."

The other tense moment was when my mom asked Theo what plans he had for me. He gave her a confused look, then said, "I don't have any plans for her."

"I mean for you and her together," my mom clarified. "As in the future?"

Theo blushed, and said "If you mean am I going to leave her anytime soon, the answer is no. I like your daughter very much."

"I mean are you serious about her? Are you going to get married someday? Are you thinking of having children?"

"Mom," I said in a warning tone. Then I whipped my head towards Theo, who was unruffled. "You don't have to answer that," I said quickly.

"I'll answer it," he said easily. He turned to my mother. "I love your daughter, Ma'am. I'm serious about her and about us. When and if we decide to make things formal between us, you'll be the first to know. That would happen, before anything else. You have my word on that."

"Good," my mom said approvingly. "Now, what about dessert?"

* * * *

Later that night, Theo sat down next to me on the couch. "I need to talk to you, Sar," he said seriously.

I was alarmed, but made myself relax. "Theo, if this is about what my mother said—"

"What I told your mother was the truth, exactly what I feel. When you are ready, we'll talk about marriage and children. Neither of us is ready yet, so we'll leave it for now."

I was good with that. "Okay. What is it, then?" I said hesitantly.

"Sar, I am going to have to change form very soon. Change form all the way, I mean." Theo seemed embarrassed or not sure how I was going to take this.

"It's okay, Theo. I expected this sooner, actually. What do you need me to do?"

"You shouldn't need to do anything," he said.

"But?" I prompted.

"I try not to change, but it can only be kept from happening for so long," he said uncomfortably. "I take a drug that helps me to keep control. Sooner or later, I have to go all the way and become a cougar. And later is now." He paused, running his hand back through his hair.

"You sound worried, yet this must have happened many times. What's the matter?"

"The longer I put it off, the wilder I become. It's been almost four months now since I last changed. I've got to do it this weekend," he said. "I'm just worried about changing with you around. Your neighbors are pretty close by."

I didn't like where this was going. "What do you usually do?" I asked.

"I usually change in the forest near Danial's home, and hunt something. I kill it and eat it. I wake up naked in the forest wherever I am, and walk back."

"Are you going to do that here?" I asked nervously. "I have over thirty acres of forest, but it's nowhere near Danial's expanse. He has over two hundred acres."

"I'm afraid to. You have neighbors with livestock around. Also, people will hear me screaming as a cat and hunters will come with guns. To them I'm a trophy," he said bitterly.

"What can I do to help you?" I said, scared.

"I want you to confine me in your barn. It's made of metal and strong wood. I should be safe there, and not tear up anything."

"What else?" I said.

"We need to buy an animal, maybe two. Rabbits would be okay, but something bigger, like a deer or small cow, would be better."

"Can it be dead already?" I said, hopefully.

"It's better for me if it isn't," Theo said bluntly. "You noticed how the raw meat affects my physique."

"I noticed," I said quietly.

"Sometimes I think the bloodlust is what builds up in me, until I have to change, that the longing to kill is what drives the change to happen," Theo said disgustedly.

"Do you have to kill?" I asked.

"I always have in the past," Theo admitted, his eyes dropping to the floor.

"Say we put an animal in the barn for you. You change, then kill and eat it. Then what happens? Do you change back?"

"Pretty much."

"Does it take all night?"

"It seems to," Theo said, awkwardly.

He sounded unsure. How could he not know? A terrible thought suddenly struck me. "Theo, when Cia was here and she changed for me, she knew who I was and understood my words. Will you know me, understand me?"

"Probably not, Sar. I don't want you near me when I change. I could hurt you, even think you were prey." Theo looked away, unwilling to meet my eyes.

"Why is it that she has control and you don't?" I asked bluntly

"Because she changes every week at least once, sometimes every night," he said in exasperation. "She doesn't take the drug, never has. None of the foxes do. The drug separates the human and animal, putting a wall between them, so it's harder for the animal and human to communicate."

The drug made it harder for the animal to get through to influence the human. The flip side was it also made it harder for the human to control the animal and its urges, when the animal finally assumed control.

"Why would you do that to yourself, Theo?" I asked. "Why cut yourself off—"

"Because I hate it, Sar! I hate it! I never asked to be this way!" he shouted. "Do you know how it feels, waking up with blood on you, naked in the forest? How it feels knowing that you have to do it again and again for the rest of your life?" His eyes flickered from blue to yellow, and then changed back to blue.

Ghost and Darkness leapt to their feet, growling. Jess and Cavity, who'd been sleeping on the couch, let out screeches and ran from the room.

I was suddenly terrified he'd change right here in the living room. "Theo, it's okay," I said quickly. "Calm down, please."

"It's too late," he said, his voice almost a growl. His body twitched suddenly, almost convulsively. He turned to me, his eyes again light yellow gold. "It's got to be tonight. I feel control slipping away. I'll leave now. Please, get whatever extra meat is in the fridge, and bring it to the barn." He quickly went for the door. "Throw it in, lock the door, and get away."

The front door slammed, as I raced to comply. I grabbed a plastic bag, and shoved the ground beef and chicken in the fridge inside, then grabbed a few packages of hot dogs. That was it. Everything else was frozen solid.

I grabbed my jacket and ran outside, careful not to let any cats out. They'd be following me to their doom. I hurried as fast as I could to the barn, let myself in, and turned on the lights. Theo was nowhere in sight.

I waited a few seconds, listening, but didn't hear any noises or see any movement. But he could be hiding in one of the old horse stalls down along the barn sides. I'd never know it until I crossed in front of them as a target. I walked into the barn a few feet, laying the meat on an extra bale of leftover hay. I listened hard, but still didn't hear anything.

I turned to leave, and then heard slow noises, but with weight behind them, padding around above me. Theo was in the loft of the barn, the upper part used for hay. It was empty now, except for some lumber, Christmas decorations, and dusty bales of old hay.

The padding sounds suddenly moved faster, coming closer. Fear raced through my veins; Theo had smelled the meat, or me.

The stairs to the loft were on the way in, right near the door. I had to get out before he came down the stairs.

I took two steps, and then a tawny head suddenly appeared in front of me.

Chapter Sixteen

Theo flowed down the steps like water, all lithe muscle. He was long, easily seven or eight feet from his head to the end of his black tipped tail. His fur was a gold buff color, and his eyes were the same yellow gold I'd seen when he had been a man, but they were huge now, gazing at me out of black edged eyes. His nose was pink, with white patches around his mouth. He bared his teeth to reveal huge fangs, easily the length of my fingers.

I was between him and the meat. I began backing away.

He turned to me quickly. I stopped moving. He paused, watching me. Then he turned back to the meat, and settled down to eat. He devoured the whole chicken, crunching the bones, fat, and gristle along with the flesh. He ate each hot dog in a gulp, and then ate the ground beef. He chewed up the plastic white container also, but when it cracked under his teeth, he spat it out in pieces.

He was magnificent, beautiful, dangerous, and terrible to behold. I waited motionless, trying to think of how to get past him. The door of the barn was unlocked. If he got loose, Theo had a better than even chance of getting shot. If he killed one of the neighbor's cows or sheep, that chance went close to a hundred.

Theo turned and looked at me for a second, then slowly padded toward me. I backed up quickly into the stall, sliding the wooden door shut as he leaped for me. He hit it hard, the wood and metal shuddering under my hands so that I nearly lost my grip on it. Theo reached through the bars, swiping at me with his unsheathed claws. One of them connected with my hand and laid it open. I let out a scream, simultaneously trying to duck, put pressure on my hand and still hold the door shut. He sniffed loudly, then screamed and swiped again eagerly,

140

wanting to get to me; real prey that was so much better than the dead flesh he'd eaten.

I crouched down and held the door, avoiding his claws. He battered the door for a while, screaming his anger that he couldn't get to me, and then swiped once more. I crouched in the dirt, praying the old door could take this abuse. These stalls hadn't been used in years. Luckily, they'd been made to withstand a kick from a horse, and the oak planks were still solid.

Suddenly, silence descended. I was afraid to get up to see what had happened, but then something fell over further out in the barn. There was a bang as several old boxes were knocked over, then a loud terrified squeal. Theo had gotten one of the rats that called the barn their home. Loud crunching noises were coming from the far end of the barn.

I peeked over the edge of the stall to look. Theo was over at the other end of the barn, a rat's tail disappearing down his throat. He licked his face and yawned, stretching. Then he noticed me and exploded in movement, reaching me in seconds, leaping to hit the door again. It almost swung open, but I held it, despite my scratched hand was bleeding badly now. The wound wasn't very deep, but it was almost six inches long.

Theo screamed again, and then padded away.

I wanted to cry. What could I do? I couldn't stay here all night. I was tired and exhausted already. I'd never outrun him to the door. Even if he went upstairs, I would have to hope he stayed there, as I'd need time to get to the door, get out, and lock it behind me. As scared as I was, I couldn't risk him escaping.

There were noises above me, to my left. A shadow was moving in the light.

Oh, God, I'd forgotten…

The stall fronts were wood on the bottom, and steel bars all the way up to the ceiling. They completely blocked anyone passing by from a horse that might bite, or kick. But the sides of the stalls did not go up all the way. There was a two and a half foot gap on both sides between the stall top, and the ceiling. Much too high for a horse to bite or kick anyone. Yet there was plenty of room for a smaller animal wanting to get into a stall.

Theo was coming over the top of the stall. First came the tips of his ears, and then great yellow gold eyes. When the front of him was almost in the stall, I threw the door back, and dashed out, slamming it behind me.

Theo wasn't going to be thwarted that easily. He jumped back up, perched on the edge of the stall, and then leaped in front of me out the open door of the adjoining stall, quickly cutting me off from the door. He screamed again, and leaped for me. I turned to run, and he hit me on my back hard, bringing me down and knocking the wind out of me. I lay there still, hoping he'd leave me alone.

He rolled on me, forcing my breath out in a rush. He was very heavy, and when he pushed down on me, I waited to hear my ribs crack. He placed his claws on my shoulders, almost kneading, then suddenly dug them in. I jerked, trying hard not to move as they sank into my jacket and my skin, the jacket taking most of the brunt. Abruptly, Theo contracted his claws, pulling backwards hard. I screamed loudly as he ripped open my back.

Theo let out a loud scream that deafened me. Then I felt his fangs close on the back of my neck, pricking me on either side. I closed my eyes and waited for him to bite me, to finish it.

I thought bitterly to myself how much Danial would love to see this. If Theo killed me or hurt me, he'd be destroyed himself by guilt. I had to get out of this. But I was afraid to move, afraid to incite attack.

Theo hadn't moved. His teeth were still on either side of my neck, pressing gently, but not biting. He was sniffing again, sniffing repeatedly, his breath hot on my neck.

Suddenly he released my neck, and began licking me instead. His tongue felt like sandpaper on my skin. He licked my neck and face, the part he could reach.

"Theo, please stop," I whispered, afraid to draw too much attention.

Theo stopped, letting out a grunt.

"Please let me up," I whispered.

Theo stepped off me. I got on my hands and knees slowly, but was afraid to move too much or too fast. He was watching me intently, the tip of his tail twitching.

I crawled over to the edge of the stalls carefully, and sat with my back to the wall. Everything hurt, and I was chilled. I'd intended to come out for a few minutes. It was only April, the temperature about thirty degrees. My back had to be bleeding, too, though maybe not as bad as my hand had been.

Keeping a wary eye on Theo, I glanced at my hand. It had dirt in the wound now, but it had stopped bleeding. I stuck it inside my jacket sleeve, cradling it to my chest.

Theo came over and sat in front of me, watching me and grunting occasionally.

After a few moments, I reached out for him with my uninjured hand.

He looked at me, and grunted again, making a kind of purring noise.

"Theo, come to me," I said softly.

He got up, and walked closer, close enough to end me with a bite. I was afraid to touch him, afraid he'd hurt me again. But what choice did I have? I had to try to get through the animal part of him to reach the Theo I knew.

I reached out to him, and ran my hand over his head. He pushed into my hand, rolling his head to follow my fingers. I rubbed his head and neck. A great vibrating sound rose from his chest, and his eyes closed. I stroked him, tears in my eyes, as he purred for me. Soon one hand was not enough for him, and he rolled himself onto me, laying his head in my lap. I was loathe to touch him with my injured hand, worried he'd think I was food again. But he found my hand anyway, smelling the blood on it. He licked it, and I cringed, worried I'd hear a crunch shortly. Instead, he just licked the blood away. This opened the wound, but he just stayed there, licking the new blood as it welled up. Eventually, the bleeding stopped, the skin surrounding the wound red where his tongue had licked away the top layers of my skin.

Theo had been purring this whole time as he pushed against me, insistently, wanting my touch. I petted him with both hands then, watching his huge eyes close as I ran my hands over him. He extended his neck as I scratched him under the chin, then rubbed his face against me, trying to get his scent on me. Then, with a sigh, he laid down on me again, still purring.

"You're beautiful, Theo. So beautiful," I whispered, petting him.

He rolled on his back, nudging me to pet him more. He couldn't seem to get enough of feeling my hands on him, stroking him, touching him.

But I was tired, and there were limits to what I could do. Finally, even his nudging couldn't get me to pet him. He lay down then next to me, laying his head on my lap. I laid one of my hands on him, resting on his fur. I was cold, but exhausted, too. With the heat of him warming me, I fell asleep.

* * * *

I awoke in the early morning light, freezing. Theo was still next to me, keeping that side of me warm. He was still a cougar, still asleep, his head on my lap.

As the light brightened, I saw him change.

A ripple passed over his body. His muscles began to twitch, and contract. Then he was changing, the hair pulling into him somehow, into his skin. His tail shrunk back into his body, and his arms and legs shortened, as his claws pulled into him. But the most amazing was his face. His feline features narrowed, as his flattened cougar nose became narrow, and his whiskers pulled in. His ears shrank until they were again at the side of his head, and human sized. All the hair pulled in, and he grimaced as his mouth was too small to contain the teeth of a cougar. Slowly the teeth shrank, too, until his incisors were like mine. His eyes remained closed, but he was human again.

He opened his eyes a few seconds later, his expression one of momentary disorientation. Then he realized he was laying on someone, and looked up.

"Sar?" He bolted up, reaching for me. "Are you okay? Did I hurt you?" Tears began to form in his eyes.

"I'm okay," I said wearily.

"What happened?" he said, his eyes searching mine.

"You don't remember?" I asked.

"Tell me," he persisted.

"Please, take me inside. I'm so cold. Then I'll tell you," I whispered.

He gathered me up and carried me to the stairs. He passed the chewed up remains of the food, but said nothing. I gave him the keys from my pocket, and he went to unlock the door.

"It's unlocked," I said tiredly. "I never got the chance."

He set me on the stairs for a moment. "Let me get dressed, Sar. I'll be fast."

He ran up the stairs. Shortly after, he came back down, dressed, his shoes on. He gathered me up in his arms, and turning off the lights, brought me inside my house.

I'd left the door unlocked last night when I followed him, but luckily, no one had used the opportunity to burglarize it. He set me next

144

to the wood stove, long cold. He took out the old ashes, and built a fire. He went out with the dogs; emptying the cold ashes in the yard as they did their business. Next, he fed them and the cats as the fire began to burn finally in earnest, warming me. Then he sat down directly in front of it, and held me in his lap, rubbing my cold hands. I hissed in pain when he touched my injured hand. He examined my wound, worry etching his features.

"I did this to you," he said. It was not a question.

I didn't reply

He went, got some bandages and ointment, and treated my wound. By the time he was done, the fire was burning brightly, and warmth had spread out to me. It felt so good to be warm. I laid there in Theo's arms and slept. I don't know how long he held me there. Sometime, maybe an hour or so later, he roused me.

"Sar, wake up," he murmured into my ear.

"I'm awake," I said groggily. "What?"

"Tell me what happened," he said pleadingly. "I need to know."

"What do you remember?"

"I got to the barn. I knew the change was close. I went up into the loft so I'd be away from the door when you came in. And then, I changed." He paused. "I can't remember anything, after that, until I woke up with you in the barn aisle on the ground."

I told him what had happened, what he'd done, and how I felt, leaving nothing out. Theo began to cry when I told him of how he'd cornered me, great tears welling out of his beautiful blue eyes to splash on my shoulders. The tears came faster when I told him about how he'd dug me with his claws.

Theo held me carefully. "Am I hurting you?"

"No," I said tiredly. "I'm sore but the wounds probably aren't that bad."

"Do you want me to leave, Sar?" he said quietly. "If you do, just tell me, and I'll go."

I turned to look at him. "I don't want you to leave."

I kissed him gently. He kissed me back, and then we were both crying, sobbing in each other's arms, all the fears we had coming out of us the only way they could. We'd both been afraid and tense for too many hours not to need this kind of release. Finally, our tears ceased, and I lay there in his arms, warm at last.

"I need to dress your wounds," he said firmly, picking me up and bringing me into the shower. He undressed me, wincing when he saw the claw marks. The jacket had taken most of it, but the bathroom mirror revealed ten vertical scratches on my back about an inch long, and about a eighth of an inch deep. He also checked my hand, but it was plain to see that the scratch he'd given me was healing nicely. I wondered if it was all that licking last night, but didn't ask.

Theo cleaned my back wounds, and put antiseptic on them. We both showered, and then he applied more of it again both to my hand and my back. We also made a point of brushing our teeth. I'd needed to kiss Theo when he'd been upset, but I kept remembering the rat and the noisy crunching. I'd had to brush my teeth three times before I felt clean. I made sure he brushed twice.

We put on clean clothes, and went to get some breakfast. I made us another huge one, with bacon, eggs, toast, waffles, and sausage and ham steaks. Theo still ate more than I, but I was starving by now and he didn't outdo me by much. I was thanking God I was alive to eat breakfast. Counting calories didn't even enter my mind.

After we put the dishes in the dishwasher, Theo brought me in to lie on our bed. He lay down next to me, and began to speak.

"Sar, I apologize again for attacking you. I shouldn't have to change for a few more months. By then, Danial will have worked this out in his mind, and—"

I spoke quickly, before I could change my mind. This was going to be our first fight and maybe our last. "Theo, you are going to change tonight, too."

"Sar, I don't have to—" he began.

"You need to, and you do have to, Theo," I said firmly. "We need to do it every night until you have the control you need, until you can recognize me when you're a cougar. I can't live with you here without you being in control of your animal side. You might hurt me, or my pets. I can't risk either one."

"I won't, Sar, I promise. The drugs give me control over my animal side—"

"No, they don't. They never did, Theo. They're keeping you from having control, real control."

"Sar, please, don't ask me to—"

"Stop taking the drugs, Theo. You tell the truth to everyone but yourself. This is who you are, what you are."

"It's not who I want to be," he whispered.

"It is that sentimentality that almost killed me last night, Theo," I said gently, if those words could be gentle. "You need to stop hiding and be who you are."

"You saw last night what I was capable of. What kind of man does that?" he said bitterly.

"The kind of man I'm falling in love with," I said to him, a faint smile on my lips. "The kind of man who doesn't lie to himself or anyone else."

The look in his eyes when he understood my words suffused me with feeling for him. Seeing him look at me like that, I wondered how it could've taken me so long to say them to him.

He pulled me into his arms and kissed me, tears again on his face. "I'll do it, Sar. I'll do it. For you, for us, I'll do it."

I kissed him back, pulling him closer. He rolled over on me, and I felt him against me, ready.

"Again?" I said to him lightly.

He knew what I meant at once, as we both snorted with laughter. That word was our joke, from that first time he'd asked to make love again so awkwardly and I'd found it endearing. I sometimes told him it was the only word that I expected to hear from him every day without fail.

"Again," he said lustily, giving me a lecherous smile and wink. "And maybe a little later, again after that."

"You're going to kill me," I said dramatically

Theo leaned closer. "Haven't you heard, Sar, it's the best way to go."

Chapter Seventeen

Theo changed for me Saturday night and every following night that next week. He showed me the pills he'd brought with him, and he had me watch as he flushed them all down the toilet. We practiced in the barn. As before, I put out meat for him to feed on before I tried to speak to him. I ended up buying an entire deer from a neighbor of mine who hunted, and he brought it to me nicely processed. It was a lot of meat, but we went through a good portion of it.

I got chased again by Theo the first night, but was able to get him to back off by asking him to. I was afraid, yet he did back off, and eventually he came to me to be touched, as he had before. The next few nights he still didn't seem to know who I was at first, but when I talked to him and he smelled me, he again wanted to feel my hands on him and mark me with his scent by rubbing his face against me. By Thursday, he recognized me before I spoke, and came to me purring. By Friday, he began to remember what had happened while he was in animal form, still just in tiny pieces of memory, but much more than he had ever remembered before. He still couldn't be near the dogs, or any other living thing in animal form, but we'd come a long way in a week, much further than we hoped.

We resolved to keep working at it together, until he got to the point where he was as Cia had been, with full cognitive memory of his time as animal. While there was still a long way to go, I was relieved that he knew me by sight and sound as well as smell now. He wouldn't hurt me if he changed and I was with him.

There was an unforeseen side effect of all this time spent in animal form, and the great amount of raw meat he ingested: Theo's age seemed to reverse. By the end of that week, he looked even younger than twenty-five, and was stronger and faster. I admitted to myself that just made me feel older, yet I was happy for him. He seemed truly at peace now, in a way he hadn't been since I'd known him, maybe in a way he hadn't been since he was attacked while still a teenager. Some part of that was because he knew I loved him, that someone could love him as he was now, fur and all.

I wondered about that, too, mostly when I was alone. I'd had so many worries about Theo and me in the beginning, and now, barely two weeks later, they all seemed to have evaporated like early morning mist. How had I come to love him so easily and so fast, when falling for Danial had taken so much longer?

I rationalized that had a good deal to do with how different the two men were, despite being good friends. I'd never felt able to trust Danial for long, and I'd always been aware on some level that he kept things from me, even when he swore that he didn't. We'd been lovers from the start almost, and I admitted that after I'd told him I'd wanted him, he had been the one who decided how and when the relationship progressed. Hell, he hadn't given the choker to me until he found out he couldn't feed from me metaphysically, and he hadn't invited me to the party he'd planned for months until we'd slept together. It was his insistence on running things, on running me, that had spelled the doom of our relationship.

But Theo had been my friend first, and I'd trusted him since he'd given me the gun. With each crisis, I'd trusted him more. What I'd said to him on New Years after he kissed me was the truth: I trusted him with my life. He'd held it often enough in his hands. He'd never lied to me, and I was open with him, because I knew what he said to me was what he thought, not what he wanted me to believe he thought. When he'd come to me that night months after we'd dreamed together, I'd been as desperate for him as he was for me, to feel again what we felt in the dream. And when the night was over, when he'd asked me if he could help me, everything had seemed to fall into place. What bothered me most is how I'd spent time with him almost every day for a few months, and not seen that the man I was looking for was right in front of me.

* * * *

That Friday night, before changing form, he'd given me a wrapped parcel tied with string.

"What is it?"

"Open it and see."

I unwrapped the parcel to find a beautifully carved cougar, made of poplar, lying atop a rock, watching below him over and out from the rock. It must have taken him hours to carve this. It was remarkably detailed. He must have started the first day I'd left for work.

"Thank you, Theo. It's beautiful," I said, kissing him.

I put it on the mantle, taking down an older picture of myself and the dogs.

"What's he looking at?" I asked.

"There's this woman he sees in the field below, and she has long blond hair and she's sunbathing naked—"

I kissed him, laughing, and he laughed too.

When we returned after Theo changed back to human form, there was a message from Terian on the machine, saying he'd be coming in Saturday night at seven or so, and to call back whenever we got in.

I called him back close to dawn. "Terian, hi. Do you want me to pick you up at the airport?"

"No, but thanks. I have a meeting first, and I'm not sure how long it will run. It may be all night."

I was very curious to know just who the "meeting" was with, but didn't ask. "That's fine. Call when you're ready, and I can come give you a ride to your truck. Or you can just drive up, if you'd prefer."

"Sounds good," he replied. "It'll depend on when my meeting ends. I'll give you a call. See you then, Sar."

I hung up and turned to Theo, who'd heard my side of the conversation. "I'll need to see him either tomorrow night or the next day. Are you sure you don't want to just stay and meet him?"

"I'm sure," Theo said, nodding. "I can leave for part of the night. We'll play it by ear, until we know what day he'll actually be coming."

I nodded, wondering to myself if I was doing Terian any favors by not having him meet Theo immediately. I rationalized that I'd tell him about Theo Saturday, and then maybe see if I could get the two of them together on Sunday. I was loathe to push them on each other. Terian might have brought Theo and I together inadvertently, but he would never have done it if he'd known what was going to happen.

Then Saturday came, and all hell broke loose.

It started like a nice enough day. After waking up, I fed the dogs while Theo fed the cats. I cooked what was becoming the Saturday and

Sunday weekend breakfast feast. We ate leisurely, watching the weather, which promised to be almost sixty, pretty good for the beginning of April. There were possible storms later, but we agreed they would probably miss us. Then I asked Theo what he wanted to do next, and he told me his favorite word. Aroused by his kisses, I let him take me back in the bedroom for a few more hours.

Theo would be going to go back to work eventually. This past week, he'd made calls to several vampires and other supernatural denizens of the nearby surrounding areas within a hundred miles, asking if they were hiring. According to him, two looked very promising. If his new job was anything like his old one had been, he might not be able to be home much, especially on weekends. Therefore, I had to take full advantage of him while I could.

We slept again after sex, until I was roused by the ringing of the phone. I looked at the caller ID which I'd set up for my bedroom phone a few weeks after Danial's call months ago. It read Solutions, Inc.

I carried the phone to Theo, nudged him awake, and gave the whole thing to him, still ringing. Theo had told me to expect this call, but I wasn't going to talk to Danial, even just to say hello.

Theo picked up the phone. "Hi, Danial," he said guardedly.

I lay back down on the bed and snuggled close to him, anxious to know what was being said, yet determined not to pry. Theo stroked my hair with his free hand as he listened

"Look," Theo said brusquely. "We both know you need me, or someone who'll do my job. Can you work with me as things stand, or do you want to buy me out?"

There was a pause of a few seconds.

"Okay, then I need assurances from you that when I'm working away from here overnight that Sar will be allowed one of your guards, or will be allowed to stay at your estate, for her safety." Theo nodded once. "Okay, I can live with that," he said, relieved.

There was a pause of several more seconds.

"She's okay, Danial, but you struck her hard. The entire side of her face was bruised. No, it wasn't broken, but it was fractured. Sure, I'll tell her you're sorry, but she doesn't want to speak to you just now."

There was another pause, this one lasting a full minute.

"I don't know. I'll tell her," Theo said in exasperation. "When do you want me back at work?"

"Monday works for me, too," he continued. "Nights or days? Either is fine, but I'd prefer mostly days, at least for now."

Another pause of thirty seconds, then Theo said, "I'm sorry, too, Danial."

Theo hung up, then pulled me to him. "Well, I'm employed again," he said, relieved.

I didn't speak, but was a relief for me knowing I wouldn't be responsible for all the bills, especially the food bill, which had tripled in the past few weeks. There was also relief that he and Danial had made up. They were a great team, best friends, and lasting relationships as good as theirs had been shouldn't be trashed because of one woman. Yet there was apprehension as well, because with Theo working for Danial, I'd most likely have to see him sometime soon.

"Can you trust him?" I said worriedly. "And what's this about me going to spend nights at his estate?"

"I trust him when he says he needs me, because it's true," Theo said easily. "I trust him that you'll be safe while I'm gone because he said he'll let me put someone on to watch the house at night when I'm not here. I included you coming with me in the event we have a situation, like we had with Turk and his men."

"Wouldn't I be safer here during an attack?" I said, confused. "They wouldn't be after me, Theo. I'm no longer Danial's girl."

"You're my girl," Theo said protectively. "I have to take care of you."

"By bringing me to the place being attacked?" I countered. "That doesn't make sense."

"I need to explain something," Theo said with a sigh. "I'm ranked now, Sar. I've never been ranked before, so no one outside the United States or even New York State paid me any attention. I was known as a friend and employee of Danial's, and that was it. I had no status, and no formal training. No one would have hired me to be anything but a grunt, and paid me accordingly. I'd have been lucky just to be security at a concert."

"And?"

"That's all changed," he said, prideful. "Being tenth puts me on a short list of the preferred bodyguards in the world. That means I'm guaranteed top pay, benefits, and I'm never out of work long, no matter what. That was why I told you that it wouldn't take long for me to get another job."

"There's a catch though, isn't there?" I asked seriously. "Tell me."

"The ranking goes from ten to one, with one being the highest," Theo said, respect and awe in his words. "The catch is that everyone in my line of work wants onto the list, to get the perks I just described. So I have to defend my rank periodically."

"What does that mean?"

"It means a fight to the death, usually," Theo admitted reluctantly. "And tenth is last place. So when someone wants to break into the top ten, they challenge me."

"Holy shit," I breathed, very afraid. "Has anyone challenged you yet?"

"Yes," Theo said. "There were two in December, two last month, and then one the first week in March. It's likely they'll keep coming at that rate—"

"Did you kill them all?" I asked, not wanting to know if he had, but needing to know all the same.

"One was a kid, barely eighteen. He didn't know what he was doing. I let him go, after breaking his arm. But yes, the others I killed."

"What do you do after?" I said, squeamish. "Is there some procedure for, um, cleanup?"

"There's magical fire," Theo said, sounding a bit squeamish himself. "That's easy, and relatively cheap, as it leaves nothing behind, just a little bit of ash. I've been using that. I'm not saying I like the killing," he added forcefully. "But if I don't kill, I'll be viewed as soft, and that will invite more challengers. I can't fight every other week for years, Sar. As it is, I was hurt badly in the second challenge."

"How?"

"The man stabbed me with a poisoned knife. You remember that blade I got hurt with on Christmas?"

I nodded. "Yes. You had an antidote."

"That was a common poison. The poison I was hurt badly by was a rare one, and it took time to get an antidote made." Theo grimaced, remembering. "Anyway, poison is allowed in these challenges. Actually, anything is allowed, though for the most part everyone I've met seems honorable, even the really vile killers at the top. Almost all fights are fair ones."

I shivered. "Would you ever have to fight any of them?"

Theo laughed. "I'm not even on their radar, Sar." He grew serious. "But you do bring up something I have to tell you. I'm going to challenge the guy ranked eighth in another few months, after I get control of my animal side and train some more."

"What?" I said loudly. "You might be killed, Theo."

"I have to," Theo said resolutely. "If I move up in rank, I'll have to fight less. The assassin I'm going to fight—"

"Assassins?" I said loudly. "You said this ranking system was for bodyguards."

"For anyone that kills in the service of supernatural beings, be they of any race, creed, or mortality," Theo said darkly. "That's the official wording. A few are like me, Sar; just bodyguards who guard particular vampires and have killed skilled fighters in that service. Others are that and mercenaries also, those who take jobs outside their main guarding one for extra pay, no matter for the cause." His face scowled, his eyes flashing yellow before returning to blue. "And some are just evil to the core, monsters that exist just to kill, to glory in murder and mayhem at the whim of whomever gives them the most money. The eighth ranked is like that."

I shivered again. "I saw you fight Danial. You beat him, even though he'd fed a lot. I have faith in your abilities, but what makes you so sure you can challenge a higher ranked being and win?"

"I have to try," Theo whispered, hugging me. "Those in tenth place have a turnover of usually a year, Sar. They get worn out because they have to fight so much. I'd be much safer at eight, or maybe even five. Though it's not a rule, most newcomers challenge the lowest ranked, then try to work their way up."

"I'm scared for you," I whispered, burrowing into him. "Can't you give this title up?"

"No," Theo said defensively. "I earned it. I suffered for it. I'm not going back to being a nobody when I can be a somebody."

"Even though you know it means you're putting me in danger?" I replied.

Theo let out a sigh. "So much for me trying to impress you. Even putting aside my pride, I'm not sure I could give up my rank, Sar, even if I wanted to. Think of this as something like the gunfighters of the Old West. Once one of them made a name for himself, he had to be on his guard ever after, because there were always young guns looking to make a name for themselves."

I opened my mouth to tell him he should find a way, but he put his finger to my lips.

"You don't have to be afraid," Theo said tenderly. "I'm going to make sure you're safe. Besides, like I already told you, these challenges are between the fighters only. All that stuff about some bad guy taking the good guy's girl to make the good guy fight him is just in the movies. The men I've fought are after a rep that they fought a higher ranked fighter and won fair and square. No one is going to hire someone to guard their life or their loved ones if they lied or cheated their way to their ranking. This is about earning power and reputation, not about just who's left standing when the gun smoke clears."

"You're sure?" I said uneasily.

"From everything I'd heard and read, yes," Theo assured me. "There's not one documented case of—"

"Then why are you being so careful to make sure I'm under guard?" I interrupted.

"I love you," Theo said, giving me look that said this should be obvious. "Just because no one looking to fight me would attack you doesn't mean I would feel comfortable leaving you alone overnight."

"I do have a telephone," I said sarcastically. "And my explosive bullets gun, in addition to my regular gun. I also have a security system, in case there's a fire or a burglar. I can take care of myself, unless it's an army or something."

"Oh, really?" Theo said, pulling me close. "And what about that guy in the truck you called me about a few weeks ago? That wasn't just a story. He'd scared you badly, by your voice that night."

"He did," I said, remembering the incident uneasily. "He said he smelled me."

Theo turned me around to face him quickly. "What else did he say?"

"Just that the intestines in the woods weren't deer," I said, shrugging. "I overreacted."

"This was in March? What did he look like?" Theo said urgently.

"No, early February," I said, thinking back. "I didn't get a look at him, really. It was snowing. There was no moon, and then the barn light went off, and we were in the dark—"

"It was cold, then?" Theo said, relaxing again.

"Very cold," I assured him, not sure what that had to do with anything. "You don't have to worry about that, anyway. The next day there was an accident reported in the paper. The men who were behind my whole scare died in a crash. They were driving around drunk, and a train clipped them."

"That's a relief," Theo said, giving me a kiss on the cheek. "I don't like loose ends."

"Speaking of loose ends," I said reluctantly. "What did Danial say about me? If I might see him in the future, I want to know if he's going to be violent again."

"He said he wanted to talk to you," Theo said. "Should I have given the phone to you? You acted as though you didn't want to talk to him."

"You said the right thing. I'm not really ready yet to talk with him."

"He said to tell you he was sorry for hurting you, that he promised you he wouldn't and he feels awful. He wanted to know if you'd forgive him, and to say he was sorry about Angelica, too."

"I forgive him, Theo, you can tell him that. But I'd rather not see or talk to him right now."

"Okay," Theo said, stroking my hair. By the way he said it, he was really thinking "Good."

The phone rang. I picked it up. It was my neighbor, Henry.

"Hi, Sar. I was getting out some gravel from the quarry to use in a construction job, and I noticed the new chain. What happened?"

"Some jerks cut it in the winter. I replaced it a few months back."

"Well, thanks. I'd like to chip in to help pay for it."

I hadn't paid for it, Danial had. "Not necessary. You can buy the next one. I'm sure it'll happen in the future."

He laughed. "You're likely right. Well, thanks. Have a good weekend."

"You, too. Don't work too hard. April's just begun."

"I won't. See you, Sar."

"Thanks, Henry."

Just as I hung up, Theo went rigid, and then swore.

"What is it?" I said, alarmed.

"I just remembered I have an appointment to get a haircut today," he said, pulling on his clothes. "I've got to get going now if I'm going to make it."

He kissed me quickly and was out the door. The front door slammed, and then his truck started up. I hoped he didn't hurry too fast and back through the garage door.

The phone rang again, and this time it was my mother-in-law. To my absolute shock, she was nice, unlike how she had been since Brennan died. I remembered the letter I'd gotten from her more than a year ago, and decided she must have gone to get that therapy that I'd recommended.

Brennan had been her only child, and she'd doted on him. I understood her loss, just not her irrational anger at me. At his funeral, she had told me it was my fault her son was dead. We hadn't spoken since then. Her calling me now to talk was a pretty big deal, both for me and for her.

When we finally hung up an hour later, I decided to go shower. I washed my hair, and dried off. Then my eyes fell on the black velvet robe on the back of my door. I hadn't worn it since I washed it. I wasn't sure Theo would find it sexy, or if I would.

I slipped it one, instantly remembering how much I'd liked it. Then I caught sight of myself in my bedroom mirror.

In my regular clothes, both Theo and I could disregard the choker. I'd worn it so long now that I really didn't notice it. The addition of the robe made me look as if I'd just stepped out of Danial's bedroom. Moreover, it brought to mind all the nights I'd spent in his cool arms.

I took it off quickly, laying it on the bed. Then I dressed in my usual jeans and sweatshirt, and sat down beside it, fingering the luxurious material.

Right now, I thought that there would never be a time I'd want to wear it again, a time I wouldn't think of Danial the moment I felt the black velvet whispering over my skin. But I'd been certain after Brennan died that I'd never find love again. Maybe all I needed was time.

The doorbell abruptly rang.

Who could that be? I got up and answered it. To my surprise, a woman stood there, bearing a huge vase of roses with a large white satin bow.

"Are you Sarelle McGarran?" the woman asked.

"Yes," I said curiously.

"These are for you, then," she said, handing them to me. "Have a good day."

As she walked off, I brought the arrangement inside, marveling at the beauty of the roses. They were unlike any I'd seen before, neither white nor red, but some mixture of both in each bloom. I smelled the nearest blossom, inhaling the lovely scent.

I made a face. These had to be from Danial.

I opened the card. It read:

I apologize for my actions. I hope to see you very soon. –D

I debated tossing the flowers outside to wilt and die. Danial had never gotten me flowers in all the time we'd been together. That he'd sent them to me now when we were no longer a couple irritated me.

Jessica jumped onto the counter, and began playfully batting the baby's breath in the arrangement. I shooed him off the counter, and then took the flowers into the bedroom, putting them on the dresser.

I smelled the blooms again. They smelled absolutely wonderful, bringing to mind spring and the warm weather that was almost here.

Screw it. This was a peace offering. I'd accept it, if just for the fact that it was better to forgive than to hate, especially when the object of ill will was someone I would have to see soon.

There was noise of a key in the lock, and then Theo calling out for me. I walked out to the door, meaning to tell him about the flowers, and stopped short.

He moved his head for me, posing. "Do you like it, Sar?" he said hopefully.

He'd cut his hair like Danial had for me, but the layers were longer, falling over his forehead and into his eyes. He had a little more curl to his hair, but the effect was the same.

Theo had been attractive before, with his hair not styled. With this haircut, he was drop dead gorgeous.

"Why did you get that hairstyle?" I said curiously.

"I know you like this style," he said softly. "And I wanted to get something shorter anyway. The stylist said it would suit my features."

"It does. How is everyone aware I like this style, by the way?" I asked kissing him.

"It may have something to do with the picture of Richard Gere by your bedside," he replied, smirking.

He was referencing the autographed picture I'd gotten from Kat for a birthday present; the only picture of a man that I still kept on display in my house. Suddenly, the hairstyle change of Danial's I'd appreciated but never understood clicked into place. "So that's it. I should've guessed."

"But do you like it?" he said insistently.

"I like it," I said, running my fingers through it. "Very much. I like you, too."

"Show me," he whispered.

I came into his arms. Our clothes were quickly tossed aside. He held me, kissing me passionately, then began to slide his hands down my sides. He stroked my side from thigh to shoulder in long gentle movements, and then reached lower.

Ghost suddenly began to bark loudly. Theo went to get up.

"Wait," I said, grabbing his arm. "Darkness hasn't barked yet. Until she does, it might be nothing except a squirrel near the birdfeeder. Ghost often barks at anything moving, but Darkness only barks at a real threat, like a strange car or person close to the house."

Theo nibbled my neck, kissing my earlobe. "But will Ghost stop if it's nothing, or keep barking?" He slid his hands to my inner thigh. "The only sound I want to hear is you moaning."

Darkness began to bark loudly, interspersing growls.

"Someone is here," I said reluctantly.

The doorbell rang, and the dogs quickly upped their barking to a crescendo.

I sighed, and disentangled myself from Theo. "Hopefully it's not my parents."

I turned to Theo, just in time to watch him produce a gun from underneath his side of the bed. He checked the chamber, then pushed in a full clip and closed the slide, chambering a bullet.

"Let's go look," he said, handing me the black velvet robe.

Chapter Eighteen

I put on the robe, and headed out to the front door, Theo following me.

"Look through the peephole," he said.

"I was going to," I replied, shooting him an annoyed look. I looked, then turned back to him, utterly shocked. "It's Tawny."

Theo's mouth dropped open, then closed with a click. "Stay right there. Don't open the door. I'll go get dressed."

He went into the bedroom, still carrying his gun. I rolled my eyes and then opened the door to Tawny, almost lost in a huge black cloak. Her eyes opened wide in shock when she saw me.

"Hi," I said, uneasily.

"Hi, Sarelle," she said stiffly. "I went to the address Theo gave me, but a woman there named Suri said he lived here now." She paused, clearly waiting to see what I would say.

"He does," I said simply.

"With you," she said, shock and jealousy in her words.

"With me," I said evenly, holding her gaze.

"I need to speak to him right now, alone," she said curtly.

"He knows you're here, Tawny," I said with a forced smile. "He'll be right out."

She turned away and started down the steps. I turned to go back inside myself.

She suddenly stopped, whipped around, and yelled, "Why couldn't you have left him alone, Sar? You had your vampire, why do you need him, too?"

"It wasn't like that. You have no idea what—"

"By that piece of jewelry you still wear, you still belong to Danial."

"He refused to take it off, Tawny, not that that's your business," I said wearily. I pitied her, especially after I'd been in a similar position not so long ago with Angelica. I knew how she must feel, finding Theo with me after she'd crossed an ocean to see him.

"How could you do this to me, Sar?" she yelled. "You knew how I felt about him!"

No one came to my door and yelled at me like this, oh no. "No. How did you feel about him, Tawny, other than a good lay when you needed it? You had months, maybe years to show up. Why now?"

"He didn't return my calls, Sar. I had to see him," she said desperately.

"Why?" Theo asked from behind me. He had gotten dressed and stowed the pistol. He walked down the stairs to her. "What's the matter?"

"I had to see you," she said, fighting tears.

"Why, Tawny?" Theo said angrily. "We've hooked up for years, and you've never taken me up on any of my invitations before."

"This is why," she said, tossing off her cloak.

I instinctively ducked, thinking she had a gun or something, but what she had to show us was much worse. Her abdomen was round, firm, and distended under her maternity dress.

"I'm pregnant," she said, looking at him. "About five and a half months. Does that answer your question?"

Theo's mouth dropped open in shock, all the color draining from his face. All the blood drained from my face, too.

"I need to talk to you alone," she said to Theo.

She went to her car and he followed her. They got in and shut the door.

I decided I really needed to walk the dogs. I pulled on some clothes, and then let Ghost and Darkness outside, hurrying quickly after them while trying not to look at Tawny's car.

The walk was terrible. I mostly stood in the lower field near the woods, letting the dogs hunt for mice, watching the car uneasily from afar. I didn't want to wait inside the house, but I also didn't really want to leave Theo and Tawny alone together while I walked a mile or more through the woods.

I didn't think Theo would leave with her, not without telling me, even if he was the father. My worry was he'd come to me and say he was sorry, but we were over, because he couldn't let the baby be born without being a father to it and marrying or mating Tawny. Theo was a do-the-right-thing kind of guy. I didn't want him to do the right thing by her, not if it meant leaving me. There was a knot in my stomach just thinking about it.

I walked back up hesitantly to the house, the two dogs trotting behind me. I was just in time to see Theo slam the door hard.

"You tell me NOW, after all the years we've been having sex, that you're married?" he screamed at her.

Oiy, this was bad…

"I'm sorry," she cried. "I needed you!"

"Bullshit!" he yelled at her. "I was just something to entertain yourself with when I was in town."

"I need you, Theo!" She cried harder, tears soaking her maternity dress. "I don't love him!"

"You don't love me either!" Theo yelled at her. "Is it mine, or his?"

"I don't know," she gasped out. "I need you to come with me for a paternity test to find out. I can't ask my husband to take one. He's so happy I'm pregnant…" She trailed off.

She hadn't told her husband the baby might not be his? This was like a train wreck. I couldn't pull my eyes away.

"I'll go with you now, but only because I need to know," Theo said angrily. "You drive your car, and follow me in my truck. I'll set up a test."

Tawny got into her car and started the engine. Theo flipped open his phone, and in a minute was talking to Dr. Camlyn. He explained the situation briefly, then arranged to meet him at Dr. Camlyn's office to get the test done.

He hung up, and came over to me. "Sar, I have no idea what to say to you right now. Saying I'm sorry doesn't begin to cover it."

Now that I knew Tawny was married, I was a little more at ease. Of course, she could always leave him. She'd told Theo she didn't love her husband. And if it was his baby and not her husband's…The knot in my stomach was back, tightening. I took a long breath, and let it out, trying to relax.

Theo was silent. He looked like he wanted to hug me, but was afraid to attempt it, in case I shrunk back from him.

"Theo, go and find out what you—what we—need to know. I'll be here when you get back," I said quickly, taking his hand in mine. "Um, you are coming back, right?"

He crushed me to him, almost bruising me. "Sar," he whispered "I'm coming back. No matter what the answer is, I'm coming back to you, tonight."

I kissed him, hating how clingy I was acting. "I'll be here."

"I love you, Sar," Theo whispered, holding me.

"I love you too, Theo," I said softly.

A wide smile broke over his face. "That's the first time you've said that," he said tenderly. "I've been waiting a long time to hear those words from you." He gave me a kiss on the cheek. "Since the night we dreamed together."

Awkwardness tied my tongue. I hadn't loved him then, but blurting that out wasn't optimal. "Call if you're going to be late for dinner," I said weakly. I wanted to add on "good luck", but it seemed very inappropriate. Instead, I blurted, "You should bring your gun."

Theo nodded, and went inside. He came back out in another few minutes. From how the jacket fit I deduced that he'd put on his holster, and the gun that shot explosive rounds.

"I'll be back soon," he said. "Lock the door."

He drove off, Tawny following in her rented car.

I watched him leave, my only thought the inevitable question: exactly how long did a paternity test take to give a yes or no answer? In all likelihood, I'd be waiting on pins and needles for the rest of the afternoon, maybe even into the evening.

I decided right then that I'd better take the dogs for a longer walk before I went crazy waiting. It was going to be agony until I knew. I went inside, grabbed a jacket and my regular gun, and left with them for the woods.

Ghost and Darkness were ecstatic to be on their second walk of the day. As we walked past the barn and down next to the field, I found myself closing my eyes, relishing the simple feeling of sun on my face. The day was still nice, almost warm, and the sky was blue, a little overcast with clouds. Its grey blue shade reminded me strongly of Theo's eyes.

I shook my head at the unfairness of it all. How could such a life-altering event happen on such a beautiful day? This day was meant for walking with Theo and my dogs, for loving him, for spending time talking and laughing with him. He'd promised to show me how he was able to make such beautiful carvings with his hands. One of those bags he'd brought with him from Danial's house contained special tools for woodcarving, and he'd been going to demonstrate some of his skill for me later this afternoon. We'd been thinking of going out to dinner tonight, had been going to make reservations. Now the carving, the dinner—fuck, the entire day—had been shot to hell.

That robe was bad luck. I should never have taken it with me; I should have let Angelica keep it. Resolving to throw it out when I got back to the house, the dogs and I went on to walk at least two more miles.

When we returned in late afternoon, Cavity was there to greet us, stretched out in the last bit of sunshine. All the cats had wanted out today, to enjoy the sun and the first hint of spring in the air. I petted his head gently, as I walked past his sprawled form.

I went into the kitchen and gave both dogs a Cheweez, trying to think of what to make quick for dinner. Even if Theo had good news from the test, it was unlikely that we'd want to go out to dinner now. I for one wasn't in the mood. Hell, I wasn't even hungry.

Screw it. I'd worry about dinner when he got back. Instead, I decided to make an apple pie for Theo and an extra one for Terian. Baking would cheer me up. I got out the ingredients, and started, switching on the weather channel to check tonight's weather. Tonight was supposed to be clear, also. Maybe we could start a fire in the outdoor wood pit, it was warm enough. Roasting marshmallows sounded good.

As I rolled out crust and peeled apples, something Tawny had said began bothering me. In my mind, I went back over what she had said; looking for what was making me uneasy. Except for being annoyed by her words, I remembered nothing meaningful. Yet I knew something was wrong, that I'd overlooked or forgotten something and it was the kind of thing that was going to bite me in the ass if I didn't remember it in time. For a good hour, I thought back over everything, trying to latch onto whatever it was that had me so anxious. Despite my effort, I still didn't make a connection. Admitting defeat, I put it out of my mind and concentrated on my baking.

At six p.m., Theo called. I picked up, holding my breath.

"Sar, we won't know today," he said quickly.

My breath came out with a whoosh. "How long until we know?"

"Stephen says that it will be a few days to compare DNA. He doesn't have the equipment, so he's going to have to send out the test to a friend he knows in New York City who has access to that kind of equipment. The virus that both Tawny and I have that makes us were, it also influences the genes, so it's going to be harder to tell than it would be with human parents. But he says he'll rush it through. We'll know in a few days, most likely the middle of next week."

"That's a long time," I said lamely.

"I know," Theo said, disgruntled. "There is some good news. Her husband is also were, and an African lion, like her, not a cougar like me. That should help to distinguish whose child it is. They're going to test her for my cougar genes. If they're there, the baby's mine."

I didn't know what to say. What if the baby was his? What would he do? I wanted badly to ask, but couldn't bring myself to.

"Sar?" Theo said. "Are you still there?"

"What is she going to do, either way?" I said roughly.

It was too late to abort the child without risk. If she'd wanted to do that, she would have already done it and not bothered us. Odds were Tawny wanted to keep it, maybe use it to get Theo back.

"If it's his, she'll go home. It turns out they've been trying to have a child for years, but she was never able to conceive."

"And if it's not his?" I said, my stomach twisting.

"If it's mine, she'll tell him about me, and they'll most likely divorce. She'll stay in Europe, with her family, and the child will stay with her. She says she wants to keep it, either way. I think that's why she waited so long to come to me. She wanted it to be too late for me to ask her not to," he said bitterly. "She had to have suspected back in January. She didn't contact me until the very end of March."

I wanted to ask about child support and stuff like that, but couldn't bring myself to. Besides, was this any of my business, if she was going to leave the country and the child was going with her?

"Sar, you aren't saying anything."

"Theo, she came here looking for something more than a paternity test from you, you know that right?" I tried to say it gently, but I was hurt and scared he would leave me. "Tawny came to see you hoping you would still want her, and your child, that you'd agree now to go to Europe with her, that she could divorce her husband and be with you."

"Sarelle, don't you think I know that?" Theo retorted, annoyed. "I told you I want you, not her. The child, I can't think about it, not until I know if it's mine or not. She said that she's going back to Europe, with or without me. It's going to be without me."

Everything had been going so well. I was scared and angry at him for putting me in this position. "Theo, you and I have always used protection. I have to ask: didn't you use protection with her?"

"Sar, she told me I was the only one and that she was on the pill. Everything was fine that way for years," Theo said, frustrated. "How was I supposed to know she'd lied to me?"

"Theo, you saw her once in a while for marathon type sex, and it never occurred to you that she might have a regular guy on the side?" I said sarcastically.

"No," he said coldly. "Did it ever occur to you that Angelica or other women sometimes went on trips with Danial that you had refused to go on with him?"

I inhaled sharply. "What are you saying?"

"Do you think she was there only to give him blood?" he growled. "The big surprise here is that you never caught on. You had to hear him screwing her to believe it."

"You asshole," I said weakly. "That's not true."

"Look, I have to go, the doctor's here to get my blood—"

I hung up, fuming.

Well, I'd been waiting for a crack to appear in his perfection and here it was. All Theo had needed to show me his dark side was for me to second-guess one of his decisions.

I sat there, incensed. Theo had been excessively trusting, and Tawny had taken advantage of that naivety. She hadn't used any protection; I'd stake my life on it. To think that they'd been lucky or whatever for years, and now that he and I were together, she'd just happened to conceive…I wasn't angry, I was furious. I hated her, but part of me blamed Theo too, for trusting her so easily. If he'd protected himself like he should have, we wouldn't be in this mess.

I looked at the pies I'd just finished baking, and wanted to toss them in the dirt outside. Trying to calm myself, I went and sat on the couch.

There was no point being mad, really. Crying and fighting with Theo wasn't going to turn the baby back into an egg. First, we'd have to make sure whose baby it was. Then, if it was Theo's, I was going to have to decide if I could accept that about him or not. In any case, I was very angry about the barb he'd thrown concerning Danial.

I called him back, but I just got his voice mail, to my surprise. Yet it made sense; Theo hadn't been monitoring security these past weeks at my house, so he hadn't needed to be in constant contact.

At the beep, I said, "Theo, I'm sorry. It isn't my business what you did in the past. I was hurt and angry. But I deserve an explanation concerning what you said about Danial. Please call me back as soon as you get this." I hung up, went back to the couch and sat down to wait.

The phone rang a few minutes later.

"Sar, I'm sorry, I shouldn't have said that about Danial," Theo said apologetically. "I got your message. There's nothing to forgive, you were right to ask how I could be that unthinking. I was angry because I had no good answer for you."

"Was it true what you said?" I said flatly.

"No. It's true that women went with him on trips from time to time. But it was always for blood, never for companionship or sex. He wouldn't let them sleep with him in the same room as him; we always got a suite, so they had their own room. Even then, whenever he was resting, I guarded his door. I said what I did because I knew it would hurt you. I'm sorry."

"It doesn't really matter now," I said, letting out a breath. "I just wanted to know."

My eyes wandered to the window. Full dark had descended a few minutes ago. To my relief, the barn light had come on as it was supposed to, its light shining like a beacon in the gloom. Suddenly, headlights on the road slowed, and turned into the end of my driveway.

That couldn't be Terian. Likely, someone had gotten lost in the dark and was turning around.

"Sar, I should be home in an hour or so. Do you still want to go out like we planned?"

"No. Let's wait until—" I cut off abruptly. There were more headlights now coming down the drive, at least three trucks worth. There were fog lights under the regular headlights, so they had to be trucks or SUVs. My danger feeling spiked. "Someone's here."

"Who's there?" Theo said, alarmed. "Terian?"

The SUV's pulled in front of the house. They were Hummers, the H3 model, all in glinting black. One went up to the start of the quarry road, blocking it sideways, the other three parking in a line, blocking the driveway.

It was then I remembered what I'd forgotten, what my mind had been trying to tell me all day. Tawny had been pregnant now for five and a half months, almost six.

Devlin had given Danial six months to oath me. My time was up.

Chapter Nineteen

An instant later, Devlin stepped out the back door of the lead Hummer, looking just as gorgeous and ruthless as he ever had. His shoulder length golden hair gleamed in the headlights of the other vehicles. Other doors began opening, at least ten to fifteen huge beefy men pouring out of them. Everyone was dressed in black, most of the men armed openly with guns. Ghost and Darkness ran to the windows and began barking.

"Devlin is here!" I said, panicked. "He's brought at least a dozen men with him!"

"What?" Theo yelled, deafening me. "He's there now?"

"Yes, he's right outside the house!"

"Sar, listen to me. Go get the gun I gave you, right now. Get all the ammunition I gave you, and load up for bear." He paused. "Those aren't men with him."

I didn't move, my mind telling me this couldn't be happening.

"Sar, get moving! Go!" Theo yelled, startling me into action.

I ran for the bedroom, the dogs running after me. The men in view from the window were already fanning out as they moved toward the house. All of them had guns. Devlin was behind them, but he'd still be at the front door in about thirty seconds. I triggered the panic button on the security system as I ran into the bedroom with the dogs, slamming the door behind me and locking it. I grabbed the explosive bullets gun from the top drawer of the dresser, and loaded it. Some bullets fell on the floor in my haste, and I gathered those up, cursing that I'd never asked Theo for more ammunition.

I had only eight bullets. I'd need every one to be a kill shot, and even then...

"Theo, do we have any more ammo here?" I gasped out. "I've only got eight bullets!"

"No. I have two clips with me, but that's it," he said despairingly.

I tried to be calm, but I could feel the men surrounding me, even if I couldn't see them. "Should I load my regular gun, too? Will the bullets have any effect—?"

"Yes," Theo said strongly. "Do whatever you have to, kill as many as you can. Remember, Devlin won't hurt you. He wants you for himself, and he can't have you for himself until he gets Danial to remove the choker. Don't be afraid to shoot him."

I let out a scared cry. For the last two weeks, all I'd thought of was how much I wanted the choker off. But Danial had been right not to remove it. It was the only thing that might give me enough time for Theo to get to me.

"Sar, stay alive, no matter what. Submit to Danial or Devlin, no matter what they ask you to do. I'm on my way now—"

"Theo, you can't fight all of them alone," I said hopelessly, realization dawning. "You'll be killed."

Theo was silent; probably trying to come up with something reassuring that wasn't a lie.

He was having trouble though, because I was right. He would be killed if he came unaided.

"You need Terian," I said forcefully. "You'll never do this on your own." I read him the number for Terian's cell from the pad beside the phone. "Call him, he'll be landing soon, he'll help—"

"Damn it, Sar, he hates me, he won't help me!"

"Tell him Devlin's got me, that you need his help! Tell him I dreamed of you, Theo, that you shared my dream. He'll know what that means, and he'll help."

Devlin yelled from outside. "She's alone in there. Don't shoot, just take her captive! I want her alive!"

There were sudden footsteps on the front stairs. The dogs barked frantically, running from one window to the other. Then they darted backwards, their tails between their legs. Glass shattered inward, shards showering the floor. One of the men in black was coming in the window.

I dropped the phone and shot him from a few feet away. The blast from the explosive bullet gun knocked him back through the window, a smoking hole where his heart had been. Another man filled his place in a moment, and I shot him, too, punching a hole in his chest.

"Watch it, men," one of the men said from outside called. "She's got one of the new-style guns."

With a smash, my other window was broken in. A man came in each window in tandem. I shot one in the heart, and the other in the leg. Despite Devlin's order, the wounded one drew his gun, aiming at me. I shot him in the heart, too, blowing him backward to fall half inside the house, blood spattering in a spray on the wall behind him.

I had a split second to thank God for explosive bullets, and then the bedroom door shuddered under a heavy blow.

As I turned to face it, it crumpled into pieces, the wood fractured. I backed away, as Devlin kicked it once more, the power of his blow twisting the metal with a screech as the hinges bent. The remaining piece fell with a crash to the floor.

In he walked, smiling happily, at once beautiful and deadly. "Hello, Sar," he said, baring his fangs.

I shot at him, but he saw it coming, and turned, blocking his heart with his body. My bullet hit him in the arm, blowing a chunk of flesh away as he ducked. I backed away from him, still aiming the gun. Ghost and Darkness had retreated to the bathroom, where they were whimpering. I backed up in front of the door, blocking it, even as I reached into my dresser drawer, my hands closing on my regular gun.

"You bitch," Devlin snarled as he lay on the floor, just his left foot in sight.

"Keep away," I said desperately. "Or I'll shoot you again."

His gold eyes peered over a piece of the door, giving me an irritated look. "Don't you dare."

I raised the gun and he quickly ducked out of sight. "Mark my words, bitch," he said melodiously. "Or I'll forget you are still wearing that collar, and drain you dry right here on your bed." His words were thick with anger, and some pain. "You can't kill me with that, only wound me temporarily."

Another two men burst in through the broken windows. I turned and shot them both, ragged holes appearing in their chests. Then my gun's slide stayed back. I was out of bullets.

I dropped the gun, and raised my regular gun, training it on the windows.

A single man came in, a ski mask across his face. He was huge, easily six feet. "Don't try it," he said flatly.

I shot him. He staggered, but kept moving, even as I kept firing. He took all six bullets, then batted the gun from my hands with a blow that knocked me off my feet.

"Clear," the man called out. He looked down, towering over me. "Don't move or get up, Sarelle. You do and you'll be back on the floor."

As I lay there on the floor, more men came in the windows. They looked at the bodies of their companions, and then at me, fury etched on their faces.

I backed up on my hands until I hit the wall. My dogs were whimpering now from fear.

"Leave us," Devlin said coldly, his eyes on me. He was standing outside the bedroom, in the hallway. The chunk I'd taken out of his arm had grown back. His shirt had a huge hole through which white unmarked flesh was visible.

His men left through the windows, taking their dead with them, leaving Devlin and I alone. The dogs whined again from the bathroom. A cool wind blew in through my shattered windows, and stirred the curtains. I shivered in the cold gust, watching him.

Devlin walked toward me. "I told you once you were a bad hostess. I'm sad to say you've proved me right with your hysterics." He picked up the phone, clicking it off. Then he reached down, offering me his hand. "Perhaps I can teach you by example."

I took his hand with my right, and with my left, I grabbed for the nearest object, my steel-toed shoe, and swung at him. He yanked me to my feet, even as he grabbed my hand in midair with his free one. He enjoyed my struggling briefly, letting me try to move my hand while he kept it immobile.

"Drop it, Sar, or I'll break all the bones in your hand," Devlin said with a smile.

I dropped the shoe. "What do you want?"

He pulled me close, holding me tightly. His golden eyes bored into my green ones, and my fear ratcheted up a few notches. I froze under his gaze, like a rabbit under the eyes of a hawk.

"Don't play stupid, Sar. I told Danial he had six months to oath you. I see he has removed the marks, so I'm surmising that he decided not to. That means you're fair game. And I can't wait to play—" Abruptly he cut off.

"You cut your hair," he said, a flicker of disappointment registering on his face. "It was so beautiful." Then he grinned, baring his fangs and brushing them against my throat. "Perhaps I'll let you grow it out again for me." He ran his fingers through my hair, pulling it a little on purpose. "My sweet Sar."

"Don't call me 'Sar'," I sneered back at him defiantly. "I'm not yours. I never will be!"

"I'll call you whatever I want to, Sar," he said deliberately. Then his eyes fell on the black velvet robe still lying on my bed. "Ahh," he said seductively. "Did you get this out to wear for me? How thoughtful—"

"No," I said coldly.

"You are going to wear it for me anyway. Put it on," he said, folding his arms across his chest, and looking me up and down. "Now."

"No," I said, backing away.

"Put it on now, Sar, or I'll kill your cats, I'll kill your dogs, and I'll torch your home to the ground. And then I'll make you put it on anyway," he said coolly. "Believe me, sweet Sar." He picked up the robe, tossing it to me.

I caught it, trying not to tremble.

The phone rang. He picked it up. "Yes?" he said pleasantly.

"She's here, just a moment," he said courteously, then covered the receiver. "Tell them the password now," he added malevolently, then handed me the phone, "or I'll make good on my threat, whether you put on the robe for me or not."

The police would never reach me in time, not to be any good to me. Not against him.

"Hold on for a second," I said, covering the phone's receiver with my hand. "Promise me, your word as Ruler, that you'll leave my pets and my home unharmed."

"Why should I?" he said, letting out a peal of laughter.

"Because you have no choice. I can't be touched, not while I wear this choker. You want it off; you're going to have to take me to Danial."

"Well now, haven't you been a busy girl since I last saw you," Devlin said, letting out another laugh. "That is correct. But there is nothing in the law about your possessions."

"I'm his," I retorted. "What I have is his. He won't be happy you reduced it to a cinder."

"True," Devlin said, looking around him. "This building has some value, even though it's so rustic. Danial does like that." He focused on me again, and smiled horribly. "But know this," he said, leaning closer. "If he doesn't oath you, I'll burn it down and kill whatever I like, however I want to. I promise you that, sweet Sar. Now tell them you're just fine."

"The password is demon," I said into the phone. "I'm fine, really. I pressed the button on accident while carrying a full laundry basket past it. The cat tripped me. Sorry and thanks." I hung up.

Devlin contemplated me, a measure of respect in his eyes. "Put it on now," he said slowly, drawing out the words.

I took off my clothes quickly, flushing red with embarrassment, and slipped on the robe. Devlin grabbed me by the back of the neck before I could belt it around me, and pushed me to the wall. He held me there with one hand, as he ran his hand up my leg with the other. I struggled fearfully in his grip, and he leaned his body into me, trapping me between himself and the wall.

"Stop," I stammered out.

"No," he said gleefully. "We're just starting." He moved his hips gently against me. I felt the male part of him hard against my lower back, and went still, utterly petrified. Knowing he was aroused terrified me in a way having him bite me did not.

I shuddered, bringing a moan from his lips. His hand reached the outside of my thigh, and then traveled upward to my naked hip. His hand clamped down on my hip as he bent his legs, and then gently thrust up against me, just enough so I could feel him straining in the cleft of my buttocks. His fangs pressed against me, as he kissed my neck below the choker. I was shaking now, both with fear and rage.

"I love the taste of your fear," he sighed. "It's exquisite, just like your blood."

"Stop this!" I snarled at him. "Let me go!"

He backed up reluctantly, and pushed me towards the door. "You're right, Sar. We need to get you to Danial. The sooner he takes off the choker, the sooner we can get to the good stuff."

I ran before him out the bedroom door and through my shattered front door, as he raced after me. He caught me easily by the back of the neck near the H3s and shoved me into the back seat of the lead vehicle. He got in behind me and slammed the door. I cowered away from him, cringing against the side door.

"Now we can't have that," Devlin purred. "The trip's a time-consuming one. Come here." He gathered me into his arms, though I resisted him as best as I could.

"Stop struggling," he said, straightening my legs so they stretched out on the seat. Then, to my surprise, he wrapped the robe over my lower body, covering me completely.

I trembled in his arms, trying to fathom what his plan was.

"Shh," he said softly. "Just relax."

"Where to, boss?" said his driver as he turned the SUV around on my front lawn. "Home?"

"Danial's," Devlin said with annoyance. "She's still collared." He looked down at me and grinned. "But not for long."

"How am I supposed to relax with your double entendres?" I said angrily.

"My apologies," Devlin snorted derisively. "It must be your beauty that's overcome me."

"Jackass," I replied angrily.

Devlin smiled faintly. "On occasion, yes. But don't fear me, Sar. I'll not hurt you, at least for the duration of the trip."

"Why are you here now? I haven't seen you since the Hallows party."

"I know; I'm a bit late. I do have a business to run, Sar, though running it is not as fun as playing with you. I have other responsibilities, too, as Ruler." His words had the same teasing quality Danial's had had sometimes, but underneath the teasing note, there was only coldness. "Surely you got my flowers this afternoon, apologizing for my tardiness?"

The roses, they had been from him…fear enveloped me again, my heart racing. "But why do you care about me?" I asked quickly. "Who am I to you? You can't be hard up for a woman, the way you look."

Devlin looked at me in shock, and then he laughed, baring his fangs. "Thank you for the compliment. The truth is I don't care about you personally, Sar." He leaned in close, kissing the tip of my nose. "Though that could change in time—"

"I don't believe you," I said angrily. "You like getting shot, and breaking into houses?"

"Then how's this, Sar? Because I can. I enjoy exercising my rights as Ruler." He leaned closer and whispered "Danial is my brother; I know you know this. You belong to him, yet you aren't with him as you are supposed to be. That is not proper behavior for a collared female, oathed or unoathed. The moment I learned of that, I came to take you back to him. I'm sure you want to go, too. You know he's the only thing saving you from me." He laughed. "All teasing aside, you could view my actions as simple ones of duty to a subject. You are not the first errant woman I've returned to a fellow vampire. You'll not be the last."

His words were a relief. He didn't know about Theo, or what had happened between Danial and I. That was something, at least. Yet he would learn of it the moment we reached Danial…I began to tremble again.

"Penny for your thoughts," Devlin whispered.

"I'd rather not talk," I whispered back. "Please."

"You do not have to speak to me," Devlin said softly. "Yet I wish you would."

Intrigued, I turned in his arms to look at him. "Why?"

"I want to know why you are not with my brother," Devlin said curiously. "You were happy with him in the fall. What happened?"

I bit my lip uneasily, wondering what to tell him. How much had Danial told him?

"Do not be afraid to speak," Devlin said encouragingly. "Tell me, why are your marks gone?"

He would know the whole story from Danial as soon as we got there. The trouble was what to tell him that would get him to take me home. It was a toss-up whether being returned to Danial or being freed for Devlin to claim was a worse fate.

"Sar, please answer," Devlin prodded. "Did Danial heal your marks?"

"Yes."

"Why?"

"I asked him to."

"Did you want out of the arrangement you had?" Devlin said eagerly.

"No," I said honestly. "I gave him my oath on Christmas Eve. He accepted and we, um, consummated it."

"Are you oathed now?" Devlin asked, his body coiled tight as a spring.

"I'm not sure," I said, deliberately acting vague. "From how Danial put it, we are taking a break from one another, though we haven't ended permanently. He still views me as his, which is why I wear the collar."

"Separations sometimes happen," Devlin said, nodding. "Did you began to get weak?"

I swayed a little in relief, clutching the offered explanation. "Yes."

"You're lying," Devlin said angrily, his expression darkening instantly. "Tell me the truth. Why did you leave him?"

"I miscarried," I blurted out.

Devlin hugged me close to him, stroking my hair. "I'm very sorry," he whispered gently. "Danial didn't tell me you'd gotten pregnant."

"You knew he was trying," I said accusingly. "Don't lie."

"Yes," Devlin admitted. "To be honest, I didn't think he'd succeed."

"Well, he did," I said brokenly. I closed my eyes, a single tear slipping out.

There was the soft brush of cool lips, kissing it away, and then gentle kisses on my cheeks and forehead. I opened my eyes and looked into moist golden eyes only a few inches away.

"You were very strong to have endured that," Devlin said, kissing my cheek again lightly. "Forgive me for causing you pain in making you remember it."

I bit my lip again lightly, wondering what to say. One moment he was violent, and the next almost loving. The most descriptive word that came to mind was sociopath. My skin crawled. I shifted slightly, turning my head away from his.

"Did you want a child?" Devlin asked softly, his lips near my ear.

"I'd never thought about it," I said, my mind racing frantically. "I was married once before, but he died in an accident very soon after."

"I was oathed once, long ago," Devlin said sadly. "She died as well. It is always tragic to lose someone you love."

"I'm sorry," I whispered.

"Thank you," Devlin said with a sigh. "Let us not speak of that. There is something that troubles me, Sar. There is more in your voice than sorrow when you speak of Danial. There is fear, too."

"I'm not afraid of Danial," I said quickly.

"Not this moment, no," Devlin countered. "But at times I hear it, unmistakably. I expect you to fear me, but I find it odd you are scared of him. Tell me why."

"We fought," I said reluctantly.

"And?" Devlin prodded.

"He hit me."

"Repeat your words," Devlin said frostily. "And look me in the eyes as you say them."

I turned to him defiantly. "He hit me," I said bitterly. Then I turned from him again.

"I would not have believed it," Devlin said slowly. "But you aren't lying. Where and when did this happen?"

"In the face," I said bitterly. "As for when, we were separated when it happened."

Devlin fell silent, thinking.

I lay there in his arms, trying not to feel sorry for myself, trying to plan of what to say next, of some way to convince him to let me go. I tried scenario after scenario, and came up with nothing.

"That you were separated does not matter," Devlin said suddenly. "You had taken an oath out of love to him, and he to you. It does not matter what you had done, or said. Oathed Ones are never to be struck."

"I guess I picked the wrong brother," I said sarcastically.

"Yes, you did," Devlin said seductively. He turned me to face him, his hand on the side of my face. "I see no mark on your skin. When was this?"

Reluctantly, I grasped his cool hand in mine, and slid it upwards. "There is a tiny scar there from his ring."

"Yes," Devlin said, "I feel it." He leaned in close, giving the scar a gentle kiss. "I'll take him to task for this, Sar. You have my word."

"Since when are you my champion?" I said sarcastically. "You kidnapped me. If you really want to help me, just take me home."

"I'd love to take you home," Devlin said meaningfully. He kissed me gently, his cool lips brushing mine.

"Stop." I moved my head, breaking the kiss. "I meant my home."

"Oh, kiss me," Devlin said longingly. "There are several miles yet, and I've learned enough to know you are not oathed to Danial." He raised his eyebrows in a meaningful motion. "I'll restrain myself, I promise. We'll wait to make love until later."

I opened my mouth to reply and he kissed me again passionately, his hand cupping my cheek. For a single second I didn't fight, then I pushed him away roughly. The movement unbalanced me, sending me backward off the car seat. With blurred motion of unnatural speed, Devlin grabbed hold of me, arresting my fall.

"Careful," he cautioned, settling me back on his lap. "You'll hurt yourself."

"If you're so concerned with my safety, why don't you let me sit up and put a seatbelt on?" I said sarcastically.

"Because I like holding you," he replied. "I like you, Sarelle McGarran. Your outspokenness is refreshing."

I didn't reply.

"My only concern is that you don't like me," Devlin said forlornly. "You reject my kisses. My promise to uphold your rights is met with derision, without a single thank you."

"What do you want me to say?" I said, frustrated. "Thanks for smashing up my windows? Thanks for making me undress in front of you?"

"I want you to show me some interest," Devlin said pointedly. "Are you not curious about me at all? I seem to somehow become Quasimodo whenever I'm in your presence."

Shifting in his arms, my hand touched the soft leather of his high boots. I seized on that. "Fine. Where did you get those boots you are wearing?"

Devlin laughed. "You like my boots?"

"Very much," I divulged, glad he was pleased. "I always meant to ask Danial where he got his."

"We have them made for us. They are authentic, like we both remember them." He paused. "It's hard, seeing everything you love, everything you know, pass away into history and dust. No one remembers but he and I, Sar. No one else really cares about what happened hundreds of years ago. It's like a movie to everyone else, hearing about what life was back then, so different from how it is today."

Maybe I could keep him talking, find some way to get him to release me?

"Why did you have stubble the night of the party, and now you are clean-shaven? I never saw Danial shave, not ever," I said curiously.

He laughed a little, but there was sadness about it, somehow. "I hadn't shaved the night I was changed. I was trying to grow a beard. Danial shaved religiously every night, so he never has stubble. I have had to shave every few days for all of my four hundred and twenty-one years."

Abruptly, the tires bumped up, the ride becoming smoother.

"We are here," Devlin said merrily. Before I could reply, he kissed me again.

Chapter Twenty

We pulled up in front of Danial's home. Devlin opened the SUV door, and helped me out. Taking my hand, he pulled me up the house steps behind him, and threw open the front door. It had been unlocked again.

"Careless," Devlin said disapprovingly, shaking his head. He strode into the house, pulling me after him. "Danial!" he shouted.

There was no one in the kitchen, or in the great room. Devlin walked into the great room, paused, then shouted, "Danial, leave off that damned computer and get out here!"

The door to Danial's upstairs office opened, and Danial came out. He was wearing some jeans and an aqua colored shirt. It was the one from the Hallows party all those months ago.

"Devlin, what are you doing here?" Then his eyes fell on me. "Sar?" he said, his eyes widening. "What has happened?"

He came down the stairs, and when he reached the floor, Devlin shoved me off balance, so I went to my knees at Danial's feet. With poise, Danial went to one knee, and helped me up. I was afraid to be near him, but I wanted him to protect me from Devlin. I hesitantly put my arms around his neck, as he hugged me.

"Devlin, what is the meaning of this?" Danial said over my shoulder.

"It's been six months, Danial. Have you forgotten your oathing deadline?"

Danial looked at me, realization dawning. My heart sank at the hope in his eyes; hope that this would force me back into his arms.

"I talk to you at least every week and you've made no mention of my oathing Sar for months," Danial said smoothly. "Naturally, it slipped my mind, with all that's—"

"Sar will oath to you now, in front of me as a witness, and you will mark her," Devlin said with authority. "Or you will take off her collar, and tell me you give up all claim to her. Then I'm taking her home to Hayden with me. Choose now, Danial."

I had hoped for an elaborate speech from him, but he clearly wanted to get moving. It had to be eight or nine o'clock by now. Reflexively, I checked my wrist to find it bare. Damn, I'd left my watch on my dresser. At least Terian's plane had to have landed by now...

"I won't remove it," Danial said, narrowing his eyes at Devlin. "You can't have her."

"Alas, poor Wisdom's chance, against a glance, is now as weak as ever," Devlin said with a sneer.

I turned and gave him an odd glance, surprised he knew poetry at all, much less romantic poetry like Moore. He gave me a sensuous look, then grinned widely. I shivered in Danial's arms. He hugged me tighter, stroking my back soothingly.

"You cannot force me to take her oath under vampire law," Danial said carefully. "She wears my symbol and that is enough for me, until she decides otherwise. There is no law that says she must be oathed to me in a particular set time, I checked. You cannot claim her so long as she wears it, nor take her for your own—"

"Ah, but I can, brother," Devlin said with a smirk. "I was in her house, in her bedroom, and I scented another male on her sheets, and on her body. A very familiar scent." He paused, seeming to savor the moment. "And I scented you not at all."

The blood drained from my face. He'd known all along about Theo and me.

"I do not need to exercise my rights to her to prove they exist, Dev," Danial retorted.

"Save it, Danial. You didn't mention to me that Theo was allowed to fuck Sarelle. The scent of their sex play was strong in her bedroom, strong enough for me to know it wasn't once they were together, it was dozens of times."

Danial looked with murderous rage at Devlin, but said nothing.

"Don't bother lying," Devlin said easily. "I know you; know you would never have allowed him to share her with you. I can smell the jealousy coming off you like mist. By vampire law I can have Theo hunted down and killed—"

"That is at my discretion, Dev, and I do not wish him punished. Do not send—"

"—and Sarelle's collar is a farce, as she is neither here with you as she should be, or confining her affections to just you—"

"I am not letting you take her," Danial snarled. "I don't want your interference in this! It is none of your business!"

"I am Ruler here, and I was witness to it. She has been fucking your bodyguard and best friend behind your back. An example must be made of her. You will be the laughingstock of the entire vampire world, if this gets out!"

"I don't care," Danial said resolutely. "She saved my life last fall. I'm not letting you take her." He let me go, moving me behind him protectively.

Devlin looked at Danial with shock, staring for perhaps a minute. Then he began laughing, rich laughter that poured out of him like water, clear as crystal and just as sharp.

"You knew," he said, incredulous. "You knew about Theo and her, and you did nothing. Have you no pride?"

Danial did not answer. It struck me in that moment that Danial did care about me, despite how he'd acted. He could have had me back at his home hours after I'd first left him, or anytime since then. All he would've had to do was tell Devlin what had happened, and Devlin would have brought me back to him, just as he had tonight. Yet Danial hadn't acted, knowing I'd hate him if he'd brought me back against my will. Even after we'd broken up, he'd used the choker to keep me safe from Devlin. His persistence and single-mindedness in making me wear it had never been out of selfishness or arrogance, but out of love.

"Even if you have no pride, Danial, as your brother, I do," Devlin said flatly, interrupting my thoughts. "And as Ruler, I decide when and where punishment must be meted out, according to the law." He paused. "I don't know when her affair with Theo started. She told me you were oathed, which means she is not free to have other lovers. So she is guilty of—"

"She oathed to me, but I released her, Dev," Danial said quietly. "She did not break her word to me."

"Fine. Then Sar is viewed under vampire law as a woman unspoken for. As such, you may oath her now, or—"

"You can do nothing while she wears my symbol. Stop trying to twist the law!"

"She is either your lover, or she is not! You can't have it both ways!" Devlin smiled, baring his upper fangs. "At least, not while you have another Ruler as an interested party. And as that Ruler, I demand that you either surrender her to me or oath to her right now."

Danial snarled at Devlin, his face livid. "That law was designed to protect Oathed Ones, so the choker could never be viewed as a simple tag of ownership—"

Devlin just smirked back at him. "Which is how you've been using it all along, to protect Sar from my attentions. But that stops now."

"She is my lover," Danial said coldly, his eyes red. "My word suffices, Ruler to Ruler. That is law."

"Not this time," Devlin said sinisterly.

Foreboding enveloped me.

"I told you, I don't care that she's been with Theo—" Danial began.

"She is not the only one who has broken faith," Devlin continued. "She has told me you struck her. Is this true?"

"Yes," Danial said simply. "To my shame."

"You are never to strike her again, not for any reason," Devlin said coldly. "You are lucky you didn't kill her."

"I will not," Danial said angrily. "I have taken steps to ensure it never happens again."

"I hope you mean that," Devlin replied. "Because it's your life if you don't." He strode over, until he was directly in front of Danial. "I, Devlin Dalcon, stand before you, Danial Racklan, concerning the woman you call your own, Sarelle McGarran. I charge you with abuse and dereliction of your Oathed One, on the basis of your own words. As such, I decree any promise that existed between you has been broken." He crossed his arms over his chest. "Now, either oath her to you anew, or set her free."

Danial held Devlin's gaze for a split second, then said, "Wait here." Danial turned, took my hand, and led me into his bedroom.

"The consummation comes after, Danial. Not before!" Devlin called after us, laughing.

Danial shut the door behind us, and sat me down on his bed. Casting a look around me revealed that the wardrobe was gone, as well as the other furniture I'd moved in months ago. His bedroom looked exactly as it had the first I'd visited him last fall.

He locked the door, then came and kneeled in front of me, taking my hands in his.

"Sar, I'm sorry for all that's happened," he said.

"I'm sorry, too," I said sincerely. "I never meant to fall in love with your best friend. I want you to know, I…I wasn't with Theo until a few weeks ago, Danial. We came to you the very next night—"

"He was right; I drove you to him, with how I acted." Danial sighed, and reached up his hand to touch my cheek, looking at the slight scar across it. "Does it still hurt?"

I reached up, and took his hand, moving it off the scar. "It doesn't hurt anymore. It healed."

Danial dropped his eyes. "I want you to know I'm seeing a professional anger therapist. I've got another two months until I complete the program." He cleared his throat. "What I'm trying to say is I've taken steps to alter my behavior, because I know what I did to you was wrong. And because I want you to know I mean it when I say what happened will never happen again, if you'd only agree to give me another chance."

"I forgive you," I said uneasily. "But what we had is done, Danial. I'm sorry."

"Do you love Theo?"

"I do," I said cautiously, unsure how he would react.

"Do you still love me?" Danial asked, his eyes searching mine hopefully.

"Yes," I said simply. "But—"

"Leave him then, and come back to me," Danial interrupted. "I'll mark you tonight. That will be enough for Devlin. He'll leave, and we can start over. You can take as much time as you want to oath to me again, Sar. What matters is that you're here with me." He took my hand and pressed it to his lips, then held it to his cheek.

To my chagrin, I was torn, wanting to hug him and tell him that we could have that happy ending, that I wanted it as much as he did. But as much as I still loved him, it was too late.

"Danial, I can't. I'm with Theo now," I said gently. "And you are with Angelica."

"Theo will be alright, Sar," Danial assured me, his dark eyes looking into mine intently. "I heard from Suri that Tawny was here, that she is pregnant, and that it is most likely his. He's loved her for years. She'll help him to get over you, and in time, he'll forgive her for lying to him, just as I have forgiven you—"

"They are finished," I snapped. "He loves me and I love him."

He stood up quickly, and pushed me back on the bed. I let out a cry of surprise.

"You know what's going to happen when Theo comes for you?" Danial said angrily, his face inches from mine. "Yes, I'm sure he's on his way. If Devlin had killed him taking you, he'd have gloated more. But Devlin won't have any problem killing him right here, Sar. Do you want that to happen?"

"No," I said staunchly. "But Theo is tenth now—"

"He got lucky getting that rank, from what he told me. Luck won't save him tonight. Devlin's guards are far more experienced and powerful. They are werebears. Grizzly bears, Sar."

"I killed at least five of them tonight single handedly," I shot back. "That gun with explosive bullets evens the playing field."

"Because he told them to take you alive," Danial countered. "And he didn't know you had that gun. Theo will have neither advantage. Dev's likely got some bears lying in wait for Theo already, to kill him the instant he arrives."

"Tell him not to," I pleaded. "He's your brother. Can't you do anything? What's the use of being a state ruler if you can't save your best friend from being killed?"

"Devlin will not listen to me," Danial said hatefully, rolling onto his side. "He is bent on getting you. Theo will be collateral damage."

"Then fight him," I said, exasperated, as I moved to face him. "Please, Danial."

"I cannot win in a test of strength," Danial said angrily. "If we fight, it will be to the death and one of us will lose. If I die, he will claim you as the spoils."

"Please, there has to be something you can do—"

"I have tried every delaying tactic I could think of in my attempts to keep him from you," Danial said haggardly. "He's called my bluff, and boxed us into a corner. There is only one path that remains, Sar: give me your oath, and let me mark you." He looked at me beseechingly. "Devlin will not kill Theo if we are oathed."

"You can't know that," I replied angrily.

"I can reason it," he replied. "If you do this, there will be no fight. Devlin will give up and leave, because he'll have no choice. Theo won't attack Devlin, either, because there will be nothing for him to fight for. You are the one who has the power to stop the carnage before it goes further, Sar, not me. Do you have the courage to act?"

I would not oath to Danial. Yet I did have the courage to act.

I leaned in and kissed Danial passionately. He groaned into my mouth, and pulled me closer. I ran my hands up under his shirt, feeling the familiar coolness of him. He slid his arms from my shoulders to my hips, then reached down to the front of my robe, sliding his hands beneath it.

I had been concentrating on acting until that moment, trying to buy precious time. Danial's touch awakened my memory of him, my longing for him. I moaned as his fingers slid over my body, caressing and rubbing sensuously. I melted into him, my skin burning up under his touch.

Danial undid my robe, pushing it aside, then covered my naked body with his clothed one. I kissed him hungrily, my conscience clamoring for me to stop.

I ignored it. Theo had said to do whatever I had to in order to survive. He would forgive me this.

Danial stripped off his shirt, throwing it aside. He kissed down my neck, running his fangs down over my throat. I steeled myself, then bit hard down into my lower lip. There was a sharp pain, and I tasted blood. I reached down with my hands, bringing his lips to meet mine. I opened my mouth on his, licking him with my tongue. He tasted the blood and let out a loud groan, his arms tightening down around me, his hips flexing against mine. He kissed me fiercely, as if he would devour me.

A moment later, he let me go, rolling on his back to remove his jeans. He slipped them off, then rolled onto me, parting my legs. The hardness of his erection pressed firmly against me.

"I'm going to mark you now, my love," he said tenderly. "Please forgive me for the pain."

I nodded, biting my swollen lip, and turned my face away.

"Tell me you love me again," Danial said softly, kissing up my throat, shifting his hips back as he poised to enter me.

I didn't answer.

Danial raised up from me, then cupped my cheek, making me face him. "I love you, Sar. We'll be happy, I promise. These months we've spent apart will seem like a bad dream."

I looked up into his eyes, so dark and dangerous, and closed mine. "Please, just do it."

I tensed, waiting for that first thrust of his body into mine. Instead, Danial let out a growl, and pushed up off me.

"No. Not like this."

I opened my eyes to see him pulling on his clothes, his expression bitter. "I'll not rape you, my dear," Danial said acrimoniously. "I'll leave that to Devlin."

"What the hell are you saying?" I asked, shocked.

"You don't want a life with me," Danial said resentfully, unlocking the door. "I don't think you know what you want, really. But I'm not going to mark you against your will. It's clear you don't love me as you once did."

I wrapped the robe back around me, belting it tightly. "What changed?" I said sarcastically, getting to my feet. "You asked me a few minutes ago to submit to your grand scheme, gave me no choice—"

"There's always a choice," Danial said arrogantly, opening the bedroom door with enough force to lodge the doorknob in the wall. "And you've made yours. Go and greet him, Sar. He's waiting for you."

I began to back away. Danial lunged, grabbing my hand, and dragged me out into the great room.

Devlin, sprawled on the sofa indolently, sat up quickly in a graceful motion. "Finished so soon? That didn't take long—"

"She refused to oath to me, Devlin. I relinquish all claim to her," Danial said angrily.

Devlin smiled so widely his fangs bared completely, his gilded eyes glowing with pleasure. "I'm taking her home with me then," he said lustfully. "I have some lessons for her to learn." He took me from Danial, pulling me into his embrace.

I stared into his eyes with raw fear, shaking a little, trying not to regret my brave words to Danial a few moments ago. Devlin leaned in quick and nicked my neck slightly with one of his fangs, even as I struggled. Then he tightened down his arms, sucking on the wound. I let out a cry of pain, and Devlin sucked harder, tightening his arms around me to the point I couldn't breathe.

I went limp in his arms, tears streaming down my face.

"That's a good girl," Devlin whispered to me, kissing my throbbing neck, as he loosened his arms. "If you don't fight, what I do to you will feel better. That is your first lesson." He kissed me gently on the lips, then my cheeks. "I'm not saying there won't be pain, sweet Sar. But I will be as gentle as I can. There will be very little, if you do as I ask, the first time I ask. Now kiss me." He kissed me again on the mouth. Trembling, I kissed him back, tears leaking from my eyes.

He kissed me long and sensuously, then drew back. "Very good," he said approvingly. "Now this time, open your mouth, so I can kiss you more completely."

I twisted quickly, looking toward Danial with imploring eyes. Devlin dug his fingers into me, turning me back to face him. "You'll find I'm a thorough teacher, Sar," he purred happily. "You'll learn fast, I'm sure. Though I hope you make a few mistakes, so I can—"

"No," Danial said quickly. "We'll take her together, Dev. Just the two of us—"

"I don't want to," Devlin said, locking his arms tightly around me, as he moved backward towards the door. "I have plans for her and me." He trailed his fangs over my cheek. "I can't wait to know every inch of her—"

"Devlin, she fucked my best friend," Danial said resentfully. "You are right in that if I let this slide, every vampire in the country will think me weak. I already have more than enough enemies. I'll punish her. Leave her with me—"

"Sorry, brother," Devlin purred, dragging me towards the door. "Sar and I have to be going. Besides, I think this is a trick."

"The trick will be convincing your subjects that you didn't just take her from me, when she is still wearing my collar," Danial said snidely. "You want me to spread the word that you did? I'll be believed, Devlin. And you'll be overthrown."

"You wouldn't dare!" Devlin snarled, turning back towards Danial, his eyes red-tinged now. "You just gave up all rights to her!"

"I changed my mind," Danial said arrogantly. "Now bring her to me."

"Fine," Devlin said coldly, each word an icicle. "You want her punished so badly, you will be needing help. I volunteer myself. Do you accept?"

"On the condition that you do not force her to accept more than your fangs," Danial said stonily.

Devlin gave me a despairing look. "Agreed," he said reluctantly, stepping back from me. "Now take off the choker."

Danial reached behind me to the choker, and with a sliding sound, the necklace I'd worn for so many months fell off my neck to land in my hands. He took it from me, and laid it on one of his bookshelves.

"You take all the fun out of bestowing punishment," Devlin said grumpily. Then his face abruptly brightened. "You want to do to her what we did to Angelica?" he said excitedly. "It will be a sweet ride, to be sure."

I'd wondered why there had been no signs of Angelica in the house, or Danial's bedroom. With a cold feeling, I remembered Danial hadn't answered me when I'd mentioned her.

"What did you do to her?" I said in trepidation.

"We drank her down together, Sar," Devlin said fondly, his expression blissful. "The shock of so much blood loss all at once stopped her heart. But it was delicious while it lasted."

Worse than hearing his pleasure-filled voice was that Danial did not deny it. I shuddered, thinking of how often I'd given my blood to Danial in those months I'd spent with him. I'd trusted him, when he said he didn't hurt women. He'd killed one he'd promised to protect. He was more like his brother than I'd ever realized.

I shrank from them both, back to the edge of the great room. "How could you, Danial?" I managed to get out. "She trusted you not to hurt her!"

"Danial said she needed to be punished," Devlin said with a shrug. "She gave him a promise, betrayed him, and then lied to him. He had a right to punish her, just as he had the right to punish you."

"I thought a vampire protected those he oathed?" I said loudly. "Not killed them!"

"She cost me you, Sar, with her arrogance, and her jealousy," Danial said bitterly. "I had told her you might come here to see me and that if you did, she was to bring you to me at once, if she could, or call me, if she couldn't. She swore that she would, as part of her oath to me. But she never even told me that you were here." He sighed heavily. "I was here that night, Sar, upstairs on a conference call. If I had known you were here, if I had answered the door instead of her." He looked at me sadly. "Everything would have been different."

He was right. I would have come back to him that night, and gotten Terian's message too late to act on it. Theo would still be alone, or maybe he would be with Tawny. But either way, he would never have been with me.

"Danial, my patience is at an end," Devlin said angrily, breaking into my thoughts. He gripped my arm. "Come, Sar, we are going to the bedroom. Danial can join us, if he wishes." He led me into Danial's bedroom, hurriedly pushing me to the bed as Danial had.

"I'm going to be inside you, one way or another, in a few seconds," Devlin said lustily, thrusting lightly against me with his hips. "God, I can't wait. Tell me you want me to be, Sar." He kissed my neck lightly, then grazed it again with a fang. "Tell me now."

"I am here," Danial snarled, slamming the door behind him. "Get off her, Devlin. This will work much better if she is kneeling, as Angelica was."

Devlin pushed up off me, and sat beside me. "Very well, killjoy. Together then?"

"Danial, don't do this," I said pleadingly.

"Sar, if he takes you with him, it will be much worse for you," Danial said, resigned. "You don't want a life with me. And by that, you've said that you'd rather die." He cupped my cheek with his hand. "This is the best death I can offer you."

He pulled the hair away from my neck on one side, as Devlin pulled it away from the other, then Danial bared his fangs.

"Wait," Devlin said. "You have a good angle but I don't. Let me get on that side."

"Devlin, this is fine—"

"Danial, the last time we did this, it was great. After I had to lose six guards bringing her here, and get shot myself, it's the least—"

"She shot you?" Danial said, surprised.

"Yes," Devlin said, clearly annoyed.

Danial laughed, enjoying Devlin's discomfort. "Where? Or don't I want to know?"

"In the arm. Move it already," Devlin said in exasperation.

Both of them moved as one, switching sides, then rearranging my hair to my back, and pushing down the collar of the black velvet robe, baring my neck and shoulders.

"Better?" Danial said to Devlin.

"Much," Devlin said, and then he kissed the side of my neck gently. Without preamble, he bit down hard. I gasped at the pain, and tried to move, but they had tight hold of me.

Devlin was swallowing me down in long draughts, but he wasn't hurrying. He was groaning, clearly aroused, and he wanted his pleasure to last. He reached one hand up inside my robe, and caressed my naked breast, cupping it as he drank me down. I struggled, but his mouth was locked on me, and between the two of them, I couldn't move.

Danial looked at me sadly. "Please, Sar, tell me you'll come back to me, oath to me. If you do I can stop him."

I looked back at him. "I hate you," I whispered. "I hate you both."

"I'm sorry," Danial said softly.

"You're a bastard," I hissed out painfully. "You're a—"

Devlin put his hand over my mouth, cutting off my words. I bit him reflexively. He withdrew his fangs, and I let out a muffled cry, as his hand clamped down tighter.

"Danial, you aren't participating," Devlin said languidly. "Go ahead. I've got hold of her. She won't be mouthing any more curse words."

"Let her speak," Danial said wearily. "I want to hear her last words, even if she curses me."

Devlin released my mouth. I let out a scream of pain.

"Shut up, bitch," he whispered in my ear, and then he bit down deeply into my neck again.

I began sobbing. Danial wiped away the tears, then said, "I'll bring your pets here to live with me, Sar," he said softly. "They'll be safe. Don't worry."

He kissed me one final time, and then bit down on the other side of my neck. The shock was almost more than I could take, as throbbing pain radiated from both of my wounds. I screamed again, and felt deep blackness suddenly, overwhelming evil snaking its way into the room, almost choking me. I began to shake, whimper, and keen with it, the evil feeling was so complete and terrifying. But hope rose in me, because it had to be Terian, and Theo would be with him.

"I feel something," Devlin said, drawing back from me, blood smeared across his face. "Danial, did you hire a demon for a new guard? You've always said you didn't like demons—"

Alarm raced across Danial's face as he turned to Devlin. "No. I thought I felt something too. Devlin, did you lock the front door behind you?"

"No. But not to worry, my guards are out there. I have at least ten left—"

"Part of the reason I punished Angelica was because of her carelessness!" Danial thundered. "You've eclipsed her in brainlessness!"

"The door was unlocked when we got here," Devlin said peevishly.

"No, it wasn't," Danial shot back. "Now go and lock it."

Devlin rolled his eyes, let me go, and jumped lightly off the bed, licking his lips. I collapsed immediately, Danial catching me in his arms.

"Fine, I'll go check. Stay here, and don't be finishing her off without me."

Devlin opened the door and strode outside. Danial shut it after him, quickly, then locked it. He ran into the bathroom, and returned in a flash with bandages and tape. He propped me up on pillows, and began to dress my wounds as fast as he could.

"What are you doing?" I murmured.

"Sar, can you hear me?" Danial said quickly. "Say something if you can."

"How could you do this to me?" I said weakly, each word a burden.

"I bit you, but I didn't take your blood. My bite is already scabbed over, but Devlin's were very deep. Lay still. If you don't lose any more blood, you'll recover."

He laid me back down carefully on the bed, holding gauze to my throat. There was a steady trickle of blood flowing out of me, staining my bandage, the robe and the sheets.

There was an enraged scream, and the sound of a body hitting the wall. The blackness had been choking before, now it was a solid thing, an entity sucking out the oxygen from the air. I labored to breathe, the sounds of bears roaring and fighting faint through the door. A cougar suddenly screamed, enraged.

"Theo," I whispered.

I heard his enraged growl a moment before he smashed through the door, and leaped on Danial, hurling him off the bed as they landed hard against the far wall. There was a wet ripping sound and then Theo bounded up on the bed, his face bloody. I reached for him, and he licked my hand. He lay down next to me, and slowly, he changed back to human form.

"Sar," he said, opening his eyes and sitting up. His eyes took in the blood and bandages on me, as I lay there, too exhausted to move. "Don't move," he cautioned. He looked under my neck bandages and grimaced, then put pressure on Devlin's bites.

He checked them again a minute later. "The bleeding has mostly stopped," he said, stroking my cheek silently. "Stay still, okay?"

He got up and rummaged beneath the bed, grabbing some of Danial's clothes. While he was dressing, it registered that silence had descended. All sounds of fighting had stopped.

Theo picked me up and carried me into the great room. There was carnage everywhere Some men that were part bear lay dead from holes in their chests. One man had been clawed up, his throat torn out, a gaping red ruin where his heart should be. At least one body looked as if it had exploded. Blood spray was everywhere, soaking the carpet in places. In the middle of it all, was my savior and friend, Terian. Devlin was on the ground at his feet, held in place by two of the bears. The vampire king was furious, cursing and snarling. The bears were holding him, though it was taking all of their strength to do it.

"Terian, I found her, she's okay," Theo said, relieved.

Terian turned in our direction, his eyes a solid red. He looked different, tanned, with hair that was longer, down to his shoulders. His hands were coated in blood, thought his clothes were unstained. His handsome face had a worried expression. "Sar, can you talk?"

"Thank you for saving me," I told him weakly. "Thank you so much."

"You're welcome," he said politely back, but he didn't move from his position. "Well, what are we going to do with them?" Terian said, turning back to look at Devlin and his bearmen. "It's taking all my strength to hold the bears. They're fighting me hard. Did you deal with Danial?"

"I ripped out his throat," Theo replied. "He'll heal, but it'll be a few more minutes. Just hold the bears, and I'll get a serviceable stake to kill Devlin—"

"If we kill him, Theo, we'll just have to deal with another vampire Ruler," Terian said with a sigh. "And that one will see us as a threat, and want our blood even more. I've shown my power now. I'd have to keep killing. I don't want to do that."

"You aren't suggesting we leave Devlin in charge" Theo said incredulously. "It would only be a matter of time until he came after Sarelle again."

"We need to go with option C," Terian said slowly. "I think I know what to do."

Chapter Twenty-One

"We'll need to wait until Danial heals," Terian said, looking down calculatingly at Devlin. "We'll need him."

I wanted to ask what Terian was planning, but I was too exhausted. Besides, I'd see it for myself shortly.

"Do you need me?" Theo asked. "I'm worried about having Sar here so close to Devlin, especially if there's danger of the bears breaking free from your spell."

"We're okay," Terian said, turning back towards Devlin. "Call Camlyn. Ask him if he'll meet you there."

"I'm all right," I said groggily. "I just need some of those blood replenishing packets. I felt like this before when Danial took too much of my blood one night last fall. Dr. Camlyn gave me one then."

Theo laid me down on the couch. "Stay right here. There are some in the kitchen." He got up and left. He was back in a few minutes with a glass of water, a few packets, and some of my vitamins. I took the vitamins first, swallowing three. When Theo opened the packets and handed them to me, I saw they had Angelica's name on them. I said a quick prayer for her, then swallowed both packets, my stomach rebelling at the horrible taste. Almost immediately, I felt stronger as the double dose of medicine kicked in.

Theo was watching me closely. "How do you feel?"

"Better," I replied. "Danial saved me, by not taking my blood."

"You have three bite marks," Theo said. "Devlin didn't make all of them, did he?"

"Danial didn't drink," I explained. "Only Devlin did. If Danial hadn't done that, I'd be dead now. As it was, you came just in time."

Theo suddenly hugged me tightly, and didn't say anything.

"I might have known that bastard had a last scheme," Devlin said vituperatively. His golden eyes glowed with pent up fury.

"Watch who you're calling a bastard," Theo growled.

"Release me, you fucks!" Devlin snarled venomously. "Do you know who I am? I am not just any Ruler! You and that demon will be hunted and killed for this, wherever on Earth you flee to!"

Terian looked down at him disdainfully.

There was the sound of a door opening. I turned to see Danial slowly coming out of his bedroom. He looked terrible, his shirt covered in blood, his skin bone white, his features haggard. He took in Theo, Terian, Devlin, and then his eyes fastened on me.

"Sar," he said in relief, and started for me.

Terian glided over to stand before him, blocking him. "Danial, I offer you a choice here and now."

Danial stared in surprise at Terian. "Yes?"

"Either you agree to my terms, or I'll kill you." Terian said coldly.

"What are your terms, Demon?" Danial said just as coldly.

"First of all, you agree Sar is off limits to you. You will cease pursuing her, for the rest of her life."

Danial looked over at me, the last hope that I would be his burning out and dying in his eyes. "I agree," he said tiredly.

"Second, that you take Devlin's place as Ruler for United States."

"I cannot, I can't make vampires," Danial said bluntly. "I have never been able to—"

"I will give you the power," Terian said smoothly.

"How?" Danial said quickly. "I have tried everything, every potion—"

"Have you?" said Terian, turning pointedly to Devlin.

Danial followed his movement. "What are you saying?" he said slowly.

"I'm saying the secret lies in him, in his blood," Terian said. "In all the time you existed together, did he ever offer you his blood?"

"No," Danial said, glancing down at Devlin. "That is Hollywood nonsense."

"No, it's very probable that is what you lack, why the power is held only by him. He needs to share his blood with you. The power lies in the older blood, as I'm guessing it always has—"

"But he shares his blood with all the new vampires he makes, and they can't make vampires either," Danial said in frustration.

"Not enough of it, and only once," Terian said bluntly. "He's keeping control that way. I suspect all the older vampires who are Rulers are."

"That cannot be true," Danial said disbelievingly. "I have drained vampires that were over a hundred years old, and I do not have the power."

"The blood needs to be much older, and it does not come at a set age, but differs depending on the vampire whose bloodline the newer vampire stems from," Terian said. "At least, that is what I believe. There are over two hundred thousand weres in the world, at least. Yet there are nowhere near that many vampires; it's theorized that the total number in the world lies under ten thousand. It makes sense that the method for making more is something only a select few know."

"That makes sense," Danial admitted. "But what proof do you have of your theory?"

"The night you were both attacked, what happened?" Terian asked. "Tell me."

"Devlin was attacked first, while he was sleeping," Danial said. "He bit the vampire in self-defense, but passed out. I woke up, and ran to his aid. I stabbed the vampire through the chest, but it bit me anyway. Some of its blood from the bite Devlin made dripped in to my mouth when it was feeding from me. I passed out then, and when we awoke, everyone was dead, and the vampire was gone."

"But it was Devlin that killed the vampire," Terian said flatly.

"No, that's not how it happened—" Danial started.

"Devlin killed him while you were passed out, Danial. He drank most of that vampire's blood, then staked him with a broken spear shaft."

"I did that on instinct, not from a set plan," Devlin said defensively. "I was not thinking clearly."

"Between the injuries you gave him, and the almost complete blood loss, the vampire died," Terian continued. "Devlin dragged him away from the rest of the bodies, and left him there. He rejoined you later, before you woke up—"

"In case the monster was not dead, idiot!" Devlin said stridently. "We'd tried with every weapon at our disposal to kill him, with no success!"

"—Devlin was the one who found a cave that night, who insisted on sleeping in it—"

"I suggested the cave because we were freezing and we needed shelter," Devlin raged. "You make me out to have known what had happened to us. I did not!"

"He is correct, Terian. Neither of us knew what we'd faced, or what we'd become," Danial said stubbornly. "I remember—"

"Do you?" Terian said. "Devlin remembers differently. The story I told you is the one I got from his lips a few moments ago." Terian turned to Devlin. "Repeat your story. And for once, speak the truth."

"Devlin?" Danial said questioningly.

"I did not know what we faced, or what we'd become," Devlin said finally. "I did drink his blood more than once, Danial, and put wood through his heart. That part is true."

"And what about the rest of Terian's theory?"

"With old blood of any kind comes power," Devlin said seriously. "But I've never heard of what he's suggesting."

"Have you ever drunk an older vampire's blood?" Danial demanded.

"Yes," Devlin said maliciously, his eyes glinting red. "As often as I can. It's full of power."

"So all this time, these past centuries, you have known that this was what I needed and you kept it from me?" Danial shouted, his eyes bleeding to red again.

"Danial, I didn't know—" Devlin began.

"You knew," Danial said disgustedly. "But you kept it to yourself, rather than lose your edge over me." He turned to Terian. "What do I have to do?"

"Drink his blood, Danial. About a pint should be sufficient, though less should do it."

"Then what?" Danial asked.

"Then you'll have the power also. Devlin will still have it, too, but this will make you equals. You will become Ruler. Devlin will become second to you, and you will keep control of him. You will keep him in line, and away from Sar."

Danial met Terian's eyes with his own. "You are saying—"

"We'll leave him alive if you do this, Danial," Terian replied. "I understand that he is your brother. I recently lost mine, and do not want to take the life of yours, deceiver that he might be. My sole concern is for Sar."

"Don't you dare, Danial," Devlin seethed. "Don't you dare do it!"

Danial acted quickly. He kneeled in one fluid motion, and bit down on his brother's neck. Devlin writhed and fought hard, but was held still by his own guards. Danial drank for a long time. When he got to his feet, he was changed. His skin shown like a pearl hit by sunlight, and his eyes shone like black opals. Danial had always been breathtaking, now he was irresistible.

Danial looked down at Devlin, lying at his feet. The former vampire king was alive, but almost drained of the fire inside him. He lay there unmoving, barely conscious, undeniably diminished. Danial must have taken much more than a pint from him. With it had gone most, if not all, of his power.

Terian spoke a few words, and held out his hand toward the two bears holding Devlin. Nothing happened for a few seconds. Then, the two bears transformed suddenly, dropping to the floor as very muscular unconscious naked men. Devlin grabbed the nearest one in a flash, and started feeding off him. Terian made no move to stop him. Soon, Devlin stopped, and turning quickly, began to drink from the other one. Within moments, Devlin's skin began to regain some of its former luster, his wan flesh brightening.

I didn't understand why Terian was letting him regain his strength. My bites on my neck ached deeply; a hurt that I felt would be best cured by seeing Devlin spitted. Leaving him alive after what he had done to me seemed a sick joke. Yet I said nothing. Terian had saved me; I wasn't about to second-guess him.

Devlin finished feeding, and climbed to his feet, looking much the same as he had. His eyes found mine, then he bared his fangs, grinning evilly, and started toward me.

Theo growled at him, but Devlin just smiled and kept coming. Terian watched, making no movement. Devlin was almost to me when Danial grabbed hold of him.

Devlin turned and pushed him lightly backward with his hand, as if to brush him aside. But nothing happened. Devlin's eyes widened in shock.

Danial pushed Devlin aside just as lightly, and Devlin fell hard against the couch as if Danial had hit him with a two by four.

"No!" he snarled, enraged. "I am Ruler! I've ruled for two hundred years!"

Devlin came again at Danial, trying to grip his throat with his hands, but Danial held him off with one hand, easily. Devlin hissed, and fought, but he couldn't break free.

"I've waited a long time for this," Danial said gleefully. Then he punched Devlin hard, knocking him sprawling to the floor.

Devlin lay there looking hatefully up at Danial. His nose was broken, as were many of the bones in his face.

"I can't believe it," Theo said softly.

"Believe it. It's done," Terian said with a note of finality. "Sar, are you ready to leave?"

"Yes," I said gratefully. Theo helped me to my feet, and the three of us went to leave.

"Wait," Danial said, walking after us.

The instant he moved, Devlin got to his feet carefully and retreated to his guards, trying to rouse them.

Terian turned and faced Danial. "You have your power. What more do you want from me?"

"I owe you for what you've done for me, no matter what the reason," Danial said.

"You owe me nothing, Danial," Terian said formally. "What you told me in anger was the best thing anyone could have done for me. I had the power to help you, and save Sarelle, because of what you told me about myself."

"Friends?" Danial said questioningly.

"No," Terian said. "But maybe allies."

"Allies, then," Danial agreed, and they shook hands.

Terian turned to go, and then turned back. "There is one thing I almost forgot, Danial," he said cryptically.

"What?" Danial said expectantly.

Terian punched him hard, and Danial fell to one knee, catching himself.

"That's for hitting Sar," Terian said coldly. "Goodnight." He walked out.

The bearmen got to their feet, acting groggy and disoriented. It was hard to tell if that was blood loss or Terian's spell. Devlin gave them a push towards the door, then turned back to look at us. His face—healed, but still covered in blood smears—drew back in a snarl as his golden eyes found mine. The hate in those eyes was so strong I shuddered, even standing there flanked by Theo and Danial. Then he turned, darting out after his guards. There was the sound of him yelling at them to get inside the truck, and then a SUV rumbled to life. There was a loud squeal of tires, then the sound faded away.

Theo turned to Danial. "Sar told me what happened, what you did for her. Thank you."

Danial looked at Theo tetchily. "You tore out my throat, or I'd have helped you fight."

"I'm sorry," Theo said sheepishly. "I heard her scream, and thought you'd hurt her. Friends?" He held out his hand.

"Friends," Danial said, pulling Theo into an embrace.

Theo hugged him back, then they separated.

Danial turned to me. "I'm sorry I didn't find a way to stop him, Sar, that events went as far as they did."

"I'm sorry, too," I said softly. "I'm grateful you did what you could, and I'm sorry for what I said."

Danial turned, and went to the bookshelf where he had placed my choker. He brought it to me, and pressed it into my hand. "Please keep this, Sar," he said. "I had it made for you."

I looked at it in my hand. The fox head choker had been something I'd loved and hated for the better part of a year now. He was right. It was mine, and no one else's, not even his.

"I'll keep it," I replied, slipping it into my robe's pocket. "I understand now why my wearing it was always so important to you. And I thank you for not removing it, that night I asked you to."

Danial took my hand and kissed it gently. "I will never stop loving you, Sar. Never," he whispered. "Devlin will never bother you again. I will see to it."

I looked for one long moment into his sad dark eyes. Then I put my hands on either side of his face, and kissed him softly on the lips one last time.

"I'll always be grateful to you, Danial," I said. "Please take care of yourself."

"I will," Danial said with a nod, smiling faintly. "Now get out of here before I let my emotions get the better of my reason."

"Wait," I said worriedly. "I have to tell you, Danial, the door was unlocked tonight."

"I know it was," Danial said, giving me a faint smile, as he let us to the front door. "I have been leaving it unlocked."

"Why?" Theo said angrily. "It was unlocked the night Sar and I came here, too."

"I'm in the middle of a forest, protected by warding spells, and by a small army of weremen," Danial said with a wry grin. "And I'm a powerful vampire. Why should I lock my door? I'd have warning long before anyone got to the door to even open it."

"You're going to start again tonight," Theo growled. "It's an impediment that can give you precious seconds, seconds you might need, Ruler of the States."

Danial grimaced. "Just Danial is fine, Theo. But I'll take your advice."

"You'd better," Theo said, opening the door. "Monday?"

"Monday night," Danial said with a nod. "Get here at dusk."

We walked out to the idling truck, stepping over more dead guards of Devlin's outside, also with large holes in their chests.

"Did you shoot all these guys?" I asked Theo.

"Until I ran out of bullets," he said, giving me a recriminating look. "Then I changed."

That explained the one clawed up guard inside. "What about the foxes?"

"I called Aran and Suri, told them what was going on, and asked them to keep everyone back. They offered to fight for you, but I told them not to get in the way, that the bears would be too big for them to handle, even three on one. They only had normal guns, which is something I'm going to remedy on Monday."

Theo helped me up into the front seat, and climbed in after me. He shut the door, as Terian said sarcastically "About time! I was wondering if you were both going to stay."

He drove out the driveway, as Danial's lights retreated behind us. But for once, that didn't make me sad.

"You know, when you rescue someone, the person's supposed to want to leave," Terian said, looking at me out of the corner of his eye. "Were you two having a moment with Danial?"

"Enough," Theo growled. "Let's go get some food. Least I can do is buy you dinner."

We stopped for Chinese takeout on the way home, and ate in the truck. Despite everyone but Theo being bloody, our mood was euphoric. I promised to make a nice dinner for everyone tomorrow, and Terian said that would be nice, so long as it wasn't health food. I let that slide, reasoning he deserved a pass from my sarcastic comments for at least a few weeks.

When we arrived at my house, Theo climbed out first, offering me his hand. I took it, then turned back to Terian.

"Do you want to stay?" I asked. "I have a spare bedroom, as you know—"

"I have someone waiting for me, Sar," he said bluntly, then he grinned. "But thanks."

I laughed. "You're welcome. Get going, loverboy."

"I'll come back tomorrow night for dinner," Terian said with a smile. Then he drove off, his taillights fading in the distance.

Theo picked me up then, and began to carry me across the lawn.

"I can walk," I protested from his arms. "I feel fine."

"You're going to have to," he said tiredly, setting me on my feet. "I've got my work cut out for me. I had no idea it would be this bad."

I nodded in agreement, looking at my home. The front door was hanging off its hinges. After we went in the open doorway, he pushed the broken door into place, closing out the cool night air.

"I'll get a new door tomorrow," he assured me. "They're easy to install."

"There's worse in the bedroom," I said with a sigh. "I was there when Devlin found me. Come look."

My bedroom was indeed the worst. There were bloodstains on the rugs and walls, and the door was off its hinges, splintered into pieces. Both windows were completely broken, and the cold April air had kicked on my furnace. Ghost and Darkness were still in my room, laying on the bed. I let them outside, where they did their business gratefully. When they came back in, I gave them three Cheweez apiece for being so brave. By that time, all of my cats had been accounted for. They were okay, if a bit scared. Most had come in through the gaping door sometime during the time we'd been gone and hidden under furniture, emerging meowing when they heard my voice.

I gathered up the rugs and put them in the laundry room to wash, while Theo carried the door pieces downstairs.

"I'll board these up," Theo said, examining the windows. "You go ahead and shower."

I grabbed a clean nightgown from the dresser drawer, went wearily into the bathroom and shut the door. I took off the black velvet robe, and threw it in the garbage. Then I took a long hot shower, washing my hair and scrubbing myself. When I got out, slipped on the nightgown, and dried my hair, I remembered the choker. Retrieving it from the robe pocket, I placed it on the sink counter. The red fox eyes winked in the bright light.

"Sar, are you done?" Theo called from outside the door. "I'll use the guest shower, if you are. I've done all I can with these tonight."

"Sure, go ahead," I called, working some conditioner into my hair.

When I went to wash my hands, I noticed fresh bloodstains on them. One look in the mirror revealed why; Devlin's bites were bleeding again, both of them. With a sigh, I got out some gauze, and held it to them. When they stopped bleeding a few moments later, I put some antiseptic on them, then a large bandage.

There was a knock at the door. "Sar, are you okay?" Theo said, concerned.

"Yes," I said quietly.

"Can I come in?"

I turned and opened the door. "I'm okay. I was just bleeding again."

"Let me look," he said, moving to lift my bandage.

"No," I said forcefully, putting my hands up to stop him. "I'm fine."

"No, you're not," Theo said softly. "I'm sorry he hurt you. I should've been here."

"You've have been killed," I said flatly, moving past him. "Please, let's just go to bed. I'm exhausted."

"Okay," Theo said tiredly, turning from me.

We got into bed. I set my alarm and turned off the light.

"I can get up with you, if you need help," Theo offered, touching my shoulder with his hand. "I'm happy to take care of things tomorrow, if you'll agree to rest here."

"Don't you have a paternity test to get results on?" I said nastily. Abruptly, I lost it, and began sobbing, tears coursing down my face.

"Shh," Theo said softly, gingerly moving me closer and putting his arms around me.

I sobbed harder into his shoulder, clutching him desperately.

"I'm not going anywhere," he said seriously. "Camlyn can call me with the results, which don't matter anyway. You matter, Sar. Just you."

"I was so sure that was it," I whispered. "I could feel myself getting weak, and I was so scared—"

"I was scared, too," Theo said, kissing my cheek. "Scared I'd be too late, or that I'd get to Danial's and find you gone. I was terrified I was never going to see you again."

"You aren't being reassuring," I said grumpily.

"I was scared we were both going to die," Theo said darkly. "We would have, if not for Terian." He tilted my chin up, his eyes meeting mine. "Danial promised to keep Devlin in check. I'm going to help him with that, starting tomorrow."

"What do you mean?" I said, confused.

"I'm going to begin training hard, at least a few hours a day," Theo said staunchly. "And I'm going to set up a challenge to the fifth ranked for a month or so from now."

"You'll be killed," I said, dissolving into angry tears.

"I don't have several lifetimes to learn magic, or the power of a centuries-old vampire," Theo said sadly. "All I have is my strength, my speed, and my skill with weapons. I need to hone them, to be the best I can be, to make sure you're safe. The best way I can do that is by helping Danial retain his crown. There are going to be more than a couple of vampires and weres who will be angry about what happened tonight."

"I'm scared for Danial," I said softly. "And I'm scared for you."

"Where is my brave lioness?" Theo said affectionately. "Someone has replaced her with a timid kitten."

I shot him a disparaging look. "I'm just being realistic. Sometimes bad things happen, no matter how brave you are."

"I know that." He cleared his throat. "That's why I have to ask you how far it went tonight."

I'd known this was coming. "Nothing happened, with either of them."

"Tell me what happened," Theo said reluctantly.

"Why do you want to know this?" I said angrily, brushing away tears again.

"I scented your desire on your skin," Theo whispered halfheartedly. "I'm sorry, but I did.

I'm worried that you're going to change your mind, Sar, that you're going to reconsider and decide you want Danial, and not me."

"Why would you think that?"

"Because he would never have put you in the position I have with Tawny. He would never have left you alone to be taken by Devlin."

"I've told you I love you, that I want you to live here with me," I said, turning to look at him. "What else do you need to hear me say?"

"That you still love me," he whispered. "I want you to reassure me we're okay."

I understood his fear. I'd felt it earlier today, wondering if Tawny would be able to lure him away from me.

"I love you and I want a life with you, Theo," I replied "That's not going to change."

He pulled me to him in a quick motion, and covered his body with mine, pulling off my nightgown. I kissed him fiercely as he ran his hands over my body. He pushed his pelvis to mine, his shaft hard and ready. I rubbed my hips eagerly against his, grinding into him. He broke the kiss, then moved onto his back, reaching for the night stand.

I stopped him. "You don't have to," I said.

He gave me an uncomprehending look. "Why?"

"That first week you were here, I called my doctor. I asked him to call me in a prescription for the pill. I've been taking it all week. I'm safe, as of yesterday night. It shouldn't have to be all your responsibility—"

With a growl, he rolled over onto me, and thrust himself inside in one smooth motion. I was ready for him, wet with desire. He head went back with a long sigh of pleasure as he entered me, at finally being inside me with nothing between us. He found his rhythm almost immediately his weight on his arms as he slowly moved in and out, in and out. I luxuriated in the feel of him, his skin on my skin, slippery with our love and lust for each other. I looked into his blue eyes invitingly, then ran my fingers through his hair, pulling him down to me. He kissed me, his tongue plunging into me with the same rhythm as his body, and I let out a cry. I could feel his heartbeat racing with mine, that heavy feeling inside me building and growing. Suddenly, he thrust himself into me as far as he could, his body jerking on mine. He let loose a roar, breaking my orgasm over me as I screamed out his name. He collapsed down onto me, still jerking slightly. After a few seconds, he rolled to his side, bringing me with him.

Theo kissed me on the forehead gently. "Sar, why did you do this for me?" He pushed my hair out of the way to look into my eyes. "You didn't have to. I was more than happy to—"

"I did it for us. I remembered how you felt in the dream, and I wanted you to know I was yours now, completely yours, that there were no barriers between us."

"I don't want there to be, ever," Theo said seriously, blushing. "I feel awkward saying this, but I want you to know I got tested yesterday, when I was at Camlyn's. I paid extra for him to do it with magic. I'm, um, disease free."

My eyes bugged out, even as I blushed.

"After Tawny said what she did, I was worried, even though we'd been, um, safe, up to then," Theo said hurriedly. "I thought it was a good idea."

"It was," I whispered, hugging him. "Thanks. I got tested, too, back when I went to check with my gynecologist, as part of the routine. I'm fine."

"Sar, I love you," he said tenderly. "I'll be here for you, no matter what."

"I love you too, Theo," I said, kissing him.

We snuggled together, and I fell asleep in his arms, relaxed and happy.

Sometime later, he said "Sar, are you awake?'

"Yes," I said, turning sleepily to him. "What is it?'

"I want to—"

"Again?" I said, unable to resist a smile.

"Yes," he said hungrily.

"As many times as you want me, Theo," I said, kissing him and smiling at the same time.

"As many times as you want me."

Epilogue

Spring finally arrived around May 1st, when the rains came, washing away the snow and ice. It was by no means warm yet, but all the trees and bushes began turning that light green brown that means the promise of spring is about to be fulfilled, that winter is really over for another year.

I stood at my kitchen window one Tuesday morning, and looked out over the field, marveling as I did every spring how good everything looked, the land breaking the cold grip of death and coming alive again. It would be time soon to plow and plant seeds, to mow and cut wood. I looked forward to it every year, and took particular joy in this one, knowing that I had someone to share it with. There was so much I wanted to show him, share with him, to see it again through his eyes and remember what it had been like for me, seeing it for the first time.

It had been a month since Devlin had taken me, since he had tried to kill me. I tried not to think about it, knowing he was still alive out there, that he wanted to hurt me now even more than he had before. But it was hard not to. Every time I looked in the mirror, I saw the twin bites he'd given me that night. Danial's bite was there as well, though the scar was much lighter, almost nonexistent. The deep wounds had healed, but the twin scars remained to remind me of what he'd done to me. He blamed me for losing his figurehead status, for Danial becoming Ruler, even though technically, Danial wasn't Ruler.

Through Theo, I had found out that Danial had requested that no one call him by that title, or any title, except his name. But that was the only part of Ruling he hadn't embraced. Upon announcement of his taking charge, Danial had demanded obedience and acknowledgment from every vampire within U.S. borders that his word was law, and executed a few of those who had refused to do as he said. What he had said before to me, about not wanting power for himself, might have been true when he couldn't have it, but it wasn't true now.

Danial had kept his word to me; I'd not heard from or of Devlin since the night of his fall from power. Danial also kept his distance from me, his only contact through Theo to ask how I was. I understood that and kept my distance, also, though I missed seeing him. I knew from Theo he was still alone, though he was by no means without female companionship. According to Theo, women showed up often, sometimes even on his doorstep, throwing themselves at his feet, trying to be the Vampire Queen to his King. In that regard, I felt sorry for him. He'd been desired for the creature he was, and not the man for a long time. Now he was desired for his power, also.

If that wasn't enough to feel badly about, there also the continuing animosity between Terian and Theo. I'd thought that had been solved when they'd worked together to rescue me, but I'd discovered that the loose ends I'd thought tied had come unraveled, when Terian had come by for dinner the night after my rescue.

I'd been setting the table with three places, when Theo had called from the door that he was leaving.

I'd turned to him in confusion. "There's no need for you to leave now, Theo—"

"I need to go," Theo said as he opened the door, his back to me, "I would have been killed trying to get to you without Terian. I didn't have enough bullets, and that was only in terms of the guards. Devlin would have killed me for sure. I am strong, but not as strong as just one of those werebears. It took two of them just to hold him."

"I don't understand."

He turned to face me. "Terian was the one who slowed them down long enough for me to make every bullet count. He was the one who forced the two guards to change, and attack Devlin. He was the one who knew the secret that gave Danial the power he has now. He was the one who defeated Devlin," he finished, acquiescent. "He is the one who saved you, not me."

"All that matters is that I'm not dead, and we're together," I said firmly. "You fought for me, so what if you didn't fight alone? It doesn't change what I feel for you."

"It changes what I feel for him, Sar," he replied. "I hated him before, but I was willing to tolerate him for your sake. Now I'm grateful, so grateful to him, and jealous that he could save you and I couldn't. I can't be around him right now; because I know I'd either be fawning over him or trying to start a fight with him, because of my feelings. So I'm going."

"Ok," I said softly, "I can understand that."

He kissed me quickly, then left, slamming the door of his pickup and driving off.

Terian had been surprised to find Theo gone when he'd arrived, but he'd said nothing. I told him that I'd made him some whole-wheat pasta, and then cracked up when his face fell.

"Just kidding," I said, bringing out some lasagna, some bread I'd baked earlier, and some of the last veggies from my garden that I'd put up last fall.

"This looks good," he said, and we dug in.

After dinner, we'd talked for a long time, finishing most of a bottle of wine. He caught me up on his doings out west since the New Year.

Terian had been out west studying with another half-demon, and his coven. He was vague as to their names, but I garnered that they were the ones who'd given him the emotional truth spell he'd used on me after Christmas, and taught him how to control animals, were or otherwise. I wanted to ask if that was the one who'd taught him how to explode enemies, too, but couldn't find a delicate way to phrase it. Finally, my curiosity got the better of me and I asked him outright.

"Terian, there were two guards who looked, um, in pieces, that night you rescued me," I said, grimacing. "What happened to them?"

"They attacked me, Sar. I ripped them apart. You know how strong I am," Terian said casually. "Weremen can't heal everything at once, especially if enough pieces are separated from one another, or destroyed."

I hadn't known he was that strong, but I remembered the wall, how he'd pushed through it with his hands. "I didn't know that, about the weremen, I mean."

"I just learned that myself a few weeks before that," he replied. "Don't feel bad."

"I don't," I said, reaching out and giving his hand a gentle squeeze. "Thanks again for helping me."

He gave me a gentle smile, squeezed back, and then let go.

"What will you do now?"

"I'm going to stay here, Sar. Not literally in this town, but a little bit south of here, I think. I could keep traveling, but I want a real home, with someone like you to share it with." He sipped his wine.

It was obvious his feelings for me hadn't changed. I took a sip of wine myself.

"I'm sorry again for what I did to you," he said, dropping his eyes.

"I told you, I'm grateful for that, Terian. If you hadn't—"

"But I didn't do it for you, I did it for me. And down deep, that haunts me. I keep wondering if I hadn't done it, would I be the one with you now, instead of Theo."

I wondered that myself. I didn't answer, and sipped my wine again.

"Sar, answer me," Terian said persistently. "Theo told me on the way to Danial's home last night about New Years, about how he'd cared for you but kept it hidden. About how you kissed him, and how everything he'd kept locked inside came pouring out. But it was the dream you shared that pulled you together in real life. I want to know, if you hadn't dreamed of him, and he of you, could you have maybe ever considered me as more than a friend?"

It was brought home to me in that moment that Terian wanted more than an honest answer to my question. He had been hoping like hell when he gave me the potion that I had been holding my feelings for him inside. He'd hoped to let them out with his spell, and hear me tell him I loved him. He'd hoped to dream with me. It was bad enough I'd dreamed of someone else, fallen for someone else. But worse than that was that he'd saved me when the man I loved couldn't, and I still wasn't in love with him.

"Was there any hope for us, ever?" Terian said softly. "Or was I always deluding myself? Tell me the truth."

The truth was I didn't know, because that road was one I hadn't ever considered. But I did know the other road I'd turned from, when I'd chosen Theo.

"Terian, if you hadn't done it, things would be different, but I wouldn't be with you. I'd be with Danial. Danial would have eventually found out from Ivan or another guard that I'd been there at night, not in the day, or Angelica would've let something slip. He'd have come here looking for me, and I would have given in to him. I was willing to forgive him, and try to make a life with him." I paused, and took another sip of wine.

"I'd be with him right now, possibly carrying his child inside me," I said, looking away and seeing nothing.

Terian let out a sigh, but he took my hand in his. "Are you worried you made the wrong choice? I hear regret in your words."

"The truth is, I feel badly, for how I acted," I said, finishing off the glass. "Danial did his best to love me, to make me happy, to protect me in every way he could. I should not have left him like I did. We should have worked through it together, and I should have tried harder. We both lost a child that night, not just me. It was not his fault, what happened. But I blamed him anyway. I regret that."

Terian sipped his wine, and considered my words. "Did you ever tell Danial this?" he said finally.

"No," I said with a sigh. "There's no point now. I'm with Theo, and all the 'should-haves' are just paths not taken. Danial would take my words as a sign that I wanted to come back to him, and I don't. I only tell it to you because it's true, because I can admit it now to myself. I don't want you blaming yourself for any of this, or thinking we missed a chance to be together. It wouldn't have worked, Terian. I'm sorry, but that's the truth."

Terian finished off his wine, and stood up. "I should be going," he said, offering me his hand.

I took it and walked him to the door. "Please be safe."

He hugged me, and kissed my forehead. "Thank you for what you said to me, Sar. It helps. I know it wasn't easy to say."

"Visit when you have time," I said affectionately, drawing back from him.

"I will," he said with a smile, then he turned and left. I waved to him, as he pulled away, and went back in, and sat down at the table.

I took out the choker from my shirt pocket, fingering the gold links. "I'm sorry," I said softly in the silence. Then I put it back, finished my wine in one long draught, and went to bed.

In the beginning, I'd carried the choker with me wherever I went, irrationally feeling vulnerable without it. Theo had noticed, but didn't mention it anything, understanding it was something I needed to come to terms with on my own. In the past few weeks, I'd been able to leave the choker in my jewelry box more and more often, not needing the feel of the fox head in my palm to feel safe.

Some of that was Theo's increasing power and skill. He'd begun training hard immediately, trying to make himself faster and stronger. I helped, supplying him with as much raw meat as he could stomach. So far, that combination was working. I believed that he would indeed win, when he fought the fifth ranked later this week.

Theo and I still tried to work on him changing form, but it had been relegated to every other night, or sometimes during the day. He was able to remember most of what he'd done, and what I'd said, but it was taking a long time to make any progress with him being with any of the pets. Cavity had gotten into the barn one night with me, and nearly been a snack, before I was able to get him out the door. Theo had backed off for me, but if Cavity had been alone, he'd be dead now. As soon as his big fight was over, I'd told Theo we were going back to every night.

Theo had shrugged at that, saying he'd do his best. Now he was back working for Danial, he wasn't around nearly as much as he had been. He had been gone almost every night all night for the first week. After that, he'd arranged to be off on Tuesday and Wednesday nights, but the others he was working. It was hard at first, going to bed without him, and—depending on when I got up, or if it was a day I worked—sometimes being without him the whole night and next day. I knew he missed me, but there was nothing to do about that. The schedule that was Danial's was his, too, and that meant nights, for the most part.

I was lonely, but I dealt with it by keeping busy, by making him special dishes, and things to take to Suri and the other foxes. They had let Theo know that now that things were okay between Danial and I, they expected some treats now and again. I knew they appreciated it, and I enjoyed making cookies and pies for them, so I did.

There was a dark side to what Theo did for Danial, too. The second morning Theo had come home, I'd gone to throw his clothes in the wash and seen bloodstains. I knew the blood wasn't his from the direction of spatter. I threw it in the wash, and didn't ask him about it. Over the weeks that followed, when I washed his clothes, there was often blood on them. Sometimes it was his, from the ragged holes in his clothes. Far more often, it wasn't. And sometimes, his clothes were drenched in it.

There was another change, too, a reassuring one. Theo had decided in the second week of working that he was taking over the household bills. I thought at first it was a territorial thing, and resented it, as I'd resented Danial's offer of money months ago. But after talking to him, I came to realize that he wanted to improve my home, make it warmer for him and me, and easier to live in. I'd met with a roofer, a plumber, and a kitchen remodeler in the last week, and all were going to be working on fixing things up over the coming summer.

The damage Devlin and his men had done was long since repaired, though that had been done by Theo. It was nice, enjoying morning sun through my bedroom windows again. I'd had to toss out the blackout curtains along with the regular curtains. They'd been completely ruined by the broken glass and blood. Making some new curtains for the room was on my list of things to do. I smiled, remembering that Theo had put in his two cents and asked that they have no bug designs on them.

He'd also come home after that first week with a wrapped package for me. Inside was a beautiful gray-blue velvet robe. I'd put it on for him, but it hadn't stayed on long…

A passing truck backfired. I came back to the present with a jolt, thinking about the one problem we had yet to find a solution to: Tawny.

I decided to make some breakfast. Theo would be home soon, he was likely on his way right now. He'd be hungry after coming off his twelve-hour shift.

As I browned the sausages and flipped bacon, my thoughts turned back to Tawny and her baby. My anger rose up almost immediately.

Tawny was back in Europe. She was due to deliver in another two and a half months, and we still didn't know if Theo was the father. Dr. Camlyn had completed his tests long since, but the results had been inconclusive, due to the werevirus being almost identical in all those who turned into great cats. Theo had asked about blood testing, but that had not helped either, as he and Tawny's husband were the same blood type. In addition, Tawny still refused to tell her husband about the baby maybe being another man's, until she knew it conclusively was.

Dealing with all this for weeks on end had my nerves ragged. I told myself to hold it together, that the end was in sight. Today, Stephen had said he would have a definite answer for us. Today, we would finally know.

Instead of feeling relieved by that, I was on edge. Theo and I were working together. I was scared that if the baby was his, it would ruin everything, despite what he said to the contrary…

There was the sound of a key in the lock. "Sar?" Theo called. "Do I smell bacon?"

"I made breakfast. Come in and sit down."

"I can't," Theo called. "Please bring me some towels."

Worried, I dropped the spatula, grabbed a hand towel, and ran to the front door. Theo was there, nude, his clothes wrapped in a ball, his shoes in his hand, blood spatters all over his chest.

"What happened?" I said cautiously, taking the ball gingerly. "Is everyone okay?"

"The fifth decided to move up our fight," Theo said arrogantly. "Or I should say, the former fifth."

"Congratulations," I said slowly. "But you don't look that bad. Why do you need a towel?"

"Get my back," Theo said, turning around. His back was covered in blood, some of it caked on him.

With distaste, I wiped most of it off. "Is this yours?"

"No, his."

That was a relief. "I think that's as good as it's going to get."

"I'll be right back then," he said, handing me his shoes. "Thanks."

I went immediately, and tossed everything in the washer, loading the soap dispenser to the maximum. Then I hurried back to the cooking meat.

Theo came out in a few moments, toweling his hair. I handed him a loaded plate.

He took it eagerly, and went into the other room. "Thanks, this is great," he said a few moments later.

I loaded my own plate, turned off the stove, and went in to sit with him. "You're welcome. How was work?" I asked, eating a forkful of egg.

"Okay," he said, finishing his sausages. "Everything had been quiet this past week. I think that the last holdouts against Danial are done fighting, and they'll be sending letters of acquiescence soon."

"That's a relief," I said. Both of them would be in less danger when that finally happened.

"I have to tell you something though, Sar," Theo said quietly, putting his empty plate to the side. "You aren't going to be happy to hear it, but I need to tell you anyway."

"So tell me," I said tiredly.

"I have to go to Europe in two and a half months. Danial has almost a whole week of night meetings to attend to then. I need to go with him."

I sighed. "Isn't that just the time that Tawny should be delivering?"

"Sar, you are welcome to go. I'd like you to come. We can have Suri or someone else come for a week and watch over everything—"

"You know I can't go," I replied coolly. "I have to work—"

"You mean you won't go," he said, just as coolly. There was no anger, just defeat.

"Tell me what you want me to say, Theo," I said, staring at him.

"I need you to say yes, Sar. I want you to come with me, because I know how you'll feel here, on the other side of the ocean, and me over there, in the same city as Tawny, with her having the baby, even if it's not mine. I've cleared it through Danial. He said if you agreed to go, he would have no problem with it."

I didn't believe that for a minute. Danial wouldn't want me along, not stuck in a hotel room with him and Theo together for a whole week. Danial was likely gambling that I'd refuse to go. He knew my predilections well.

The phone rang. It was Dr. Camlyn. I handed the phone to Theo.

"Tell me," he said quietly. "Is the baby mine?"

I held him around the waist, my head on his back. The moment I felt the tremor go through him, I knew without him saying the words.

Theo hung up the phone and turned to me. "It's mine, Sar," he said.

There was so much I'd practiced to say if this happened. Instead of saying any of that, I did exactly what I promised myself I wouldn't; I burst into tears.

"Sar, please don't cry," he said softly, hugging me. "Please."

"I'm just scared," I said, the words distorted and hard to get out. "I'm sorry—"

"I'm scared too, Sar," Theo whispered, hugging me tightly.

I pulled myself together enough to stop crying. We stood there for a few minutes, just holding each other.

"Theo, will Stephen tell her?" I said finally.

"By now he's told her," Theo said, upset and a little angry.

On cue, the phone rang again. Theo picked it up.

"Hi, Tawny," he said guardedly. "Yes, I know. He just told me. No. I told you, no."

There was a brief pause while he listened.

"No, I don't love you," he said finally. "I know you don't love me, so stop lying. It's not going to happen. But yes, I'll come. Good-bye."

He hung up and turned to me. "Tawny wants me there when she is having the baby. It is my baby, and I think I should be there. I'll be there in Europe, anyway, if she has it when she is supposed to…" He trailed off, watching me hopefully.

I took a long shuddering breath. "I'll come with you."

* * * *

The next few weeks passed quickly, maybe because I tried to pack as much happiness and work into them as was possible, before we left for overseas.

In mid-May, with Theo's help, I got the small garden plot tilled up, and ready for seeding. The following day he took off work, and helped me plant seeds. He was amazed that something so small had the potential to become something so much more.

"Are you sure, Sar?" he'd said, looking at the radish seeds and carrot seeds that were almost too small to pick up with anything larger than tweezers. "These aren't for miniature vegetables?"

I cracked up laughing, and then managed to say, "I've planted a garden for the last four years, Theo. Yes, I'm sure. They just need a little care and nurturing."

We got the garden planted, and finally two weeks later, small green sprouts begin to push their way out of the ground. I showed them to Theo, drinking in the look on his face.

"They're growing, Sar," he said in wonder.

I also showed him the flowerbeds, which I'd weeded. The daffodils were blooming, and the later plants were beginning to put forth new shoots. Some of the roses already had buds.

I stood there with him, and in that moment, I realized that I had gotten my wish. I'd longed for a new life, and now I had one with Theo. I no longer felt broken, or on the fringes of life, looking in. My personal winter had left with the ice and snow, and spring was in my heart, as well as all around me.

"Sar, what are you thinking?" Theo said, wrapping me in his arms.

"I'm happy, Theo. Happier than I've been in a long, long time," I said with contentment.

"Me, too," he said, hugging me. "Say it will always be like this between us, Sar. No matter what happens, what life brings us?"

I looked up into his blue eyes, suddenly so serious, and swallowed the lump in my throat. I was still worried about what would change for us after Tawny had the baby, just as he was likely still worried I'd change my mind, and leave him for Danial. But that didn't matter. He'd always been strong for me when I'd needed him to be. Now it was time for me to be strong for him.

"It will be Theo," I said, smiling up at him. "I promise." Then I kissed him.

The End

Coming soon

Taken in the Night, Book 3 of the Promise Me Series